Til Morning

■ ■ ■

A Novel

Bonnie Hearn Hill

Larry Hill

TIL MORNING

ISBN-10: 1502592185
ISBN-13: 9781502592187

Authors' Note

He was one of the world's biggest singing stars. She was the most renowned female journalist of her time. Johnnie Ray and Dorothy Kilgallen. They had fame, power, money, connections. The last thing they needed was love.

In 1952, an American singer named Johnnie Ray dominated the charts with "Cry" and "The Little White Cloud That Cried." Deaf in one ear, he produced heart-wrenching vocals that influenced celebrated entertainers including Elvis, The Beatles, and James Brown. But Johnnie Ray was an enigma. Some said he sounded black, some said he sounded like a woman. Was he gay? Bisexual? Most shook their heads and just listened in wonder.

"Just Walkin in the Rain" shot to No. 1 in 1956, right around the time he met journalist and "What's My Line?" game show panelist, Dorothy Kilgallen.

Eleven years Johnnie's senior and married, Dorothy co-hosted a long-running radio talk show with her husband from their brownstone on East 68th Street. She had risen to prominence after covering the Lindbergh kidnapping for Hearst's *New York Evening Journal* when she was nineteen. Her coverage of the Dr. Sam Sheppard murder case, on which the television series "The Fugitive" was based, helped secure a new trial for Sheppard. With her "Voice of Broadway" gossip column, she rose even higher.

Dorothy and Johnnie's very public love affair—the alcohol, the *pillskies*, the gossip, and the often delirious, sometimes cruel times—almost destroyed both of them. Yet they seemed to provide each other with an intoxicating rush neither could find with anyone else.

Johnnie was arrested twice for soliciting men for sex, and although he was found not guilty in 1959, the publicity surrounding his trial damaged his career. Dorothy's drinking threatened both her radio and television shows. Convinced that the government had hidden the truth about the Kennedy assassination, she believed her exclusive interview with Jack Ruby would reestablish her as a serious journalist. She published his testimony to the Warren Commission in the *New York Journal American* before the report was released to President Lyndon Johnson.

Almost all who knew about the two thought their union dangerous and confusing. "Johnnie Ray and Dorothy Kilgallen?" they'd say. "I can't imagine them together."

Was her bond with Johnnie as relatively uncomplicated as sex? Was it just a shared appetite for excess? The lure of great fame? Was it love?

Please read – and decide for yourself.

Bonnie Hearn Hill
Larry Hill

*Yet, as only New Yorkers know, if you can get through
the twilight, you'll live through the night.*
–Dorothy Parker

*A hundred times have I thought New York is a catastrophe
and 50 times:
It is a beautiful catastrophe.*
–Le Corbusier

Johnnie

New York could be a cold bitch when she wanted to. The town was especially bitter this February of 1956 when I stumbled into CBS Studios. Making my way through a maze of hallways, I searched for *What's My Line?*, this TV panel show of stiff-necked New York assholes playing their parlor game. Most uppity member of this select group? Dorothy Kilgallen. The little purse-mouthed social queen had been bum-kicking me in her newspaper column.

At a corner, I bumped into my favorite blues singer Jimmy Witherspoon, who seemed as lost as I was.

"Johnnie Ray," he said. "Hear you been tearing 'em up, man, since you opened the shows for me at The Flame Showbar."

Detroit City. Yeah, I thought. For me, that was a few gold records ago. "What's happening, Spoon?"

He gripped my hand, pulled me close, and wrapped me in his arms. Both tough and tender, Spoon could make you feel safe from the fiends in this business.

"The Flame," he said, looking off like the hallway was a train and he was waiting for one. "We had us some good times in that place."

"You threw me onto the stage and hoped the crowd would eat me alive," I said, and remembered how I was the only white singer to perform there back then.

He eyeballed my blue suit, and I felt his gaze linger on my hearing aid. "Where y'all headed dressed up like that?"

"The *What's My Line?* show." I said, feeling that usual apprehension about my wired up left ear. "I'm their mystery guest tonight."

He slapped my palm and glided away. "You the mystery, all right."

Standing in front of what I hoped to be the right door, I regretted not asking Witherspoon what he was doing here tonight. His rich voice lingered in the hall. What I would've given for that kind of timbre in my pipes.

A few minutes later, the make-up guy warned me, "Watch out for Kilgallen. She's liable to ask you your brand of condoms."

I acted shocked. "Thought they wore blindfolds."

"Dorothy can see through hers."

I waited in the wings, checked the volume on my hearing aid, and tried to remember what I was told in the green room. The show's host, John Daly, would call for me to enter and sign the blackboard. I'd sit next to him while the blindfolded panel, a few feet away, tried to guess my identity by asking questions.

"Change your voice when you answer them," a stage manager advised me.

I noticed a young assistant in a bright yellow shirt talking with the older guy who did my make-up. The kid turned covertly to him, eyed me, and hid a canary-eating grin with his hand.

What the hell? I had at least a minute to burn. Passing harried glances, I walked over and stood in front of Yellow Shirt, laid a close-up on him, and watched him sweat. Then I pressed my index finger on the cleft of his mouth and held it in a hush-hush position.

"Careful," I said softly. "I read lips, man."

Dorothy

It was all Sinatra's fault.

Dorothy sat in darkness behind her satin mask as the guessing game took place around her. Blindfolded in public, a metaphor for her life. She felt the studio audience's vibrations race against her pulse. Were people across the country scrutinizing her profile, pointing at their televisions, and snickering? She squared her shoulders and felt the rustle of her taffeta wrap.

"Will our mystery guest sign in, please?" John Daly's deep baritone made the memorized command sound ominous.

She tried to concentrate. In her mind, she heard only Frank Sinatra and pictured him in his last Las Vegas engagement. "Dotty Kilgallen, couldn't be here tonight," he'd said to the crowd. "She's out trying to buy a new chin."

Had she missed her cue from Daly? Down the line to her left, Bennett Cerf asked some question that caused the audience to titter. Then Arlene Frances jumped in, her melodic voice enthusiastic.

"Are you in show business then?" Arlene asked.

"Yes," the mystery guest replied, voice disguised.

Behind her blindfold, Dorothy focused her thoughts. Was the voice male? Female? An image of a man, tall and blond, hovered beyond her blindfold.

Arlene asked something else and got a no. Fred Allen's stupid question went nowhere, and it was back to Dorothy too soon.

"An entertainer?" The camera was probably lingering on her mouth. She tried to smile, make her face less stiff.

"Yes." That voice!

"Are you known for your work on the stage?"

"No."

"That's four down, six to go," Daly said.

"An actor in films?" Cerf asked.

Daly must have gone into one of his whispering huddles with the guest. This usually resulted in chuckles from the audience and always infuriated her.

"Sometimes."

"Five down, five to go."

Arlene's turn. "Singer?"

"Yes."

The voice was clearly male. A singer like Sinatra. Dorothy straightened her spine. It couldn't be Sinatra. No, but from the audience's reaction, as big or bigger.

Arlene was still on the hunt. "Could you be—" she asked in a smug tone, "the man who made crying a national institution?"

Applause surged. Arlene went no further. Damn her. Dorothy needed only a moment more.

"Panel, you may now remove your blindfolds," Daly said, giving all the glory to Arlene, as if he'd planned the course of questioning from the beginning.

Dorothy removed her mask and blinked into the light.

Applause continued. "Ladies and gentlemen," Daly said, "let's welcome Mr. Johnnie Ray."

In the bedlam, Dorothy allowed herself one quick look past the other three panelists to the young man smiling directly at her. How dare he? He stared right back as if waiting to see who glanced away first.

Minutes later, Dorothy slammed the door, and her dressing room closed around her. She should have guessed him by his voice. "*Endsville*," she had written of his style. As easy as it was to make fun of him, few could wring the emotion from a song the way Johnnie Ray did.

Marie held out a tumbler of vodka from the decanter she kept there.

"Figured you could use this," she said.

"And how." After primping her, Marie always watched the show from the wings, and the sympathy in her expression left no doubt that she'd done so tonight. Dorothy clutched the glass. "What a debacle."

"Remember," Marie said. "You have more right guesses than all of them combined."

The vodka was warm and friendly going down, and Dorothy began to relax. Marie fluttered about her, tiny but sure-handed. Facing herself in the narrow mirror, Dorothy caught sight of a stack of unopened fan letters on the table. She picked one up, then let it drop. No, she couldn't deal with more insults tonight.

"Don't bother setting these out for me."

"You've always enjoyed them."

"Not anymore." Dorothy spread her hands and leaned against the table. "This overdone dress. I feel trussed as a turkey."

"It's the boning. Now, let me unzip you."

"I'm foolish allowing the show to upset me." The evening was, however, tarnished. P.J. Clarke's tavern wouldn't be the same tonight, nor would the Copa. People would know she'd been bested by Arlene, especially those already snickering about Sinatra's running barrage against her. "What did you think of our mystery guest?"

"That voice," she said. "I think it's true what they say about him being almost deaf in both ears."

Dorothy wagged her finger at Marie's image in the mirror. "You're reading Sheilah Graham's gossip rag again."

"Am not. I only read you. Anyway," she said, making a sour face, "he's nervy showing up here after you took him apart in your column."

Had she really been so vicious about this famous singer? "I've seen him perform," she said. "I should have guessed his identity."

"If he didn't sound so much like a woman, you might have." Marie ended her sentence with a gasp.

Dorothy turned from the mirror. Marie's arms flapped away from her. "Oh, excuse me, Mr. Ray," she stammered. "I was just leaving."

Johnnie Ray politely moved aside and allowed her to pass. He stood tall at the door, his blue suit almost muted away from the set's harsh lights. The small hearing aid in his right ear, with its wire disappearing into his collar, upset the symmetry of his angular face. He appeared less sophisticated, more untamed than he had out in the studio. In the small room, Dorothy backed away.

He stepped toward her, loose gaited, and surveyed the tidy liquor display.

"I got time for a drink," he said, "if you're buying." His voice sounded raspy, a bit unsettling.

She picked up her vodka. "I'd prefer not to contribute to your notorious habit."

He brushed past her and helped himself to a drink. "Why not? Your readers dig it."

"They dig your music. I'll give you that. And I admitted I liked *Please Mr. Sun.*" She purposely did not mention his earlier hits *Cry* or *Little White Cloud.*

"Big of you."

Dorothy felt an urge for a cigarette but made herself stand rigid. "I saw your act at the Copa. I meant every word in my column."

"That I'm Endsville?" His smile contained a bit of sweetness that surprised her. "Some people aren't hip enough to know that's a compliment."

"My readers got it."

"That was 1952." He tossed his head back as he drank. She watched his throat move. He returned to the liquor, poured another, and held up the bottle. "You?"

"Why not? It's been a dreadful night."

The splash of vodka into her glass sounded luxurious in the tight space.

"Look," he said. "I don't want a war."

"Nor do I," she said. "One public enemy is enough."

"Sinatra?"

"Who else?" She'd found her voice and was feeling stronger.

"Some say you asked for it."

So his appraisal of her feud with Sinatra matched the way most of New York felt about it. "I'm a journalist," she said. "I don't answer to him or anyone else."

He chuckled. The slight space between his front teeth made him look even younger than, what—twenty-eight, twenty-nine? The hostility in his eyes paled. "You pissed off a man don't nobody piss off."

"I wrote the truth. I didn't ridicule him personally, and I didn't do it on stage at the Copa, for Christ's sake."

"Don't let it get to you." He drank, then lowered his voice. "You got too much class."

She smiled, the first honest smile in a long time, she thought. Perhaps, in spite of his youth, his fame, his armor of arrogance, he was wiser than on first impression.

"Thank you," she said.

"Sinatra shouldn't be knocking anyone's looks," he added. "He's not blessed with a strong profile himself."

"He's blessed with a strong one below the belt," she replied and immediately regretted it.

His drink paused at his lips. He looked her up and down, as if searching for some secret she might be hiding. "How would you know?"

"That's my understanding," she replied, carefully. "Everyone's heard the rumors."

"He ain't as blessed as some of us."

"Oh, spare me," she said.

"According to Ava, that is."

So the stories about him and Ava Gardner were true. Her rival columnist, Sheilah Graham, had scooped her again. Sheilah, with her overused British accent, was still trading on her famous love affair with Scott Fitzgerald. But he'd been dead for years now. How many more books about him could she write? Sheilah's successful reporting of Ava and Johnnie Ray bothered her more than his boasting. This entire encounter with him was a bother, come to think of it. She'd suffered enough indignity for one evening.

"It's late." She glanced up at the clock. "We've given those on the other side of the door ample time for conjecture."

He gazed past her shoulder and smiled. "Haven't had time to conjecture that."

She turned abruptly and stared into the mirror at her naked back, even her garter belt, the tops of her stockings. He'd had a clear view the entire time. She whirled back around to face him.

"You son of a bitch."

The animated smile didn't leave his face. He reached into his jacket and took out the battery pack for his hearing aid. With a flourish, he switched it off. Without another word, he sauntered from the room and closed the door firmly behind him.

"You son of a bitch," she repeated, shouting this time, in spite of herself.

Johnnie

Friday, broad daylight, and I was still pondering my exchange with Dorothy Kilgallen last Sunday. A few fans buying early tickets for tonight's show spotted me. That's all it took, and a bunch more followed in hot pursuit. I sprinted from the stage door to Morrie Blaine's Cadillac.

I dove into the sedan's backseat. "Hit it, Morrie."

Fists pelted the Caddy's roof. Faces splotched against its windows. Tires crunched ice.

Checking to see if I was in one piece, I allowed my mind to wander back a decade to those low, roving hills back home, and I saw myself hanging onto our Holstein cow Dinah's tail. My feet rested up on her flanks. She clomped along behind Rover, my shepherd mix. Back then, I never doubted that life would always remain that complete and full of freedom.

Place a blade of grass between my teeth, and I was exactly the Norman Rockwell portrait my manager, Morrie Blaine, wanted me to be.

"Hit it, Morrie," I yelled again at the back of his balding head.

"I'm flying this ship fast as she'll go, Johnnie," he said.

My devoted fans, mostly kids, dropped from the moving car like bees drop from a hive jostled with a long stick. I turned to see their figures in the gray afternoon then concentrated on Morrie.

"You look like an owl with those specs of yours," I said. "Stay in the right lane, man."

Morrie spun the wheel like a great sea captain lost in a storm. "Call me owl again, you fucking radical, and I spill you out and let 'em cut you to ribbons."

I jerked my topcoat around so I could examine it. "Shit, next thing you know they'll be using razors. I'm lucky they didn't take a kidney."

Morrie found a groove in the traffic. "Where's his majesty going?" He shot me a glance. "And what's in the sack you're carrying," he asked. "Dope?"

The bag carrying some of my record albums had been slashed, but the discs seemed to be intact.

"Records I snatched from backstage," I said. "Got me a birthday party gig, East Sixty-Eighth and Park."

Morrie's percentage of my earnings had put fifty pounds on him, and he bounced like a beach ball in the driver's seat. "You're crazy," he said. "I ain't staying to chaperone you in some posh penthouse for Chrissake."

I spotted a tavern I knew and decided that I'd better line my stomach. Besides, I was a little antsy. The Voice of Broadway had ended our first meeting by calling me a son of a bitch. But then she'd also phoned my record company to request the platters for her daughter's sweet sixteen party. Maybe I just liked being sworn at by classy women, or maybe I was correct in assuming that Kilgallen kind of dug me. Either way, I realized what I needed right now. "No chaperone required," I said. "Stop up at this corner."

Morrie's head bobbed, and he tried to catch me in the rearview. "It's past noon, Johnnie." Playing the concerned manager now, the old song-plugger went on. "We got a matinee in four hours."

"Four and a half hours," I corrected him. "And I still need my breakfast."

"Booze is more like it. You should be arrested for your choices."

I had to laugh at the guy. I loved him was the sad truth. "They serve cold beer and hard-boiled eggs, don't they?"

I heard the shriek of brakes, and after a long second, I was thrown damn near up in front with Morrie. Then came the bam! And I realized that Morrie's car had climbed the back end of the little Studebaker ahead of us.

Studebaker guy jumped out. I took off running. When I glanced back, I saw that Morrie had eased out of his Caddy and was squinting up at the buildings like a lost hick, his first time in Manhattan.

Two minutes later, I sat in the tavern, drinking breakfast and thinking about the lady who'd requested my records for her kid's birthday party. She was married to some show-biz type named Kollmar. I'd have to be on my best behavior.

Dorothy

At Dorothy's insistence, the dining room in the Sixty-Eighth Street residence had remained without a clock for years. Dick at first found her aversion charming. Years passed, and so did the charm. Finally, he demanded that she explain her problem with clocks.

"They tick," she had told him.

He pointed out that they also kept her from being late, to which she replied that she wasn't the one who missed appointments. As with most of their conversations, this one had drifted into polite sniping. Dorothy had since ignored a defiantly ugly pendulum piece on the wall of their bedroom, which, after her move to the fifth floor, was really Dick's alone anyway. Another timepiece, a bell jar, appeared in the dining room a few weeks later.

It rested today as always on a buffet behind them. As she and Dick prepared for their daily radio show early that morning, Dorothy had been conscious of its soft whirring. Sitting at the dining room table, the WOR microphone before her, she watched Dick settle across from her. His business suit lacked its hard edges. His actor's good looks had grown mealy from heavy drinking.

For once, he was on time, but that was about all. No doubt she'd have to carry the show again, and she would. Their lifestyle depended on it.

The director signaled, and Dorothy breathed deeply. It was important that she stay in character. The tow-headed technician watched pensively, as if it were his first time recording the program.

Dick responded on cue. "Good morning, darling," he said in his rich baritone. "It's time for *Dorothy and Dick*. My, this is great orange juice."

"It's Juicy Gem, our favorite," she responded with exaggerated enthusiasm. "Would you like some toast?"

He clinked his champagne glass against hers and gave her an evil wink, "No, darling, but I'd like to toast you." Again he rang the crystal. "Eleven years of *Breakfast with Dorothy and Dick*. Can you believe it?"

Eleven years. She had been in her early thirties, both she and Dick vital and excited. "We've certainly had a marvelous time," she said, managing to keep a sigh out of her voice. "And we've met many wonderful people along the way."

"Interesting ones, wouldn't you say?"

Now what? Lately he'd been meandering off their mutually agreed upon subjects. "Yes."

"Your mystery guest Sunday night on *What's My Line?* for instance."

She hadn't expected that one. "Yes?"

"The Prince of Wails."

She almost laughed at how Dick must have read Johnnie's nickname in *Variety* and looked up how long the song *Cry* had been number one on all the charts. "You must mean Johnnie Ray."

"The Nabob of Sob."

She jerked her head up and caught nothing but Dick's placid smirk. "Mr. Ray is a talented performer."

"The guy with the rubber face and squirt-gun eyes."

Enough of this, she thought. Their listeners would be angry about Dick's attacking the country's leading pop singer. "There is an indefinable something in Johnnie Ray's voice," she said. "An articulation of his loneliness."

"But sweetie," he countered, "Elvis is the one with art in his pelvis." He offered his signature chuckle.

She bit back her anger. Their banter today lacked the sparkle of years past. She promised herself to hold their bickering to a pace the listeners might enjoy. Right now the show was all-important. If their audience moved away, so would Juicy Gem and the rest of the sponsors who contributed to their sixty thousand-dollar yearly reward for conversing with each other five days a week.

She straightened her shoulders and continued to talk into the mic, forcing a smile, as if the world could see instead of hear her.

⬛ ⬛ ⬛

Still upset about the show, Dorothy managed to finish her column before the courier picked it up around noon. She changed into a black dress for the birthday party and tried to relax before the teenage guests arrived. Over a cup of coffee, she watched Dick devour his food at the table they'd broadcast from earlier.

"Really, Dick. Eggs Benedict in the afternoon?" she asked.

He sat as still as a discarded movie show card while Julian poured him champagne. Julian held the bottle above an empty glass and raised his brow at her. She shook her head.

Dick cut into hollandaise-drenched Canadian bacon, and she reminded herself that as long as they kept the show and their family together, all would be tolerable.

After Julian was out of earshot, she said. "I could have done without the Johnnie Ray dig."

"Just trying to breathe some life into the show, darling." He put down his fork and reached for the champagne. "Besides, that column of yours badmouthed the guy more than anything I've ever said."

"Perhaps." Johnnie had told her in her dressing room after the show that he didn't want a war, and in spite of the exchange with which they had ended their meeting, neither did she. "But that doesn't matter now. We've declared a truce."

He cocked an eyebrow ever so slightly. "Since when?"

"We chatted after the show last night. It's fine." The coffee and conversation made her pulse pound. She glanced at the bell jar. "Are you going to miss your own daughter's birthday party?"

"Afraid so," he said. "I'll be back late. I'm meeting with some people about the club."

For an actor, he was a poor liar, or maybe he just didn't care enough to make the role he played at home believable. Looking into his eyes was like trying to gauge the depth of a glassy pond.

"I know how late your meetings run," she said.

"Money people," he put in. "Must quell the nasty rumor that I'm Mr. Dorothy Kilgallen."

She pushed away from the table. Tired, she thought, already bushed, and the evening hadn't started.

"Gosh, Mr. Kollmar," she said. "You mean being the voice of Boston Blackie on the radio isn't enough for you?"

"Don't knock it. Blackie's bought us both a drink now and again."

"So has *Breakfast with Dorothy and Dick*." She circled the table and stood behind him. "Try to be back at a civilized hour. We've much to go over for tomorrow's show. It's been flat lately."

"Not so today," he said with a self-satisfied smile.

"I'm sure we owe that to you."

"Now that you mention it."

"But what about tomorrow?" *After you've had a few more bottles of that*, she added silently.

"Tomorrow will take care of itself if you just relax." He held up a finger. "You've got to quit giving Sinatra the satisfaction of getting your goat. Our listeners hear it in your voice."

"Nonsense."

"Okay, okay." He heaved a dramatic sigh. "So we get a few more letters addressed to the Chinless Wonder."

Hearing Sinatra's expression escape her husband's lips reminded her how vile and cruel he could be. "Dick," she said in a small rush of breath.

"A few letters. A dozen is all, not hundreds, not thousands, for Christ's sake. But it's driving you crazy. You've played right into the mobster's greasy little hands."

"Please." Her legs wobbled. She leaned against the table and picked up the champagne bottle.

"You don't sound natural anymore." Dick continued.

A quick turn of her hand and the remaining champagne streamed from the neck of the bottle and fizzed like a tiny brook in his gray hair.

"At least," she said, "I sound sober."

As he left the table, wet head and all, he shouted, "Hubba-hubba, darling."

In that departing catch-phrase, once a term of endearment, she heard a thin, sad echo of gaiety from their yesterdays.

Johnnie

The five-story townhouse was located on East Sixty-Eighth, between Madison and Park—final neighborhood on the Monopoly board. I told the cabby to drop me, then counted out his fee and tip from the bar change in my suit pocket.

He whistled through his teeth. "Thanks, pal." I showed him my Hollywood choppers. His eyes got big. "Hey, ain't you the *Cry* guy?"

I dashed for the steps. The air smelled ashy and felt cold against my throat. As usual, I began to worry about the vocal chords. An uptight butler answered my ring and cooled on me like he was bored to death. I took a swipe at the egg crumbs and salt on my upper lip and gathered my record albums to my chest.

"Johnnie Ray to see Dorothy Kilgallen," I told the guy. With his white hair and chocolate skin, he looked like the butler straight out of *Gone with the Wind*.

"Is she expecting you?"

"Tell her I'm an errand boy running over some records she requested for her daughter's birthday bash."

This got me a ride up an elevator that groaned like an old man. The butler ushered me down a hall that reflected our walk off every surface. Cold, man.

Doors opened, and I stepped into a sea of teenage pastel. In the bright parlor, lots of jailbait moved around in rustling taffeta. Young boys stood in stiff poses, afraid to flare their acne. A white Steinway baby grand sat in the center of the action, its lid agape.

Before I actually saw her, I sensed her coming near me. The honest-to-god delight in her voice rang in my hearing aid. She mumbled something to the butler, then took hold of my sack of record albums.

"I had no idea you'd come in person."

She spun in front of me in simple black, kind of a noir look with her dark hair and Betty Boop eyes. Her skin was alabaster but soft-looking. Standing still, she seemed to be confident on her own turf, and she sent little sex waves. She looked different from the Dorothy Kilgallen in the CBS dressing room, whose rank fan mail had been strewn all over her table. Don't tell me about rank fan mail. I'd been buried in it for months.

I headed straight for the Steinway. The kids were in shock. With my name on their whispers, I tried the keys, and it was in tune enough for me.

"Ready to raise a little hell?" I asked louder than I meant to.

Kilgallen looked tiny and pale among these teen animals as she sent me a brave smile.

I gave them a crash course in boogie woogie, and don't tell me about boogie woogie. Then I settled down and gave them some Louis Armstrong. I'd always had him down pat. I put him with Jack Teagarden on *St. James Infirmary*, a duet, but I doubted the kids knew that. I felt like I was dragging them down, so I gave them some Edith Piaf to punish them more. Then I figured, hell, why not, since I invented the motherfucker? I stood up and gave them Elvis, complete with bumps and grinds.

"My favorite," shouted the lady's daughter.

Later I chatted with her and the rest of the kids. Then for a while I watched them dance to my records. Kilgallen brought me a spiked punch, and for some reason I didn't ask her to dance, though I knew she would've liked an invite.

Finally it was time for me to go. "I got a show downtown," I started to explain.

"I'll drive you," she insisted. "After your kindness, it's the least I can do."

Kindness or no kindness, women like her didn't play chauffeur to guys like me. I had nothing to add to that, so I just stood there. Then

I thought of some smart-ass answers but stayed buttoned up. She looked at me with those huge, soft eyes, and I couldn't hold back what I did next. I reached out and touched her bare shoulder, then her cheek with the backs of my fingers.

"I'd like that an awful lot," I said.

Dorothy

In the weeks following the party, Dorothy found herself phoning home more frequently. "Just checking in," she'd say to Julian, sensing in the silence before he spoke the impropriety of her behavior.

Johnnie Ray had said he'd call, and she knew he would, although she still wasn't certain why. He was impressed by her power, she knew. As she waited for the message that would surely come, she collected anecdotes for him. She'd tell him about her spontaneous dance with Bobby Short at Eartha Kitt's opening at the Plaza, and her privileged coverage of Grace Kelly's wedding the month before.

At times, she tried reminding herself that she was a journalist, not just New York's finest woman Broadway columnist. The Lindbergh kidnapping in 1932 when she was a nineteen-year-old rookie, the Dr. Sam Sheppard murder case in 1954. She counted her major scoops like beads. She didn't need any distractions, she told herself, not even a friendship or whatever it was with this odd young man. She resolved to do nothing, no sweet note of thanks, no more innocent calls to his record company. If she appeared indifferent, then she wouldn't be disappointed and wouldn't be humiliated.

Besides, maybe the rumors about Johnnie being with other men were true. Maybe it was more than swinging both ways, a sticky subject she always chose to avoid in her column. But then what about Ava Gardner, *The Barefoot Contessa* herself? Ava had made it clear to reliable insiders that her relationship with Johnnie was more than platonic.

Dorothy had never been the type to kid herself. Even when, years before, she had hoped against hope that Tyrone Power would marry her, a solid part of her had known better and steeled her softer self against the truth. She felt no such protection now, only the pleasant flow of anticipation. Johnnie Ray had said he would call.

A month after the party, to the day, he did just that.

They agreed to see *An Affair to Remember*, Johnnie's idea. She told him about her misunderstanding with Vic Damone, who sang the title song, and how they were now great pals. It seemed important that he understand that not everyone she wrote about hated her.

Although she and Dick had long since pursued other interests, she felt almost clandestine as she dressed for her movie date. Silly. She had many male friends. Was ermine too much for a movie? Well, they would surely stop somewhere after. What about a hat, that cute black cloche that dipped below her eyes? No, hats were for dowagers. Better to brush out her hair and let the wind take care of the rest. Did she need more perfume? At least on her wrists, and don't forget the backs of her knees. As her father always said, she might be a journalist, but she was feminine to her fingertips. And for tonight, to her toes.

In the end, she decided to tuck the folded cloche hat into her purse. For once she was grateful that Dick had left the house before her. Julian barely looked up as he summoned a cab for her and bade her goodnight.

The glaring New York cold made her grateful for the ermine and knit dress beneath it. The rest of her apprehension vanished when she spotted Johnnie's face. He waited for her outside P.J. Clarke's, standing under the flashing Michelob sign in a black topcoat and suit. As she stepped from the cab, he took both of her hands in his. "Would you look at that?" he said, as if boasting to someone else about her.

They crushed against each other in the padded seats of the theater. He smelled of lime aftershave that complemented rather than covered his own brisk outdoor scent. He turned, and she felt his breath on her cheek.

"You smell gorgeous," he said. "Want a drink?"

"Here?"

He shushed her softly as the credits began. In that frenetic way of his, he reached into his jacket and came out with a leather-covered flask.

She looked from one side of the row of seats to the other and wondered what the penalty for such an act would be and how Sheilah Graham might report it in her column. To hell with Sheilah. This was a rare night, and she intended to enjoy it.

She tilted her head back and thought of Prohibition, speakeasies, underage kids huddled and drinking at football games. The liquor carried that same illicit pleasure in its soft burn. She handed the flask back to him and settled in to watch the film.

As a journalist, Dorothy seldom lost herself in any performance. This film was an exception. She couldn't remember the last time she'd seen a bona fide love story on the screen.

She fought to keep the tears from her eyes, a task that grew more difficult each time she took her turn at the flask. Beside her, she heard a loud sniff. She turned and watched Johnnie blow into his handkerchief. The dim lights from the screen illuminated his face, shiny with tears. She touched his wet cheek and found it unexpectedly soft, almost delicate. He placed his palm over her hand, squeezed it, then pressed it against his lips. She turned back to the film wordlessly, and they sat like that, sobbing in earnest now, cheek to cheek, drunker than two people should be in a theater, her fingers pressed to his lips.

Outside on the street, she clung to his arm and leaned into him as they walked. "What an absolutely marvelous film," she said. "I'm going to plug it in my column."

People in all manner of dress hurried down the sidewalk toward their own destinations. Some gave them second looks. A pair of what looked to be young lovers smiled at them and waved. The girl must have recognized Johnnie.

Johnnie Ray, she thought. She was walking with Johnnie Ray, his arm around her waist, and someone had noticed.

"That'll be the day," he interrupted her thought. "Dorothy Kilgallen plugging a love story."

"No, I'm serious." She inhaled the thin, giddy air, and tried to catch her breath. "It's a boon, I'll say, to those of us who are getting tired of pictures about dope addicts, alcoholics, unattractive butchers, and men who sleep in their underwear."

He took another swallow from the flask, and the scent of vodka lingered in the cold air like perfume. "I'll drink to that, although I liked *Marty*. Cried all the way through it."

"I believe that," she said. "You're impetuous, you know and very, very sentimental. I always thought you faked the tears on stage."

His arm tightened around her. "I don't fake anything."

"Wish I could say that."

She expected a laugh in return, a smile at least. She got nothing but a lingering, unreadable look. Well, she could play the stare-down game too. Better to meet his gaze this way than to let him focus too long on her now infamous profile.

In a moment, he chuckled softly and turned away. "I love to walk," he said. "You?'

"A waste of valuable time," she replied, grateful for conversation once more.

"If we head north long enough, we'll reach Central Park."

It sounded like an invitation. Above them, nearly full, the moon glowed. She remembered the hoedown beat and corny lyrics of a terrible song he'd once recorded. "Didn't you sing something about walking home, other than the obvious one, that is?"

"A duet with Doris Day, god bless her. *Let's Walk That-A-Way*. Don't judge either of us by it."

With every step, her feet were shredded by the frivolous shoes in which she'd never walked farther than the distance between a maître d' and the best seat in the house. "Well, don't get any ideas about trekking through the park tonight. I never have, and I don't intend to start now."

"What kind of New Yorker are you?"

"One without sore feet."

He laughed and slid his hand to her elbow as they crossed the street. "Someday, you put on a pair of pants, I'll pick you up, and we'll stroll the park."

"You'll see me in hell before you see me in slacks." Her voice brushed over the words, stopping just short of a slur.

"You okay?" he asked.

She shrugged and tried for a bright smile. She longed for a warm room, a cold drink, and some time to reflect on this odd night, this man. "A little high, I'm afraid."

"This is the time I get started."

A challenge. She took it. "I'm Irish. I can keep up."

He nodded approval and steered her through the couples crowding the street. "Then follow me, girl. I want you to hear a cat who's a friend of mine."

"Anyone I know?"

"Count Basie." He said it almost shyly.

Now he was the one trying to impress her, but she was having too much fun to care. At least everyone at the Copa would be as drunk as they. And if they weren't, if she showed up in Sheilah's piss-poor excuse for a column, it was better than everything else they'd been printing about her lately.

She grinned up at the glowing moon and hurried to keep up with him, her fragile heels clicking on the sidewalk.

"I'd love to see the Count with you," she said.

Johnnie

By the time we arrived at the Copa, I was higher than Mount Everest. Brilliant lights dueled the black sky as we glided under the marquee. Inside, a hatcheck girl took Kilgallen's ermine and my topcoat. I scared up Umberto, the maître d', and he threaded us through the crowd. I held Kilgallen's hand, wondering who was pulling whom. Heads turned, mostly because of me at first, then her, the fact that we were obviously together, *an item,* as Dorothy herself would report it.

I faded back and watched her pass ahead of me, smooth power in her carriage, moving as if she were sure of herself. Basie's band rocked the six hundred-capacity room by its subterranean balls and swayed its ten-foot palms.

She slid into a crimson banquette. I started to follow, then she stopped me with her hand and said something about dear friends. A couple crossed the sunken dance floor. Pals from her privileged status in New York society's Four Hundred, not mine. It showed all over this pair. She presented them. "Clarice and Roland Fairchild." That was all I heard as Basie pushed the beat. The woman looked fortyish like Kilgallen, only her curves had flattened. Roland was fat, with a round face full of barracuda teeth.

He ignored my hand. "Dorothy," he said. "People are staring."

"Nice to meet you," I told him. "Getting stared at is nothing new to me."

"Nothing new to Dorothy either." Roland flashed his sharp fangs. "But she needs to be careful of the company she keeps."

"That's up to the lady," I replied, and started to walk on past.

Kilgallen popped up Irish angry, which surprised even me. "That's enough, Roland. You're way out of line."

Clarice tried to apologize. Roland flung a right cross. I ducked and came up smiling. I read in him every heckler who'd pitched me a bitch in every joint from Detroit City to Sydney, Australia.

Umberto stepped in like a ref and attempted to escort Roland to a table. Clarice helped. Kilgallen bristled. I played the whole scene like a journeyman.

"Fuck him," I told those within earshot. Then I joined Kilgallen in the booth and sent a thumbs-up to Basie.

A server brought us a bottle in a bucket of ice and presented the booze for my inspection. "Your brand, Mr. Ray."

I smiled at Kilgallen. "Hope it ain't grape."

"Potato," he said, and poured us chilled vodka, straight up.

The Count took a break. After the applause, Kilgallen launched into an apology for her friend's behavior.

I held up a hand. "No need," I told her. "I get that stuff all the time."
Her eyes grew moist, like in the movie earlier. "Yes, I guess you do."
"I've always been the weird kid," I added. "Even before the blanket toss."
"Blanket toss?"

I pointed to my hearing aid. "I was twelve, in the Boy Scouts. Landed on my head when someone dropped his corner of the blanket."

Her hands fished through her purse. She lit a cigarette, then found a pen and began taking notes on a Copa napkin.

"Don't do that," I told her.

The pen and bunched napkin flew back into her purse. "Sorry," she said. "Force of habit. From now on, everything is off the record."

"Then I might tell you my awful secret."

She waved away smoke and watched me. "Knowing you'd never ask, I feel I better tell you," I said, reaching for her hand. "I'm not really from Dallas, Texas."

She gave me a relaxed look. "No?"

"I'm from Dallas, Oregon."

"You sly bastard," she said, and changed her eyes again. "Next you'll be on *I've Got a Secret.*"

We drank hard. She scoped the place and spoke of the patrons with a razor tongue. I lit a filter, tried to act cool, and began to feel the booze.

Basie returned to the bandstand. When I saw his vocalist dawdle and grin at me like he didn't mean it, I felt a storm of adrenaline hit and knew what was coming. In the back of my mind, I heard Morrie say, "No! Last time we stepped on contracts in that room, Frank Costello's Mafia was all over me and so were the musicians' union goons."

"See a friend of mine out there tonight." Basie growled into his mic.
Kilgallen brightened under a spotlight.

"I've been jammin' with the Count now and then," I let her know.

"Ladies and gents," Basie announced, "let's hear it for the incomparable Mr. Johnnie Ray." Basie's drummer laid down a soft roll. "Get up here and acknowledge your fans, man."

Now the applause was deafening, and don't ask me about deafening.

"Johnnie," Kilgallen said, "Do something."

Trembling like a rabbit, I attempted to scoot out of the booth, stumbled, but finally gained a bit of composure on my way up to Basie.

On stage, I gave the vocalist, a new cat Basie had been working with, a palms-up gesture.

"I'm cool with it," he assured me.

To Basie, I whispered, "I'm awfully drunk, man."

"Ain't you the cat who never drives sober?" He jabbed my stomach with a huge fist. "Give 'em the Mary Jane song, then *Whiskey and Gin*."

"Mary Jane?"

"The *boo* song, marijuana," Basie said.

I nodded my head up and down, grabbed the stage mic and waited for the big man's soft, single notes to form an intro. Most of the band had been on this trip with us before, and they chipped in.

So I squared my shoulders and gave them *Sweet Lotus Blossom* impersonating Billie Holiday's voice. Basie dug it. The crowd wasn't so sure.

When I finished, the mob, if they were truly around, hadn't started to riot. I turned to Basie. "They want some blood and thunder, Count."

He nodded and began to bring up *Whiskey and Gin,* a song I wrote. I started it torchy and then let it go. The crowd and Basie's musicians felt it. In order to gratify the beast in most, I offended some, and that's when I broke the thermostat. I peaked the vocal while jumping off the stage. Then I strutted over to kiss the cheeks of Clarice and even the asshole Roland, both of them shrieking now with the rest of the crowd, born-again fans. Having wrung the song dry, I finished up in front of the mic.

I threw Basie a hand, fiddled with my hearing aid, and groveled my way to the booth. Kilgallen stood, applauding, her small hands in a frenzy. There was something in the proud way she held her head, a grandeur about her posture that made me lightheaded. Sweat dripped off me as if I'd tried to drown myself in the East River.

The lady put her arms around me and drew me close as if I belonged to her alone.

Dorothy

On the street once more, they stood facing each other. She felt like a teenager trying to make conversation before her date kissed her at the door, or didn't.

"You were wonderful," she said. "Better than your records, better even than the night I saw you open here. You sounded like Billie Holiday on *Sweet Lotus Blossom.*"

He rubbed his cheeks, warm from the cold and the vodka. "Lady Day taught it to me. It's about loco weed, as we used to call it back home."

"You didn't write it then?" She was chattering, couldn't help it. Keep him talking and maybe he wouldn't notice that the evening was over.

"No," he said, "but someday I'll sing you one of my songs, maybe later tonight."

"Tonight?" Not even her deliberately flat voice could make it a question.

He touched her cheek then reached for her arm. "Come on."

His bachelor flat at Fifty-fifth and Broadway looked like a brownstone flophouse. They stumbled up the narrow stairs as if they came home this way together every night. *What am I doing?* thought the sane side of her. They'd cuddled in the red leather booth, clung actually. But they hadn't even kissed. Now here she was, trudging up the stairs beside him, smiling as he stroked her arm. He didn't seem to notice her hesitation. Humming a few bars of *Walking My Baby Back Home,* he fumbled with his free hand for his keys.

"It's a dump," he said, as he unlocked the door. "I'll move if you hate it."

The interior of his apartment had the chilly scent of a bar after too many ashtrays had been emptied and too many glasses rinsed. Neon from the signs outside washed the wall with fuchsia light, illuminating a chesterfield and imposing oak coffee table. She pulled the fur close around her and maneuvered around something that had to be an overstuffed ottoman.

"Where's the lamp?" she asked.

"Up ahead. Can I take your coat?"

"Let's find the lamp first." She couldn't give up the fur, not yet. Just then she heard a menacing growl and saw the shape of a huge dog as it descended upon her. "Mother of God!"

"Don't worry." Johnnie wrestled to control the Doberman. "Sabrina's a sweetheart."

Dorothy stepped back into the ottoman and felt the heel of her shoe break off. She cried out and struggled to regain her balance as pain cracked through her ankle. "My shoe."

"Take them off, and I'll buy you new ones." He reached out in the flashing light. "Here, give me your hand. Show Sabrina you're not afraid."

"But I am. My Underwood relies on all ten fingers." Slowly she put her hand out and let him take it. The dog responded with a sloppy sandpaper kiss. "Ick. Her tongue's wet."

"Most tongues are." The dog tagged behind him. "Careful up ahead here," he said, and led her deeper into the shadows. "Morrie might be flaked out on the divan."

"Morrie?" she repeated. "Another dog?"

"More like a nearsighted owl. The guy's my manager." He let go of her and cupped his palms around his mouth. "Morrie, if you're in here, give us a hoot."

Dorothy could hear her own shallow breathing. No answer. They were alone. He took off his overcoat and tossed it in the empty chair, then his jacket and bow tie. He wasn't at all awkward here in his own environment, she realized. He just had his own rhythm, and it wasn't like anyone else's. Pain shot through her ankle again. She leaned against him and removed what was left of the offending shoe and its counterpart. Her eyes got used to the dark and the neon-washed wall.

He looked down at her and smiled. "You're short."

"Shoeless," she said.

"Well, that's okay." He led her to the ottoman and sat down. "Here," he said, and motioned to her foot. She lifted it, and he took it into his hands. "You have cute feet."

No one, drunk or sober, had ever called her feet cute before. "My second toe is too long."

He pressed his fingers into her arch, a light touch that radiated the length of her legs.

"Stop it." She tried to pull away.

"Beautiful feet," he murmured, pressing his lips against her hose.

"No," she pulled back. He was moving too fast. She needed a minute, a drink.

She felt his tongue against the sensitive skin of her instep. "Johnnie, please. This is the first—I mean, I've never done..."

Her voice trailed off as his fingers closed around her toes. "Didn't figure you had."

He rose from the ottoman and leaned down, slid his hands into her coat, and slowly pulled her into a kiss. The sound of their quick breaths filled the room. Dorothy pressed her body against his and wrapped her arms around his neck. It was time to take off her coat.

They didn't bother to pull down the bedspread, didn't pause to discuss what they were doing. He threw her ermine on the bed and unzipped her dress.

"I'm scared," she said.

They eased onto the bed. Neon bathed the wall and tinted their flesh—his spectacular body, her breasts—purple and green. She heard his intake of breath as he pulled the last lacy scrap of fabric from her. "You're beautiful."

"Johnnie, wait."

"It's okay." He snaked down alongside her on the bed, kissing her as he went. Dorothy tried to twist away from him, to pull him onto her, but he held her firmly.

"What are you doing?" she whispered.

"Taking my time," he said.

■ ▩ ▩

"Still scared?" Johnnie stretched out his long arm and handed her the cigarette he'd lit. She lay nude on the satin lining of the ermine. His head still rested against her ankle.

"Not really."

"How do they hide that body of yours on television?"

She moved closer to him. He had no idea what he'd done for her. She'd been cheated her whole life, and she hadn't even known it. Hadn't even realized that it wasn't her fault. "God, you're different," she said.

His eyes changed. He looked less vulnerable as he took the cigarette from her. "As in weird?"

"No, that's not what I meant."

"Morrie's had me checked by a shrink," he said with a laugh. "Until most people see me, they figure from my recordings that I'm either black or I'm a woman."

She took the cigarette back, inhaled deeply, and sighed. "I never thought that, but Johnnie, I had no idea."

He gave her a lazy smile. "What?"

"You know. You must."

"Tell me."

"Do you know how old I am?"

"I don't give a damn," he said.

"Forty-four. I'm forty-four and I've never really, I mean that's the first time I ever…"

He slid his hand along the bare flesh of her leg. "Want to try for an encore?"

Johnnie

I watched Dorothy raid my icebox.

"Your fridge is a disaster," she said, waifish in my robe, naked and showered under it.

In nothing but my suit pants and suspenders, I approached her from the rear and pressed into the soft terrycloth.

Her smile was a raspberry splotch on her alarmingly pale face. "Keep that monster away from me. My hangover is terminal."

I fetched some pillskies from a cabinet and a cold beer from the box. She didn't hesitate to throw them back. Holding her palms to the sides of her head, she stared at me in a way that reminded me of my sister when we were kids and she wanted to skip school. I moved past the counter and out into the living room, where I stepped over Sabrina and turned table photos Dorothy's way.

"Hazel and Elmer," I said. "Mom and Dad. This one's my sister Elma and me."

"Nice."

"Hardscrabble farmhouse behind us." I jumped Sabrina again and made a fuss straightening gold record plaques on the wall. I put an early Ellington on the turntable and heard Dorothy sigh deeply. Sabrina yawned under me. I heard the soft fall of cloth, and Dorothy's red toenails came up next to my big feet.

Sun slanted in and striped her body with light. I looked at her and couldn't believe she was a mother of three. I thought briefly about those kids, her husband, life around the townhouse. "You're putting a lot on the line," I said.

"I know what I'm doing." She ran her fingers through my hair.

"You're the only one here with plenty to lose," I told her, and really meant it.

"Or gain," she said.

I just stood there listening to Duke's band, wishing I could explain to her who was gaining and who was losing.

"Ellington," she said, and the name sounded like a lover's words against my better ear. "Do you jam with him too?"

"I have," I said.

"Any records in store with him or Basie?"

"Hope so."

"Who would stop them?"

"Morrie," I said. "Him and the Beard's determined I stay with bubble gum stuff."

"The Beard?" She took a step back.

"Mitch Miller," I said.

She pinched her nose, either about Mitch's music, the stale odor that always lingered from Morrie's cheap cigars, or maybe Sabrina, who was out like a light across the room.

I threw a thumb at the plaques on the wall behind me. "Morrie had a lot to do with those."

She moved closer, and then I saw Sabrina prick her ears. Beyond Dorothy's flawless forehead and dark coffee-colored curls, I saw my front door knob turning, and I thought, shit, hadn't I locked it?

Moving fast, I threw terrycloth around Dorothy nearly in time.

Morrie swung the door open. With him, garbed in leopard-print capris and a blond-streaked wig, stood Miss Cornshucks, my old pal from the Detroit days. It was her, all right, her dark skin shiny, both she and Morrie looking frightful in the window's curtained light.

Cornshucks dashed past Dorothy and bear-hugged me. "Wow," she said, pressing her pelvis against me. "You must be feeling happy."

I broke away, stuttered a greeting, then turned to Dorothy, who clutched my robe around her. "Dorothy Kilgallen," I said, throwing out an arm. "Meet my manager, Morrie Blaine. And this is Miss Cornshucks," I added. "We go way back to The Flame Showbar in Detroit."

"Way back," Cornshucks echoed. Her grin showed more gold than I remembered.

Dorothy placed fingers to her temple, and I could almost feel the hangover raging inside her skull. "How do you do," she managed.

"I do what I can," Cornshucks placed her fists on her hourglass hips.

Morrie beamed at Dorothy as if she was royalty. But it wasn't long before he began screeching at me, something about the Copa last night, about the Mafia.

"They'll cut your tongue out with their greasy hands," he shouted.

Dorothy became a white blur. She kicked my robe out in front of her shapely legs, strode into my bedroom, and slammed the door. We all flinched.

"What's her line?" Morrie said, and hee-hawed at his own wisecrack.

I beat my fists against my own bedroom door. "Dorothy, please, for Christ's sake. Open up, would you?"

Dorothy popped out, last night's fancy garb a mess on her. "I thought you said this was your apartment."

I followed her, finally caught up with her in the hall, and grabbed a fistful of the ermine she had gathered around her like some kind of armor.

"Dorothy, wait up," I pleaded. "We haven't even had breakfast."

"Have it with your friends," she said.

Her dark blue eyes were beautiful in the dim hallway. "Damn it to hell," I said. "You mean something to me."

She screamed right back, "And you mean something to me."

Turning on her broken shoe, she almost went down. A black floppy hat I didn't remember from last night was angled on her dark hair. As I watched her march away, I realized I was hurting for her dignity as much as she was.

5

Dorothy

The black room, adjacent to the master bedroom they never used, had always been her sanctuary, which was the reason Dick kept insisting they change the decor. It was as wide as the entire apartment and had matte-black walls and a white ceiling. The only color came from the red furniture, the kelly-green carpet, and a huge painting depicting a scene from the Revolutionary War that Clarice, her gallery owner friend, had told her had to go.

Dorothy collapsed against the back of the settee and watched the candlelight flicker around Billie Holiday's ethereal voice. *Lover Man, where can you be?* Before her, on a cocktail table shaped like a drum, sat an untouched drink. The soft wash of rain on the windowpanes only made her feel more alone.

She'd allowed herself to be humiliated, a graver sin than the adultery she'd committed. She still felt every step of that sharp, broken walk down the hall of Johnnie's apartment building. But he'd chased her, shouting, almost weeping. How about that, Dotty? It didn't console her. Johnnie Ray would weep at a change in the weather.

He had said she meant something to him. How could she believe him, sleeping with another man's wife, shaking her out like laundry in the morning? Then ushering in those people, that awful woman.

"Lonely?"

She jumped at the sound of Dick's voice. He leered at her from the doorway.

"Please, Dick. Can't you announce yourself?"

He moved closer. "Thought that's what I was doing, darling."

His bloated face made his teeth look smaller and shrunken. "You've been here all day. Julian says you're not taking visitors or calls from anyone, not even Jack Kennedy."

He settled on the other end of the settee, and she realized he had been drinking.

"Aren't you starting a little early?"

He drew back as if struck and nearly knocked over a candlestick on the table behind him. "I never take a drink before five-thirty. You know that."

"And you never rise before four, do you?"

"Hubba hubba, darling. I'd watch the sarcasm if I were you."

He thought if he repeated the term he had invented enough times, he could make it part of the lexicon. She was sick of it. "I'm not trying to be sarcastic," she said. "I just need some time to myself."

"As do I." Even in candlelight, his once-handsome face lay flat and gray. "I'll be late tonight."

"Of course."

"Very late. We're putting the last touches on the club, moving in the piano. Maybe your friend will sit in with the band some night."

Her temples throbbed. "My friend?"

"The Prince of Wails. I'm having various entertainers drop by, do a few tunes. Cheap labor and all. So now that you and the prince are pals—"

"I'll mention it to Mr. Ray if I talk to him," she said.

"I hope you will. Considering the condition of his career, he ought to welcome any opportunity to perform he can get."

"Last I heard, he wasn't begging for any singing jobs," she said. "Just check out the ticket lines at his show sometime."

"Is that what you were doing last night?"

So that was why Dick had sought her out, to argue. "I don't care if you spend the night at your club or anywhere else," she told him. "You needn't pick a fight about my nights out to justify it."

He rose from the couch as if trying to muster a degree of dignity. "I didn't say I was staying out all night. But there is a small apartment above the club, and if you're going to be so testy—"

"Just be here by seven for the show tomorrow morning, and be careful. People do talk, even about us."

He stopped at the door. "Yes, darling, they do."

Billie's song had ended. Except for the rain, the room was silent. Dorothy put on Johnnie's record and listened to every word. Perhaps she should have taken his phone calls. He couldn't help it if those people showed up at his apartment on that particular morning. She'd been mortified at the time, but now, she just missed him. She turned up the phonograph and let his voice blare through her.

"*Tell the lady I said goodbye,*" he sang. "*Tell the lady I'm through.*"

She didn't want to be through before they had as much as begun.

For a second, she thought she heard the doorbell. No. The courier had already come for her column, and nobody ever dropped by unannounced. She rushed to the phonograph, nevertheless and lifted the needle. The bell chimed again, clearer this time.

Was it Johnnie? It must be, she thought. He'd come, and Julian would turn him away. She rushed to the stairs in her stocking feet. No time for shoes. No time to wait for the elevator. As she ran down the carpeted hallway, she could see Julian, shaking his head, making a commotion.

"No," she shouted. "Wait."

"Mrs. Kollmar," Julian began. "Please."

"No. I've changed my mind," she said.

Before her stood two strangers wearing the innocuous clothing of delivery men. Between them, they held a large object, perhaps a piece of sculpture.

"I don't understand," she said to Julian. "Is this something Dick ordered?"

"No, ma'am." Julian moved in front of the object. "Leave here at once," he said to the men, "and take that with you."

"What is going on?"

She glared at the men. One looked down. The other smirked.

The decent one raised his eyes. "It's a gift." He paused as if asking permission to go on.

"From whom?"

"From Mr. Sinatra."

She moved around Julian and started to speak, but when she saw what the men had delivered, her voice died in her throat. It was a tombstone with only two words on it. *Dorothy Kilgallen.*

■ ■ ■

The son of a bitch. What a sick joke. Dorothy tried to hug some warmth into her body as she watched the cab's windshield wipers blur the neon-drenched street.

"Should I wait?" the cabdriver asked, as if he knew that she didn't belong to this neighborhood, nor it to her.

"No," she said. "I'll be staying."

Trying to duck the rain, she ran up the slick stairs. Johnnie would understand. He'd dismiss Sinatra's disgusting gesture for what it was and keep her warm all night. Yes, all night. She'd stay all night if he asked.

She rang the bell and pounded on the door. On the other side, a dog barked. Sabrina. She heard the lock click, and the door opened. Before her stood the black woman. She wore the same robe Dorothy had put on. Her head was almost shaved and covered in soft fuzz. With one hand, she restrained the growling Sabrina. In the other, she held the gold-streaked wig she'd been wearing the day they met.

"Oh." Dorothy couldn't move, could barely even speak.

"Don't look so scared." The woman shook the wig. "It don't bite." Then she glanced down at Sabrina, "Neither does she, unless you make her real mad."

Dorothy forced a tight smile and tried to regain her composure. "Forgive me for intruding. Something happened, and I just jumped in a cab without thinking."

"Well, come on in," the woman said in a proprietary tone.

A chill set over Dorothy. She needed to get out of there before Johnnie came to the door. "No thanks. I shouldn't have come."

"He ain't here, if that's what you're worried about."

Dorothy sighed in relief. "I'm not worried."

"Could have fooled me. I have a gig in Harlem. He's out in Hollywood recording. Said I could flake out here."

"Yes, of course." She pulled herself up to full height beside this giant-sized woman.

Cornshucks shrugged. "Why don't you help me get this dog inside and come on in? You look like a lady could use a friend."

The words touched her. She felt a tear creep down her cheek. She reached out to pat Sabrina's head. "I could use a drink."

The woman chortled. "Me too. Let's go in and raid the booze cupboard. Then you can phone up Johnnie. I got the number."

"I could never call Johnnie." She said. "Never."

"So don't." She handed Dorothy her wig. "You take this and let me get Sabrina under control. Her smile showed some gold as she grinned. "And don't worry about calling Johnnie. I'll do it for you."

Johnnie

I woke up parched on a short divan, my head splitting. California, I thought. The Garden of Allah Apartments again. The sunlight came through the blinds like sliced cheese. Unfamiliar cologne and the smell of chlorine tangled in my nose along with the reek of Camel butts and beer cans.

I raised up like a corpse from its coffin. The bed, a few feet away, looked so tight you could bounce a quarter off it. I also noticed someone had hung an Army uniform on the bathroom door. I must have insisted that my old pal Mark Wakefield take the bed, and then I remembered that I'd offered him my wardrobe for a lunch date with his girlfriend. Mark and I went way back to high school in Oregon, and I wondered if he was hurting as bad as I was. We'd pounded it pretty hard last night catching up.

My wristwatch said two-thirty. It was guaranteed waterproof, but I shook it and stared at the numbers. My session date was less than an hour away.

My scraped knee throbbed. My boxer shorts on the floor caught my attention, and I recalled skinny-dipping with Mark and a bunch of other hotel guests who were as drunk as we were. Nothing improper. Bathing suits were outlawed here after dark.

A key scratched the door. Mark coming back? No, it was Morrie, wheezing and panting his way rudely into the room. How did this fucker find keys to my every hideaway?

He coughed and waved his straw fedora in front of him. "Holy god, this shithole should be fumigated." He rattled the blinds.

I shielded my sore eyes. "Yikes."

"It's called daylight," he said and watched me struggle upright. He looked hard at the bed, the hanging uniform. "Who's been here? The military police?"

"Clean your glasses," I said, and pointed to the door. "And clean up your thoughts. That's the uniform of an officer in the United States Army."

"Fuck, what is the guy?" Morrie inspected the decorations, the silver bars. "A hero?"

"Yeah, from my hometown. He dated my cousin."

"Tell him Korea wasn't worth it, and he should desert before they send him into another fiasco." He spotted a towel on the floor. "Holy god. Blood."

I rolled off the divan, used one hand as a fig leaf, and placed the other over my kneecap as I hobbled for the bathroom. "Swim party last night. Scraped my knee."

Morrie covered his face with his pudgy paws. "You're insane."

Under the shower, my thoughts started to take some shape. Wakefield's questions about my life since school seemed innocent enough. He knew I'd been married for a short time, but he'd heard enough about me swinging the other way to make him tentative, and don't ask me about tentative. Over drinks at Ciro's, a nightclub in West Hollywood, I told him about my relationship with Dorothy without divulging her identity. "Right now," I said, "I'm wigged over a lady back in New York."

Dorothy was heavy on my mind as I toweled off. Staggering out of the steam, I told Morrie, "Kilgallen keeps refusing my calls."

On the divan, he ranted behind yesterday's *Hollywood Reporter*. "She's got too much brains to get hooked up with the likes of a switch-hitter like you."

So much for managers offering solace.

While I dressed, he yanked my chain about being late for the session.

"Wish it was Columbia's studio on East 30th," I said. "The vaulted ceilings, those great acoustics."

"Well, it ain't." Morrie peered like a bullfrog over the paper. "It's Radio Studio in Fag City."

"How you talk."

"Speed it up."

"If you let me sleep once in a while, I'd be sharper."

"When you do find a bed," he growled, "you should be certified, the acts you commit."

This got my back up. I threw on my favorite shantung sports coat and said, "I want a vacation."

"You wouldn't know a vacation if I handed it to you on a gold record."

"I need time to compose."

"I've been telling you for months to take off and write more songs," he said.

"But you're always booking me."

"Only way to keep you out of jail."

I moved into his myopic view. "You ain't working on another movie deal?"

"God forbid." He jumped up as if partaking in some ancient vaude-ville drill. "You get a couple grand for fifteen minutes on the set."

Morrie was right about the easy pay, but I'd seen myself on film. As an actor, I was nowhere. I adjusted my dark shades and hearing aid and strode forward as if I were born on Sunset and Vine.

Surprisingly, Morrie lagged behind. "Give me a good session today, Johnnie," he said in his softer voice. "And we'll leave for New York tomorrow."

"Solid," I said, and shot him a grin. "I'll rest back there, get into shape."

"You'll drink and fuck your brains out."

"No, I won't. I'll have Dorothy."

He lifted his heavy brow. "So?"

"She's different, man."

"How?"

I forced myself to ignore the fact that she had refused to speak to me since she limped out of my apartment that morning and told him what I knew in my heart. "She wants to give me something for nothing in return, and that's about as rare a thing in this world as anybody can hope for."

In his salesman suit, he waddled past me on the sun-splashed tiles. The air smelled like citrus and the coconut oil from the starlets basking poolside. I put a hand on his shoulder and pointed back at the room.

"Errol Flynn shot his wad back in the room we're staying in," I informed him. "You missed the plaque on the wall."

"So did Ernest Hemingway," he said. "Let's hope they did it with a couple of broads and not with each other."

I watched him assume a bodyguard's lead and couldn't get over how old he looked compared to the earlier days. He was losing a bit of his hustle. Hell, I was too. I glanced at the marvelous sky. How did a town so full of beauty and youth mark you up so bad?

Looking back once, Morrie held his arms out in a beholding gesture. "Garden of fucking Allah," he said, reading the old hotel's sign. "God save us."

"Amen, Brother Lane."

■ ■ ■

I recognized Radio Studio from a few years back. The legendary orchestra leader and music producer, Mitch Miller, had sent me home after a couple of takes, first song out of the chute. I looked for our engineer Frank Laico, but he evidently wasn't at this gig. Mitch sneaked up on me as I was looking things over.

I went for a smile that almost broke my face. "What's happening, Beard?" Everybody called him Beard, so I knew he'd be okay with that, maybe even take it as a compliment.

He still looked like he could explain Einstein's theory to you in two languages. "We're going to make a hit today, kid." He pulled at his whiskers. "Ready to get back to being Number One?"

He'd done it for Tony Bennett and for Rosemary Clooney. He was even beating the rock 'n' roll crowd with his sing-along TV series. My eyes wandered. Ray Conniff and his band of musicians were a bright sight as they sent me smiles and hand gestures. This felt good. Conniff had been working on a bolero beat for me that I really dug.

Miller noticed my appreciation. "Pour your heart out for him, Johnnie."

We started out with *In This Candlelight*, and my voice glided nicely on last night's screwdrivers. Next came *Weaker Than Wise*. Miller went for a laugh and said it was the story of his life. I backed him down, laying the song out full of sugar. Then we swung into *If I Had You*.

Three on the menu offered and served, I thought, so good you could taste them. We were all happy at the break. The musicians jived, and the back-up singers joshed. Conniff sent a thumbs up to his orchestra and wiped my face with a purple hanky from his lapel pocket. "You really do let it rip, don't you, man?" he said.

■ ■ ■

Everything became a blur after the session. Mark Wakefield and his gal drove me back to the hotel. We popped beers in my room, poured them over ice, and toasted the times. Mark's girlfriend showed me her smile and told me she'd never had such an exciting trip.

"Jeez, you're a great singer." She beamed.

I uttered my *ah, shucks* and told Mark he needn't return my clothes. "They're from my sports line," I told him.

"Really?"

"Keep 'em." I didn't tell him they weren't selling like they used to. I blamed the lukewarm venture on Morrie. He had blamed it on Saul Rosen, our accountant. On the plus side, I owned more silk shantung from Hong Kong than Charlie Chan.

After they took off, I crashed on top of the bed in kind of a coma. I saw colors of ungodly intensity, heard sounds like huge cymbals falling from a great distance, ringing as they spun like coins in my head.

Ringing.

The phone.

I probably caught it on its last scream, because I had to say hello twice.

"'Bout to give up on you, Bones." The voice was a dark, vampy rasp.

"That you, Cornshucks?"

"It's the Shucker, sugar. How you doing?"

"Getting by. Where are you?" "The Apple, baby. Still at your place. Got a lady here wants to talk to you."

"Oh man, I ain't got time for games."

But she'd already put the phone down and was talking to someone else. After a silence, I heard a tiny "Hello." That clipped speech like she was afraid to let it out.

"What? Who is this?" I couldn't believe what I was hearing.

"Johnnie?" she said.

My throat closed up on me. "Dorothy?"

"Yes." I heard a nervous cough, muffled by a hand over the phone. She was calling me. My lady was calling me. I wanted to howl, but I could barely speak.

"My voice is gone," I said. "Gave it up in the studio today."

Silence. Then, "It's raining here in Manhattan."

"Reach out and grab some." I felt the strength of my voice return. "And hold on to it for me until I get there."

Dorothy

The Voice of Broadway, 1956. *"Elvis Presley just released his first gold album, and everyone knows it isn't going to be his last. His hip movements on The Milton Berle Show caused a frenzy. Marilyn Monroe legally changed her name, although no one thinks of her as Norma Jean Mortenson. And when will she become Mrs. Arthur Miller? Soon, I'd wager."*

Marilyn did marry Miller, the most unlikely of her unlikely matches. Grace Kelly gave up her film career for Prince Rainier III of Monaco. Dean Martin and Jerry Lewis broke up their comedy act. Johnnie did come back to Dorothy.

Their continuous partying only added to her joy, a desperate joy at times to be sure, but one unlike any she had known before. On *What's My Line?,* she continued wearing the mask in more ways than one. Her answers were quick, her questions clever. In The Voice of Broadway column, she reported the gossip as she always had and longed to write more serious pieces.

She and Johnnie attended *My Fair Lady,* the musical based on George Bernard Shaw's play *Pygmalion.* The Mark Hellinger Theatre appeared packed to capacity that night, probably fifteen hundred people ringing their applause and laughter through the place. Poor Johnnie kept fiddling with his hearing aid as if trying to dial out the static on a radio.

Afterward, they stood in the rotunda lobby with its fluted Corinthian columns and debated about whether the play were a true love story. Johnnie appeared oblivious to the stares from other theatrego-ers.

"It was perfect," he said. "Henry Higgins realized he had loved Eliza all the time."

"That's so like you," she replied. "Ever the romantic."

"Better ever than never. I had tears in my eyes at the end of the play, and I know they'll get married."

"Because Henry told her to fetch his slippers?" she asked.

"He was just kidding."

"What about the age difference?" She baited him a little. "Henry Higgins is old enough to be Eliza's father, and he's pretty bossy."

"We both know age doesn't matter, Dotty. Neither does bossy." He grinned. "And remember, Higgins panicked when he thought the girl had left for good. Couldn't live without her. He'd grown accustomed to her face." He sang that line softly and touched Dorothy's cheek. "She almost makes his day begin—"

"Shaw would be rolling in his grave," she cut him off, "if he had to witness what Broadway has done to his beautiful play."

"Well, Miss Kilgallen." He faked an expression of disapproval. "You're sounding about as cold and put-offish as some people say you are."

She knew what they said about her and wished he hadn't tried to tease her about it.

"Is that what you believe?"

"You know better." He grabbed her hand. "It was a bad joke because you hurt my feelings. I really do want Henry Higgins to marry Eliza."

"Well, maybe he will."

They left the theater and began walking down West 51st. The fall air barely turned their breaths into plumes, and they braved the climate coatless.

"The people who say I'm cold aren't used to a woman being as serious as I am," she said. "They think I'm a bitch because I want more than most of my fair sex will admit to wanting."

"I understand all that, Dotty."

"Do you really?" she asked. "Because I do want to win, I'll admit it. On the TV show, even in the parlor games we play at P.J. Clarke's. When I don't, I wonder why I didn't do better. Most people find that unattractive. They're more comfortable with Arlene."

"Arlene wants to win too."

"But she can hide the fact. I can't. Furthermore, I don't even want to hide it. My father always told me I could be anything I wanted to be, and I still think I can. I just got sort of sidetracked, I guess."

Johnnie wrapped his arm around her waist. "Do you feel sidetracked now?"

"Not when I'm with you." She looked up and realized she didn't have to explain anything to this man.

Taxi cabs honked. Their tires rushed along the avenue. Voices cheered, perhaps at them, for them. Yes, for the two of them. Dorothy and Johnnie had scored against the night. They had beaten the game again.

She found her breath. "Please," she asked, "hail us a cab."

He moved fast toward the curb.

"Johnnie Ray," a voice shouted.

"And Dorothy Kilgallen," another voice added.

Johnnie stood amid the Manhattan traffic. A cab stopped, and he held the door open for her.

"P.J. Clarke's," Johnnie said, and they were off.

They walked in, hand-in-hand and passed Roland Fairchild. He was talking to a couple of guys we didn't know.

"Keep walking," Dorothy whispered into his good ear.

She had explained to Johnnie that night at the Copa, that Roland was an art critic, and Clarice owned a well-respected *avant garde* gallery in the Village. Always overprotective of Dorothy's reputation, Roland had apologized for "going overboard," as he put it, and he'd promised to keep a check on his behavior in the future. She glanced at the empty glasses on his table and hoped he would remember that promise tonight.

Two drinks arrived at the table moments after they did.

"From Mr. Fairchild," the waiter told them.

"Send him and his buddies a round from Miss Kilgallen," Johnnie said.

Once the waiter left, Johnnie squeezed Dorothy's hand. "Why do your friends hate me?"

"Clarice doesn't," she said. "Roland is just more concerned than he should be. And, by the way, what about your friends?"

"Babe and Cornshucks consider you family. Saul says you're smart for a chick."

"But your hangers-on, especially Morrie, see me as the evil older woman."

"Let's not talk about Morrie tonight."

She lifted her drink. "A fabulous idea, Johnnie Ray."

He clinked glasses with her.

"Hey, Johnnie." Roland had managed to sneak up behind her. She turned and noticed that his hair passed his ears now. He had tried to grow a mustache to cover his thin upper lip and possibly tried to fill it in with some kind of pencil. "Thanks for the drinks, man."

"They're from Dorothy," Johnnie told him.

"Sorry we got off on the wrong foot, John." Roland shot Dorothy a blurry smile. "My wife and I, we just love this woman."

Johnnie squeezed her hand on the tabletop. "So do I. Love her a lot."

"Yeah, well, take good care of her."

Roland walked carefully in the direction from where he had come, and Dorothy kissed Johnnie on the lips in front of anyone who cared to watch.

"You just get better all the time," she said. "Where to next?"

"What about the Regency? My friend Rafael plays there. It'll help him a lot if I show up at the piano bar."

The Regency, where they could get a drink and later a room high enough to look down at her townhouse not far away.

"Let's end our night there," she said.

Outside, Dorothy leaned against Johnnie as they waited for a cab. The fresh air refreshed her.

Roland followed them out, drunker now. He stood on the other side of her, beefy in his khaki trench coat. "So." He narrowed his eyes at Johnnie as if taking aim. "Got any new records planned?"

"I sure hope so," Johnnie said. "I might be making another movie. My manager thinks it's good for my image."

Jailhouse Rock seeped out to the sidewalk from the tavern and seemed to drive the point home.

"Oh yes," Roland said. "The music business is so unpredictable these days. You ever think about doing another musical film?"

Johnnie nodded. "If the right one comes along."

"It's been a long time since *No Business Like Show Business,*" Roland said.

"Maybe *My Fair Lady* will set a new trend for musicals in the fifties. I bet it will run for a long time."

"Too bad Mary Martin beat you to *Peter Pan.*"

Bastard, Dorothy thought and shot Roland a nasty look.

Johnnie only grinned."I don't mind. I've never really liked Shakespeare a whole lot."

Roland gave Dorothy a noncommittal glance. She pretended to dig for a cigarette to keep from laughing. "I'd better be going now."

Roland took the first cab, she and Johnnie the second. She loved the intimacy of weaving through the congested streets tucked next to him.

"You look happy," he said.

She slid her hand into his and snuggled closer. "You were wonderful, darling. That line about *Peter Pan* was the best."

The mischievous glint in his eyes could mean anything or everything. "But I really *don't* like Shakespeare," he said.

Johnnie

I started to want more with Dotty, started to wonder if it was something I could pull off. She accepted me for who I was, even if I hadn't been able to accept myself. She gave me pure goodness that made me realize that a woman like this wouldn't care for me the way she did unless I was a whole lot better than I thought I was.

After the holidays, I felt sorry about not spending more time with my folks and my sister. I wanted them to meet Dorothy, but some things didn't always work out the way I hoped. I'd not caught up with Dotty since New Year's Eve, and today was January 10, my thirtieth birthday. Cornshucks came up to my apartment out of the snow, and we were having a taste when my drummer, Babe Pascoe, knocked on the door. As I started to open it, I told Cornshucks to hurry up and finish her drink.

"We're going bowling," I told her.

She and I joined Babe up in the front seat of his Fairlane. Morrie Blaine and my accountant, Saul Rosen, had been waiting for us in the backseat. Within minutes, we were tooling down Broadway.

Saul Rosen gave Babe directions to the bowling alley. Snow fell silently.

"Babe," I said. "Best you turn on your wipers."

I soon learned that Saul didn't know bowling from lacrosse. Morrie and Babe kept using the wrong lanes. A skinny-necked pinsetter popped up way down the lane and waved a tattooed arm. "You're on the wrong alley."

"They in the gutter," Cornshucks screamed.

For the fifth time, the bowling gestapo asked could I please control the colored lady. Her pink pedal pushers were so tight they appeared dark fuchsia where she was divided. The noise killed both my good and bad ears. I suspected a motive behind this venture, but what? Had I agreed to this torture when I was too drunk to refuse?

Saul Rosen clapped his hands and yanked his pants up above his waist. "Way to pick up that spare," he congratulated Cornshucks. Most of us were just having fun, but Saul, always truthful, tried to keep an accurate tally of each player's efforts.

Projected on a screen above us was my score pad with the lipstick kiss Cornshucks had planted on it. In coarse printing, she had added for all to see: *Bet you a blow job who'll win the next frame.*

I grinned and sang her some Lady Day. "Love will make you gamble and stay out *all* night long."

"Treat me right, baby, and I'll stay *home* every day."

People in nearby lanes stopped their deliveries and acted stunned. My voice broke loose, husky and wild. How I wanted to let it out of its cage.

"Crazy," Babe said, and shook his head.

◼ ◼ ◼

In the bar above the alleys, Saul Rosen's son-in-law joined us. Right away I smelled fish. The kid lacked his father's integrity. In his Brooks Brothers suit, he made Morrie look like a virgin when it came to hustle.

"We didn't forget your birthday, Johnnie." Morrie stood up in our booth and raised his glass.

The whole gang sang the song.

"Give him his present," Morrie told the son-in-law. Babe and Cornshucks scatted "Happy Birthday." I kept smelling carp from the East Side.

Son-in-law handed me a leatherette folder. "It's a prospectus," he said.

I gave the contents of the folder a proper gander. Most of it bore the mark of Saul. Numbers, projections, business shit. I spread out what they wanted me to see.

"Looks like something out of Madison Avenue," I said.

"Keep looking, Johnnie." Saul grinned. "We got the best illustrator to paint the rendering, finest graphic artist to design your logotype. See the sign in front of the building?"

"Johnnie's Bowl 'n' Bite," I read aloud. "I get the bowl. Where's the bite?"

"It's a bowling-dash-delicatessen," Saul said, without any real enthusiasm. "Combination-type place."

"You can see," Morrie said, throwing out a hand as if to display the building we were in. "How television has resurrected the sport."

The place filled up. Early evening, and the alleys thundered.

"We start a chain," son-in-law yelled into my hearing aid. "It's called franchising."

"Place where you can bowl a few lines," Morrie shouted above the roaring echoes. "Then relax with some lox and bagels."

"Say what?" Cornshucks jumped up. Her enormous teeth flickered gold and ivory. "Sounds like a fool scheme to me."

Babe Pascoe stood as well. "Let's get out of here, Cornshucks" he said, "and let these guys talk business."

I sat back down and wondered how much this birthday was going to cost me.

"It will only take me a minute, Babe," I said. "Wait for me outside."

■ ■ ■

A minute was about all it took to get me in the Bowl 'n' Bite business. Saul had always done his best for me, and my clothing line had sold well, at least at first.

Babe and Cornshucks took me to their favorite tavern, a place called Tabby's on 52nd. People came in shaking snow and ducking in out of the swirling rush hour. Night had started to fall, but the sky had that odd cast like it was about to turn solid white.

Babe bought me a birthday shooter and introduced me around. I started looking for a phone to call Dotty.

"This is your year, Johnnie," Babe said. "Morrie's got us lined up for a world tour."

"Gives me nightmares," I said.

Two broads walked in smelling like French perfume and winter. They adjusted their furs and flicked their hair. I caught them smiling at me and gave them my all-knowing look. They both raised their eyebrows like how did I know they were together—really together?

In no time, Babe began to tell them a story how over in London at the Dorchester, I ended up naked, pounding on the door to Paul Douglas's room.

"You were nude?" one dish asked.

"Buck-assed," I admitted, although any memory I had of that night had been enhanced by fiction.

"Paul Douglas, the actor?" the other one asked. Then, out of the side of her mouth, "You were interested in him?"

"You ever see Paul?" I asked.

"Not in real life."

"You take the biggest bear in the woods," I said. "He mates with the wild witch of the north. And you got your Paul Douglas."

They cracked up. I moved off to find a phone. In the tavern's doorway, I thought I spied Liz Montgomery and her new actor husband Gig Young. Maybe I was drunk or hallucinating, because they looked right at me, then danced back onto the sidewalk as if rehearsing a scene. Then a shiny, shaved head appeared. The guy could be a twin of Yul Brynner, fresh from his performance in *The King And I*. Something felt off here. Too many coincidences.

Then I saw Dotty. My eyes filled up, and I felt for a moment like I were flying through space. Less than two weeks since we'd been together, and I already missed her like crazy. Next to me now, she threw her arms around me. "Happy birthday, darling," she whispered. "Surprise."

I buried my face in her dark hair and looked past her out on the street. There stood Liz and Gig. They and others, her friends, my friends, jumped in and out of a bus, laughing, drinks in their fists.

"Get in your shuttle, Johnnie," Dorothy said.

I looked at Babe and Cornshucks. "You knew all along, didn't you?" I asked them.

"Just get your skinny ass onboard," Cornshucks said. "We're right behind you."

Liz Montgomery grabbed one arm, Yul Brynner the other.

"First stop, the Colony," Yul said.

"Then Le Pavilion," someone added.

Dorothy took my face in her hands. "Then the St. Regis, the best for last. All your favorite places."

I didn't tell her they were her favorite places, not mine. I was too happy. I could sense that she was waiting for my reaction. I paused on the shuttle's step-up and took a cocktail from an outstretched hand.

"I'm all yours," I said, and I watched her smile in the falling snow.

Dorothy

The Voice of Broadway, November 3, 1957:

Whatever's happened to the year? In 1957, we've embraced West Side Story, a musical about street gangs, no less. We've added words like Sputnik and Frisbee to our vocabularies and removed (not a moment too soon) others like Edsel. It must indeed be true, as Jack Paar says, that time flies when you're having fun. Jack's having fun, taking over the Tonight Show from my former What's My Line? cohort, the multi-talented Steve Allen. In entertainment as well as in world affairs, this year has been a veritable whirlwind.

Speaking of whirlwinds, Johnnie Ray continues to wow audiences in Europe, causing as big a stir over there as French import Brigette Bardot is causing over here. In June, he wowed England, then Rome again, now Germany. He did find time between trips to catch "The King and I" three nights in a row. I understand that he and Yul Brynner came up with hand signals so that the Cry guy could let the king know from his seat whether or not the Yankees were winning. Only in show business!

Johnnie

I came back from my '57 European tour on top of the world. Morrie had me on an itinerary so crazy even *Confidential* magazine couldn't catch me. Still, the mongers linked me to sex-crazed sirens, swishy counts, every sheik and Sheba wanting their face on a scandal sheet: "Half-ass Celeb So-an-So, shown here with singer, Johnnie Ray, the Prince of Wails."

The term, "rock'n'roll," was being tossed around, and I figured like most everything else here, it originated underground, probably at The Flame.

"Hardscrabble honky come to Detroit City," the great Jimmy Witherspoon had chided me back then when I was opening for him. "Sings the blues like Al Jolson crying for his mammy."

"Who's Al Jolson?" I'd asked. Not for laughs, but because I really didn't know.

Last week some stiff-assed Brit stuck a mic in my face and told me I was the father of New Music. "Shucks," I said. He wanted my opinion of Elvis. "Al Jolson, crying for his mammy's grits," I told him.

Morrie called while I unpacked. "Today's *Times* has your pic and says you broke the Palladium's numbers," he said in salutation. "By the way, you're booked Friday and Saturday in Chicago."

I felt lost in my own flat. Traffic noises drifted up from 55th and Broadway. I started flipping stuff back into my bags. "You and Saul," I shouted into the phone. "Dig up some of that money from your backyards. I need the bread."

"We got no backyards," Morrie reminded me and hung up.

Sitting bedside, I worried. Blue devils rang in my hearing aid. I needed a drink. I needed Dotty. I dialed her townhouse. Her butler answered the ring. "You wish to speak with Mrs. Kollmar?"

"Come on, Julian, get the lady," I said. "I'm falling apart over here."

After a silence, her heels on that cold marble, then her soft "hello," and I could smell the lavender.

"I'm back," I announced. "Flying to Chicago tomorrow. Come with me."

"When is our flight?"

"That's my baby." The closet mirror sent me a look that must have matched my boyhood smile back when life was full of freedom.

"One condition," she said.

"Ask."

"We can catch Lenny Bruce. You're friends, aren't you?"

"I knew him before he was considered a satirist," I told her, "back when the only way a comedian could use language like that was at a stag party. What do you want with poor Lenny? Everybody's been trying to bust his balls since he started."

"Is that what you think of my column?" she asked.

"I remember how rough you were on me."

"That was before."

I threw an honest-to-Christ laugh at my reflection. "Well, all reet. Maybe I can warn the poor boy in time."

■ ■ ■

In Chicago, Dorothy and I imbibed a tad heavily after my Friday gig. After making it through the back-to-back performances Morrie had committed me to on Saturday, I sprayed my throat with a vodka atomizer and popped aspirin for my tin ear. Strange, the noises one could hear from one's deaf side. By the time we caught a yellow and headed for a small club called The Cloisters, I was motating on fumes. Next to me, Dorothy lifted my hand and guided it under her skirt.

"Touch me," she whispered. I sneaked a feel. Her hazel eyes watched mine. "I can't wait to see Lenny Bruce," she said, her breath warm against my face. "He's post-existential."

"Post-existential," I repeated. Lenny would need a hand job himself over that.

Inside the club, we drank doubles served by a cocktail girl, hair in her face, runs in both net stockings, and no idea who we were in the darkness.

I winked at Dorothy. "Not my kind of town."

"*Sawr* a man dance with his wife here once," she sang. "And it wasn't that bastard Sinatra."

Not wanting to get into that sore issue, I excused myself.

She caught my sleeve to stop me. "I've heard that Lenny Bruce can be venomous," she said. "Please come back soon. Protect me."

"I'll do better than that," I told her. "I'll let him know we're here and ask him to keep it cool."

Backstage I found Lenny in a suit that looked metallic, no tie, and a polka-dot shirt with a big, high collar like Billie Eckstine wore.

"Twerp," I said. "Last guy I met named *Bruce* tried to kiss me."

He gave me a peck on the cheek. "Unfuck you, man. Last kiss you turned down was from Ethel Merman."

Two wrinkled suit types tried to pamper him.

"House is loaded with law," one of them said. "Best lay off the fag shtick, or they'll arrest you for outraging the public decency."

"Unfuck them too," Lenny said. "If I planned every word that came out of this mouth, I wouldn't sound the way I do, dig?" He leaned forward and kissed my cheek again. "Thanks for coming, baby."

"I'm here with Dorothy Kilgallen tonight."

"What the fuck?" He made a face. "Can't picture you in that square scene."

I flinched. "Easy on her, Lenny. She's cool. Keep her on your side, okay?"

"That ain't the way I work." He smiled, and the gray suits shoved him toward the wings.

I rushed back to Dotty, most of the people in the darkened club aloof to my six feet of ungrace. A few rubes spotted me and buzzed. Obviously they had picked Dotty out of the crowd too.

She seemed upset when I joined her at the small table. "You were gone a long time." Her face looked tight with tension. "Did you tell him I'm here?"

"Yeah." I brushed back my hair and gave her my cornpone expression. "He promised to tone it down."

Then Lenny found the spotlight. Furious applause greeted him. I knew that kind of applause. Standing sideways to the house, he turned his face, full portrait as if amused to catch three uniformed Chicago police officers leaning against the far wall.

Lenny shaded his eyes. "I'm gonna get shot, burned, and hanged for this," he said. "But give 'em the light over there."

Everyone followed the spotlight until it landed on a dick in plainclothes who'd joined the lineup of fuzz along the back wall. Then their gaze returned to the lighted stage. Lenny bared his chops like a Bronx pimp.

"Granite." He popped the word into the mic. Most of the patrons knew he meant the cops' faces. "A Mount Rushmore of cocksuckers."

Even I ducked at that word. Dotty blushed. Under the table, her hand felt warm in mine.

Lenny removed the mic from its stand with a swipe. His delivery became machine-like, too fast to follow. People sat still as stone, as if in a sort of rapture, a deep concentration to stay aboard the rapid train Lenny had put them on.

"My tongue," he said, "has just outrun my mind." He seemed pleased by the applause. "Some of you must know what I'm talking about over here." Then he began to rant.

"Look at him," I said to Dotty. "His voice is popping like Babe Pascoe's drums."

"Unreserved," she replied, as if writing a column in her head. "Unrehearsed, and uncensored."

Lenny's gunshot delivery suddenly stopped.

"Speaking of cocksuckers." He moved across the stage and pointed them out to the crowd. "Let's have the light on the incomparable Johnnie Ray and his lady, the Voice of Broadway, Dorothy Kilgallen."

The joint split its seams. Even the cops thawed and started clapping. Lenny had won them over.

I nodded at him, heedful there was a price for taking his thunder. He would want payback. In his mind, he had immortalized us. Dotty flashed a grin at me, then at Lenny, and the heart of the night began beating rapidly again.

But Lenny wouldn't let go of the roll he was on.

"Hey, Johnnie," he called out. "Have you heard that bisexual is the new faggot?"

I shook my head. Lenny continued his diatribe. "Gays claiming to be bisexual. Holy shit. Next thing you know, Shirley Temple will be calling herself a virgin." He grinned at me again, eyes pure challenge.

Dotty shifted in the booth and didn't meet my eyes.

"Hey, that's just Lenny," I whispered to her. Still, her smile looked forced.

At noon the next day, I gazed down at Chicago's Loop district from our room in the Morrison Hotel. Forty stories down, anonymous people scrambled toward the deep blue of Lake Michigan. In the early fall glare of the window, I thought about our partying the night before and tried to remember if I had subjected Dotty to anything too outrageous.

Let's see. At an after-hours joint on the Southside, we had caroused with Lenny and his wife, Hot Honey Harlow, part doll, part gangster moll. Then, far into the early morning, I had sung *All of Me* and *I Can Dream, Can't I?* Then, *God Bless the Child*, feeling as much like Billie Holiday as Johnnie Ray. After that, I channeled Billie non-stop and got most of the group who had gathered round the piano to sing along.

A moan from the bed joined mine. Dotty, lips parted, raked at her hair, an onyx-colored halo on the pillow.

"My fault." I pressed fingers into my skull.

Her eyes opened, laced with panic, then she seemed to relax.

"Good morning." Her voice sounded smoky and dry. She propped herself up and stared at me for a long time. Then, out of the blue, she asked, "What's it like being with a man?"

I froze. Played it deaf and dumb without my wires.

She straightened a pillow behind her. "What I mean, of course, is what is it like for you? I know what it's like for me."

I just looked at her, speechless.

"I know you can hear me, Johnnie. I'm just asking if you think the business you're in gives you the license to behave bizarrely in any way you wish?"

I felt my cheeks heat up, but I kept my voice calm. "You want to know what it's like for me, or you want to know if I think I have a license to be bizarre?" I asked. "Which is it?"

"With those people last night, I saw something." She ignored my question. "A desperation you all seem to share."

"Yeah," I agreed. "I saw some of that too. I saw Lenny pretty desperate to make a three-way with his wife and the black chick from the Sunset Club. And I saw some desperation in those talented musicians snorting heroin through pink cocktail straws." I didn't embellish this with how Dotty had destroyed the career of tenor man Tiny Walsh in print for doing just that.

"Spare me," she said.

"Hey, I'm agreeing with you. Out amongst 'em, without a gig, without a dime, without a hope—sometimes it can get a bit bizarre, as you put it."

"You're saying it goes with the territory?" she asked.

"I'm saying last night you saw nothing compared to how it can really get." I knew I'd better shut up, but I couldn't stop the flow. "Sometimes we want to be loved so bad we love each other. Maybe that's it."

She pulled the sheet closer. "But last night wasn't about that. It will take years before people catch up with Lenny's brutal type of satire."

"That's the way it happens for the real innovators," I said. "In the meantime, every comedian will be influenced by him from this point on."

"He really needs to be careful. They've got laws against innovators in this country."

I knew she meant me as much as Lenny.

"They've got laws about a lot of things in this country," I said, "including what you and I are doing right now."

"There are no laws where we're concerned, Johnnie." Light struck her flesh. I couldn't believe her marriage to someone else, her kids, her other life. "With us, there are no rules."

I moved inches from her face. She reclined against her pillow.

"Are you going to prove that?" I asked.

"Oh, yes."

Below me, a smile teased her lips. Our hangovers would hit really hard soon, so I didn't wait.

■ ■ ■

Dotty's friend, Clarice, had come to Chicago with us and spent most her time visiting galleries. Lucky for us, she showed up at the hotel with our return flight tickets. In the air, Dotty and I drank tiny bottles of Smirnoff, enough that Dotty became bleary and nauseated.

"Maybe we should slow down," I told her. "You have to make *What's My Line?* tonight."

"That's why I have no intention of slowing down," she said.

As we stepped off the plane, we got looks from people, as if they hoped we'd lose control and make their sighting of us bigger than life. Roland waited at LaGuardia to pick up Clarice and offered us a ride. I caught one look at his barracuda grin, refused his offer, and waved down a taxi.

In the cab, Manhattan loomed, its sundown glinting off limestone and glass. Dotty was antsy, hyperventilating, and don't ask me about hyperventilating.

"Wish I had a pill that could help," I said, "or a paper bag for you to breathe in."

She rummaged through her purse, found a small vial, and shook out four capsules. "Doctor Feelgood," she murmured.

I glanced at the cabbie's pencil neck. He seemed oblivious to our sinful ways.

"How do we get them down?" I asked her.

"Voila." She came up with a two-ounce Smirnoff. "The incredible shrinking Russian."

CBS Studios waited minutes away. Skyscrapers split the air, and dry-cleaned suits rushed everywhere. I still felt drained from trying to explain my randy ways to the lady this morning. Cars passed in the evening, and their lights formed a swirling galaxy of stars all around us. Dotty almost nodded off next to me, her face serene, as if satisfied life would go on for us, although I was an old thirty-one and she eleven years older, more than keeping up in her high heels.

Pencil-neck cabbie turned and flipped his words back to us. "I got some dynamite pot I'll let go cheap," he offered, and I realized nothing ever really ended.

Dorothy

They returned from Chicago, and again Clarice suggested that she and Johnnie needed to be "more subtle."

"Is that your concern or Roland's?" Dorothy asked.

"We both love you," Clarice said.

That Sunday, Dorothy held up the Kilgallen end of the panel on *What's My Line?* The following week's show didn't go as well.

After being notified that she'd been chosen to ride in Queen Elizabeth's procession from City Hall on the weekend, Dorothy had a closed the Stork Club with Ernest Hemingway the night before the panel show.

Simply put, she was exhausted. Her head buzzed throughout the show. She blew two easy guesses, giving one to Arlene, the other to Bennett Cerf. On her way backstage, somebody mentioned that Alistair Parker, the show's producer, was looking for her. That couldn't be good.

She took a seat before the makeup mirror and smiled at Marie's stern reflection.

"I wasn't that bad, was I?"

"Anyone can have an off night."

She smoothed a drape over Dorothy's beaded gown. "Mr. Parker was back here looking for you tonight. Himself."

"Indeed." Dorothy gave herself a moment to regroup and watched her own image in the mirror as Marie began removing the heavy stage makeup. She needed to cut her hair again, do something about the puffiness beneath her eyes. "Let's hope he didn't catch my humbling performance."

"He said he'd be back after the show."

"Let's leave on the rest of the war paint," she said. "And thanks for the warning, Marie. Arlene has had a bad day or two, and no one utters a peep. Let me screw up once, and they're out to get me."

"It's because they're jealous of you." Marie handed her the box of tissues. "If you're going to keep the makeup tonight, I'll leave a little early. Is there anything else I can do before I go?"

"Perhaps we could go through the fan mail. Anything good?"

"I peeked at a few of them," Marie said. "That club owner from Dallas sent flowers again. Over there."

Dorothy turned to look at the extravagant carnation arrangement. "What's his name, Rudy?"

"Ruby," she said. "Jack Ruby. The flowers should cheer you up."

"Did you read what Hemingway said about me?" she asked, addressing Marie's reflection again. "How much he loved my work on the Sam Sheppard case? We drank champagne all night and closed the Stork Club. Jack Kennedy was there, but that's, as we say in journalism, off the record."

Marie glanced at the clock. "What do you want to do about Mr. Parker?" she asked. "Are you sure you don't want me to stay?"

"You run along now," she said. "And to hell with Parker. I'm going to meet Johnnie at the Regency."

The Regency's lounge was packed, but when the bar manager caught sight of her, he seated both Johnnie and her at the piano bar. When their drinks arrived, they clinked glasses.

"To us," he said, his face almost boyish.

Murmurs ran along the half circle of patrons seared around the piano, and she realized some of the voices buzzed about her and Johnnie. This was her territory, her turf. She had met men here before, friends and colleagues involved in her career. On a few occasions, when the drinks numbered too many, and the night stretched into morning, she had slept in one of the hotel's rooms. Always alone, except now when Johnnie shared her room.

Now Raphael sat at the keyboard. His hands began to move along the keys, and a smooth line of what she thought of as martini notes began to riffle along the bar. He acknowledged her with a bright smile.

"Good to see you again, Dorothy," he said in a soft accent. "May I play something for you?"

On the other side of Johnnie, a pair of young men laughed, and Johnnie turned to smile at them. "*All of Me.*" She drank the rest of her vodka tonic as her requested tune came to her, plaintive and oddly from far away.

Piano music blended with their voices. *All of Me*, one of the songs Johnnie wanted on the new record. When they finished, and Rafael played with a final flourish, all at the piano bar applauded.

"Lovely," she told Rafael, testing her voice.

The Regency was closing. It had to be close to two. She'd lost a chunk of the night. The help milled about, no one paying much attention now that the music had stopped. Only Rafael acknowledged their existence.

"Encore," he said. "One more, JR. Let's sing."

All the pretty boys, they all loved her Johnnie.

"Not tonight, man." Johnnie turned his attention to her. "Had enough, Dotty?"

"Never." Her black bra strap slipped over her shoulder, and she tried to push it up. "Have we eaten?"

"No, and we need to get you something."

"I'm fine." She gave the stubborn strap a solid yank, a tacky maneuver, she thought, adjusting one's underwear in public. She slid gingerly from her seat at the piano bar, and sought out the floor with uncertain feet. Oh great, she had taken off her shoes again.

Rafael left his perch at the piano, and in moments, was at her side. "Freshen that for you?" he asked, and took her empty glass.

His voice was soft and friendly, his eyes dark in the dim room. Only his defiantly shaven head differentiated him from all the other young hopefuls sitting at pianos in clubs all over town. That smooth, tan slope of his head gave him a masculine look that belied his delicate hands and slender pianist fingers.

She gave him the public-Dorothy smile, the prim one she used when asking if she might examine the label of one's jacket when guessing an occupation on *What's My Line?* "How very thoughtful of you." She turned to Johnnie. "Want a nightcap before we go home?"

"I'm game if you are." He rose from the bench and turned to Rafael, who had somehow become, in this unreal world of afterhours people, their bartender. "One for my baby and one for the road, right honey?"

"All the way," she said. Life was good when they could joke about Sinatra lyrics. Life was good, period, although a little fuzzy around the edges at the moment.

She longed for the narrow, firm mattress of Johnnie's bed, the cool wash of pink neon over her flesh.

"Let's finish this and go home," she told Johnnie.

He pulled her closer. "Well, *all reet.*"

Rafael returned with a fresh drink. "Had to make it myself," he said. "Bartender's stoned out of his skull."

Dorothy took hers carefully in both hands, and sipped.

The very act made her feel better. They could always go home, and they would. The night didn't have to end yet. Morning would arrive soon enough.

She sank back down on the piano bench. "Join us?" she asked Rafael.

"I don't want to intrude." He eyed Johnnie, who still stood beside the bench.

"Your choice, man."

Rafael went his way. They went theirs. They walked out into the night, holding hands. "We could make this better," she told him. At that moment she mustered enough courage to tell the truth.

"Better how?" he asked.

"Simple," she said. "I'll try to put up with Rafael, Morrie, and anyone else you toss at me, if you try to put up with my friends too."

For the moment, it was as true as anything she'd said all evening.

"I'll try," Johnnie said. "Even that asshole Roland."

Johnnie

Somehow I managed to make it into 1958 alive. Mafia boss Albert Anastasia, had got bumped off in the barber shop at the Park Sheraton Hotel, same chair I sat in a few days before. Morrie said it was me they were after, and they just got the day mixed up. The Soviet Union launched Sputnik into space, using a dog to pilot its orbit of the earth. President Ike survived a stroke. In May of last year, I lost a shoe on the Ed Sullivan show between *All of Me* and *Yes, Tonight Josephine*. Then later, while performing a medley of *Cry, Just Walking in the Rain*, and *Should I Reveal*, the wire came off of my hearing aid a half dozen times. Sullivan told me he'd never seen a more gutsy performance and invited me back on the show.

Dotty was proud, and that got to me. Nobody, not even Morrie, cared more about my career than she did. No one believed more in my music.

In January, a team of sawbones wanted to do some surgery on my right ear, and I checked into the hospital. The place was a dump. I had Babe Pascoe smuggle me a taste of gin, and the staff got upset.

Surgery was a blur. I woke up punchy and asked for my lady.

"Who?"

"Dorothy Kilgallen," I mumbled. "This is my surprise for her."

"Earl Wilson's in the waiting room," a voice said.

"Who's Earl Wilson?"

"Hollywood reporter," the attendant said. Then, "You know that."

"There ain't but one reporter, and that's Dotty."

Another voice. It was Morrie, and don't tell me I don't know the owl's hoot.

"Morrie?"

"Yeah, pal?"

"Speak up." I freed a trembling hand and touched a turban of bandages. Soaked in a rush of terrible pain, I felt terrified. "Oh, God, Morrie. Now, I can't hear out of either ear."

■ ■ ■

After a few hours, I got a bit of my hearing back, and my panic subsided. Dotty visited later that day.

She kissed my cheek. "You could have at least checked into Mt. Sinai," she said, "instead of over in this borough."

Walls spun, then came into focus. "I wanted to keep it a secret." I smelled her lavender and the thin whiff of vodka on her lips as she kissed me again. "Jesus, Dotty. I'm still the weird kid. I'm hearing harmonics, dinosaurs crunching up trees in some prehistoric recording."

"You'll be making your own music again, Johnnie," she said. "I'm working on lining up a session with Billy Taylor for you. Jazz standards. If Morrie can't make the deal, I will."

"Oh man. Let's hope I can hear Billy's piano."

Later they tried to keep her in the hall while they told me the surgery failed. She stormed past the nurses and conferred with the doctors.

"What's going on?" I asked her. "Give it to me straight."

"They want to try it again." Tears filled her eyes. "Another surgery."

"Oh fuck."

The doctors chattered. I attempted to read their lips. The room kept fogging up. They waited like a ghostly jury for my permission.

"Go ahead," I said, "but make sure you knock me out better than the last time."

■ ■ ■

A week after my second operation, I walked onstage at Philadelphia's Latin Casino, winging it without a hearing aid. Earl Wilson wrote in his column that show biz believed in miracles again.

Dorothy Kilgallen's column said my audience dug the drama. When I sent a grinning wink and snapped my fingers at the band, and when I came to the lyrics about dark clouds passing in time, there wasn't a dry eye in the house, she said.

In truth, I did it all by rote. By instinct. By mirrors. Dog-and-pony show with a one-trick star. Deaf as a post.

■　■　■

Cold day, light snow blowing with cinders. Winter birds scuffled in the downtown doorways. At my side, Cornshucks lifted her yellow galoshes out of the slush. Not wanting to lay all my woe on Dorothy and still determined to find a new ear, I had asked the Shucker to be my scout.

"Slow down." She almost slid off the sidewalk into the gutter. She swore a blue streak and refused my hand. Passersby gawked at her. Her manner of dress was indescribable. Think bazooms that could bring down Jericho. "Where we going?"

"I need amplification," I said.

"One thing you don't need baby, more amps."

"In my ear," I said. "First they took what was left of my left, then stole half of my right."

Cornshucks touched my left ear with her mitten. "Let's get you the most powerful tin ear they make."

I placed her mitten on my other ear. "My only hope now is this side."

"What are people going to think when you switch sides? They'll say you don't know your left ear from your right."

"What?" Clamor of traffic and street hubbub crested like the Lost Sea in my head.

She shot me a sweet smile. "Let's head over to West 52nd. I know a place that allows white guys."

"Bet you do." I worked on a grin. "Now you're coming in loud and clear."

We continued along the wet sidewalk, and I scatted a free-flowing chorus of *Whiskey and Gin*. She joined in. I had forgotten how pure she hit those high notes. Then to my astonishment, she pulled a joint from some fold in her garb and set fire to it with a big Zippo.

"What are you thinking, girl?"

"No big thang. Used to be, you could do this along here, no hassle."

"You're kidding."

"Don't be all hinky now."

We walked the midtown stretch between Fifth and Seventh. Brownstones were modified into street-level clubs. Under dark marquees, they sulked in the cruel daylight.

She halted and stomped her galoshes. "Sang here in the Club Onyx the first night Joe Helbock moved it from over there."

I followed her pointing finger.

"Used to be a speakeasy that side of the street." Her gaze turned dreamy. "First night booze was legal after Prohibition. First night they'd bust you for this." She held up her reefer.

"How old were you?"

"It was the summer of thirty-seven. Guess I was 'bout fifteen."

"Lord." I reached for her.

Her grip on my hand could have been a small girl's. She looked off and moaned low in her throat. "Club Onyx. The Famous Door. The Hickory House. All mostly for whites, but there's still a bit of my voice around here."

We looked at each other, both of us lost in yesterday's echoes. I tried to imagine all she had sacrificed to just get in front of a microphone and tell the world who she was. With luck, maybe I could muster up just part of the courage she possessed. If I could get the session with Billy Taylor, I'd lay out everything I had.

Dorothy

Late that afternoon before the Queen's arrival, Dorothy took Johnnie to the Cedar Tavern, a Greenwich Village drinking hole Clarice had introduced her to. Johnnie was instantly charmed by the dark interior and friendly bartenders. It was obvious from the smiles and double-takes that everyone in the place recognized them.

Morrie called the next morning as she was leaving to cover Queen Elizabeth's visit. Johnnie, she thought. Something must be wrong. One white glove on, the other still in her hand, she almost yanked the phone from Julian.

"Is he all right?" she demanded.

"Oh, he's just fine, thanks to you," Morrie said. "Couldn't you have picked out a bigger hearing aid? He'll have to push that one around in a wheelbarrow."

She felt the tension leave her chest. Johnnie was fine. He and Miss Cornshucks had gotten high when they were supposed to be shopping, and she had no choice but to step in and help in the hearing-aid quest. Although her selection was a bit cumbersome, it was supposed to be the best on the market.

"At least he'll be able to hear when he records *'Til Morning* with Billy Taylor. I should think you'd be pleased by that."

"Got the album named already, do you? That's why I'm calling." Morrie's nasal voice took on a wounded quality. "We need to talk, you and me."

"I'm sure we will," she said. "I can't imagine how we can avoid it."

"I'm just concerned." His voice rose, then she could hear him force it down, trying to mimic her frigid tone. "Concerned about you butting in on this latest recording deal you set up for him."

"Butting in, my ass," she said, before she could stop the profanity. "I created the deal. If it were up to you, he'd still be throwing his money away in that stupid bowling business. You should be glad I'm not taking a cut of this opportunity I've secured for you."

"Oh, you're taking one, all right, lady. You're taking a big cut, and we both know it."

She started to tremble. This nonsense had her wishing for a valium to quiet her nerves, but it was too late for a pillsky now. Julian appeared in the doorway. If he'd heard her outburst, he gave no indication.

"The driver's waiting, ma'am."

She nodded, then spoke icily into the phone. "I want what's best for Johnnie, and you'd better just get used to it. I'm going to be around for a long time."

"We'll see about that."

"Yes," she said. "We will. Now, if you'll excuse me, I have a queen to meet." She handed the phone to Julian, without waiting to hear Morrie's response. Still working her right hand into the glove, she hurried out the door.

Johnnie

I walked onto the *Dick Clark's Saturday Night Show*'s debut wearing the new hearing aid Dotty had gotten for me. First star I glimpsed was Pat Boone, doing the bump and grind with a plastic ring around his hips and a grin on his Sunday school teacher's face.

"Hula hoop," he said. I walked by him, showing him nothing but boredom. "Yoo-hoo," he hollered after me. "Earth to Johnnie."

Before show time, Jerry Lee Lewis horsed around on the piano and kicked the bench behind him. Bam! Right into Dick Clark's shins.

All in all, the show was a hit, and I joined Dotty at Trader Vic's for a quick one. We ended up breaking our old record for Scorpions—dark rum, light rum, and triple sec, a little orange juice thrown in to help it go down. Before we got too smashed, she told me about my upcoming disc for Columbia.

"Billy Taylor has agreed to produce." She said his name as though she'd appointed him my new manager. "March third and March sixth. I got you two days between so your voice won't be taxed."

"Who negotiated that?"

"Not Morrie."

My little lady was getting tough over there.

■ ■ ■

Billy Taylor was a genius at lulling the best out of everybody. He greeted me at Columbia, those smiling eyes through windowpanes. "Hey, Slim."

"Hey, professor."

"You sane and sober?"

"Certified."

"Solid," he said, "because we're doing the real thing here."

Adrenaline splashed into my veins as he set up. He ran Gershwin over the keys, cigarette in his right hand, and soon, with his easy way of communicating his ideas, I'd scribbled out my own lead sheets.

In three hours, we laid out Gershwin's *They Can't Take That Away from Me*, Johnny Mercer's *Too Marvelous For Words*, and Sammy Cahn's gems, *Teach Me Tonight* and *Day By Day*.

Digging deep, Billy layered color hues on those standards that dissolved the static in my head and left it clear enough that by the end of the day, I was proud of the job I'd done.

After work, we smoked and chatted. The studio was dark, full of old voices and old refrains.

"You are blessed with a most distinctive voice, Johnnie." Taylor leaned against the wall so he could view the entire room. "Your *Day By Day* will ring in my head forever."

I felt my face turn hot. "Thanks for getting with Morrie. This session means a lot to me. Last week I thought my hearing had split for good."

"Morrie would have us doing *Hi Ho Silver,*" Taylor said. "It's Dorothy Kilgallen you should be thanking. She says she'll have you fronting Ellington before she's done."

"That would be a reach for a hayseed like me."

"You *are* a reach, Johnnie Ray." He rose from his dark corner. "One hell of a reach." He extended his hand. "See you in a couple of days. We'll wrap this gig in gold."

Right about then, I was feeling pretty good.

Dorothy

The Silver Wraith Rolls-Royce that Mr. Hearst provided her for the queen's visit was rumored to have set him back more than twenty-five thousand. Dorothy perched stiff-backed in its massive rear seat, slid off her shoes, and soothed her aching feet against the Persian lamb's wool. The sensuous gesture made her think again of Johnnie. He'd love this car with its gold fixtures and French walnut bar. Even more, he'd love watching her in this procession creeping past City Hall, just two cars behind Prince Philip's party and three behind Queen Elizabeth herself.

Tonight she would tell him all about the parade. She needed to keep his spirits up, get his mind off the failed surgeries and whatever propaganda Morrie was feeding him. At least Johnnie wasn't threatened by her involvement in his career. Quite the contrary, he loved it, and there was nothing Morrie Blaine could do about that.

Cheering crowds lined the streets as the royal procession passed. Clever the way her driver had inched in right behind Governor Harriman's group in a position of prominence. Sheilah Graham and the other reporters would be beside themselves. Randolph Hearst would know she'd done him proud again in print, and just maybe the publicity would keep Alistair Parker, her producer, at bay about her streak of bad luck on *What's My Line?* It was merely television, after all.

The crowd pressed closer and reached out in imploring gestures. They cheered as if grateful to witness such an event. Dorothy lifted her hand, palm facing her, in the slow circular wave of the Royal Family. At that moment, she felt like royalty. In her own way, she was royalty.

She met Clarice the following Thursday at the new apartment she'd found for Johnnie. Even the address was musical—163 East 63rd Street. Sunlight from the row of floor-to-ceiling windows greeted them, and Dorothy rushed to gain a view of the street below. One glance to her left, however, stopped her in her tracks. The wall she had hoped would be painted an earth tone appeared coated in an ivory white. An enormous abstract painting of black and white covered most of it.

"My god," she said, unable to hide her shock.

"Big, huh?" Clarice replied.

"I should have known you'd nix my idea of using a warm ochre for the wall."

"And how about the painting?"

"I wish you'd asked me first. I was thinking of something more subtle."

Clarice cocked her head and smiled. "You told me to use my judgment," she said, her voice soft and even. "So that's what I did."

This apartment for Johnnie would be her spot too, and she had been looking forward to choosing everything in the space, everything perfect for the two of them. She turned her back to the painting.

"We can change it, Dorothy."

She scoped the entire space. Maybe it wasn't so bad.

"I hate to second-guess you, Clarice. You're the one with the gallery. I just want to make this place perfect for Johnnie."

"Everything will work out."

"Truly?" she asked.

"Hell, probably not."

Their light laughter sounded like whispers in the large room. She stared again at the canvas and realized that it must be the work of one of the rising abstract expressionists.

A knock on the door broke into her thoughts.

"Who could that be?"

"Max the decorator, I should hope." Clarice threw open the door. "Max," she said, "it's about time."

Although he looked like an overweight undertaker, Max was considered the finest decorator in New York. Also the tardiest. Behind him, two workmen balanced a large carton.

He glanced past her at the wall. "Ah," he said, "The Kline looks marvelous. Does it not Miss Kilgallen?"

"I was just telling Clarice how much I love it."

"It's what this part of the room needs," Max said, with enthusiasm. "Graphic strength. It looks like a calligraphic oath against all that's mundane, don't you think?"

"I can't seem to take my eyes off of it." But how would she ever afford it? Franz Kline was the definitive abstract expressionist.

Clarice seemed to have read her face. "I'll need it back one day," she said. "Meanwhile it's insured to the gills."

Max's helpers went down to the street and toted up another monster-sized carton.

"The chandelier." He gestured toward the workmen and wiped his face with a handkerchief. "I wanted you to see it inside and be sure it's what you have in mind."

"Put it there." She pointed to a spot on the ceiling above where the table would go. To Clarice, she said, "It's absolutely massive, all cut crystal and burning candles."

"Well, not burning yet," Clarice said.

Dorothy again felt anxious. The chandelier had been her choice and hers alone. "Clarice," she said, "what do you think? Will it really work the way I'm hoping it will?"

"Sure it will."

Encouraged, Dorothy decided to show her the sample of fabric Max had designated for the sofa. "Now here's the test!"

"Did you choose the color?"

"Johnnie chose it."

"Then salmon pink is in," Clarice said.

Her own laughter could have been chimes in the vacant room. Max, Clarice, and the workmen stared at her. The color was perfect for the room, perfect for Johnnie. "It arrives tomorrow. We'll put it here." She extended her arm. "And the piano right there." Her heart raced as she walked across the hardwood. "The short wall here without any window is his personal gallery." She pointed out the several black-framed photos of Johnnie and the Queen, Johnnie and Lady Day, autographed photographs of Marilyn Monroe and Noel Coward that were stacked on the floor.

Max returned to the chandelier. "You couldn't find anything more dramatic," he said. "The dining table will go beneath it."

"A solid oak table," Dorothy told Clarice. "It's costing Johnnie a fortune. The chandelier's a gift from me."

"Do you want the bill sent to the same address?" Max spoke in the understated tone that people in his profession used to discuss large sums of money.

"That will be fine." Her secretary would just have to do some juggling this month.

"Of course," he ventured, as if sensing her hesitation, "we do have other styles, if you think this one's a little too large."

What he meant was *too expensive*. "What do you think, Clarice?" she asked.

"I think having what you want is half the battle."

"Would Roland like it?"

"Heavens no."

"That settles it," she told Max. "I'll take it."

"I know you won't be sorry," he said. "Marilyn Monroe and Arthur Miller bought a similar one."

"Indeed." She flashed him her *What's My Line?* smile. "I'll still take it."

■ ■ ■

Dick waited for her in the dining room when she got home. He held a drink in his right hand and stared at her with the squinting half-smile of someone who had spent too many hours in the dark.

"Where have you been off to?" He circled her like a large animal checking for scent.

"Out with Clarice."

"Spending a lot of time with her, aren't you? That trip to Chicago? All these afternoons?"

Her worn-thin patience snapped. "I have no time for games today. Say your piece, if you must. Just be sure you can sit down here in front of the microphone tomorrow and resume our show with a semblance of sobriety."

"Say my piece?" He drank slowly and watched her face. "Okay, then, I came home only because I heard something this afternoon that I thought might interest you."

"Such as?"

"Tyrone Power."

"What about him?"

"He died today. I thought you'd want to know."

His statement knocked the air out of her as surely as a physical blow would have. She gripped the chair in front of her and tried to steady herself. She once dreamed of marrying Ty. How different would her life be if she had?

"How?" she managed to ask. "He's so young." Her age, she reminded herself. He was her age.

"Over-exertion, they said, doing a fencing scene for his new film. His heart went."

She shook her head, barely able to speak, remembering the idol she'd often praised in print. "He tried to teach me to drive," she said.

"I know."

"He was just a sweet man, not at all the Hollywood type." She felt the threat of tears again, not just for Ty but, damn, for what? Dick looked helpless, awkward now with the extra weight he'd put on, his facial muscles working as if searching for something to say that mattered. "Thank you for letting me know," she told him.

He nodded, stone faced, and took another drink. "Don't worry about this." He tilted the glass toward her. "I'll be fine in time for the show tomorrow."

She looked at his lips, still wet from the liquor, his hunched shoulders and swollen belly, and felt an inexplicable rush of tenderness. "Good," she said. "I appreciate that."

She waited until he left, then poured a drink of her own.

Johnnie

Columbia let me know how happy they were with the results of my new album. Dotty was ecstatic. Morrie told me the beatniks would like it. I didn't ask him to explain that. The songs must not have been corny enough for "regular folk" like him. He had jumped aboard his own ship lately, thinking no doubt I'd become Dotty's puppet. As for me, I was proud when people I respected told me that Billy Taylor and I buried Sinatra's version of *Day By Day.*

Dotty and I celebrated by opening my new apartment. We'd walked through it before and made love at twilight on a boat-long sofa of pink velvet. Max, her two-ton decorator, had thrown enough earth tones around that I began singing *September Song.*

This hot Sunday in July, a bunch of us partied as we waited for Dotty's show to air. When I saw her off earlier, she looked bushed, and I had become apprehensive. *What's My Line?* could be a stiff work-out with those lights and close-ups. I drank cocktails double-fisted to relax. Morrie, who'd found his photo on my gallery wall, gave me a look and shook his head at my drink.

"That picture of me looks like a wanted poster," he said.

"Yeah, yeah." I rattled my ice. "That's the police wagon down on 63rd."

He lit one of his cheap cigars and gazed seriously out the floor-to-ceiling window. "Why do you throw these big parties?"

"So friends can drop by bearing gifts," I answered, "except you, you cheap screw."

He looked crushed. "Gladys brung that clay thing."

I turned and saw his washed-out wife nibbling at the spread I'd set up on the oak table. "An ashtray, Morrie," I reminded him, "you brought me a fucking ashtray."

He cleaned his glasses against his paunch. "Whatever. It's a Picasso."

"Yeah, and Sabrina over there is Rin Tin Tin."

Party time arrived. The air conditioner hummed. Hi-fidelity blasted away. The big black-and-white painting Dotty liked so much had everybody talking. TV was warming up for the show. I prayed for my lady and hoped she'd have a winning night.

Christopher George, who was trying to break into TV doing shaving cream commercials, strutted into the den and threw his arms around me. Morrie turned all prim and shook his wrist as George walked away. "Another Hollywood pansy?"

"Good friend is all." Knowing truth didn't always prevail, I pointed out the actor's gorgeous wife.

"Maybe he throws from both sides of the mound," Morrie mumbled. "Amby-dextry, like you."

I did what I didn't do often. I flared. "And maybe you pitch a bitch when your opinion ain't needed."

He turned around abruptly and bumped into Yul Brynner. Sabrina bolted from a nightmare and bit Morrie's pant leg. His wife jumped up and clutched him before he became an unintentional suicide out one of my widows. She sent me an anxious look. I took the opportunity to thank her for the Picasso piece.

"Really nice, Gladys," I told her.

She released Morrie. "It's a fake," she whispered.

"Don't worry," Yul said. "Nothing is real."

About then, Carol Channing bellowed, "*I've Got A Secret* is about to come on."

"*What's My Line?*" Fifteen people corrected her. She eyeballed us, looking like the Al Hirschfeld drawing of herself on my gallery wall.

I prayed again for my lady. Nothing in this racket came easy.

Dorothy

When Dorothy returned to her dressing room after the show, Alistair Parker awaited her, a picture of solemnity in a dark suit, oiled-down hair, and a scent to match. At least she had been able to ace the last guest before Arlene could get another question out of her mouth.

"Good evening," she said. "Did you catch the show?"

"Never miss it. I just wanted to say hello. We so seldom get a chance to chat."

They stood facing each other. Chatting was not something this man did well. His fair skin paled in the bright light of the room, and with his arms stiff at his sides, he looked mechanical.

"Forgive me, but I'm in a bit of a hurry tonight," she said.

"I know you're busy."

"Terribly busy. I'm covering Khrushchev's trip in September, you know." She gauged his reaction, unable to read beyond the expression of mild interest.

"Your schedule must be very demanding." He made it sound like an accusation.

"If you have a problem with my schedule, perhaps we should set up a meeting to discuss it," she said as pleasantly as possible. She'd promise anything, say anything, just to get away from him right now.

"Oh, this isn't an official visit." He moved closer to the door as if he too wanted to get out of this stifling room. "I just wanted to be sure nothing is bothering you."

"Implying?" The question slipped out, icy and swift.

"Dorothy." He now stood only a few feet from her, so close she could see the beads of sweat on his smooth forehead and smell the unctuous odor of his aftershave. "You know I have only the highest regard for your work." The insincerity in his words irritated her more than his presence. She crossed her arms in front of her and tried to ignore her throbbing temples.

"My work," she said, "isn't pleasing you?"

"You've been off, Dorothy, you know you have."

"As we all are on occasion." She hesitated, then went on. "If Arlene has a bad night or a bad couple of nights, no one says a word."

"That's not true. You know that I pride myself on my fairness. Both you and Arlene make your individual contributions to the show. You have different styles."

Now she had him on the defensive. She tried to sound hurt, injured. "Every time I open my mouth, everyone's hoping I'll make a mistake. I'm resented because of who I am, because of my competitive spirit, even because of my religion." Sweat glistened on his forehead now. Good. She hammered a little harder. "I'm the John Kennedy of broadcasting, discriminated against because I'm Catholic."

"Oh, come on, Dorothy. You're the one who kissed Bishop Sheen's ring on national television. You flaunt your religion."

"Why shouldn't I?"

"It's not your Catholicism that concerns me," he said. "And you're right. We probably need to talk about this later. I just dropped by to see if there was anything I could do."

He reached for the door. In a moment, she'd be rid of him and his sweet barbershop smell. "I appreciate your concern," she said. "But I do find it a trifle odd that you, this paragon of fairness, aren't equally concerned about others on the show."

His pasty face went pink as if she'd pinched it. "Others don't have problems with their speech, Dorothy."

That did it. How dare this sniveling little man in a cheap suit criticize her? "You're questioning my diction?"

"I'm questioning what it is that sometimes slurs your speech and makes it difficult to understand you, such as tonight, for instance." His face was now florid. "We can talk about it next week in my office. I'll have my secretary contact you to set up a time. Goodnight." He all but whispered the last word.

"Goodnight," she said, enunciating clearly, as he left.

She'd deal with his veiled accusations later, and if it came down to it, she'd walk off the damned television show. Her diction was flawless. He'd said it only because she'd bested him, as she always did, in their little battles of words.

Her makeup felt as if it were melting into her skin, and her parched throat ached for a cool drink. She'd deal with Alistair Parker later. Right now all she cared about was getting back to where she really belonged, back home with Johnnie.

Johnnie

Dotty's show was like watching the seventh game of last year's World Series. I kept pulling for the Yanks against the Braves, but each inning got worse. Finally, when the show was over, and someone had turned the music up, I thought only of how I might greet her, maybe console her if she needed it.

She arrived late. We all rushed to compliment her, to tell her she was marvelous. I suddenly realized how much of her weekly job was bona-fide performing. I'd considered it such a simple feat, not really an art, but that half-hour viewed by millions was one intense gig.

"I need a drink," she said, her small jaw tight, her lips a straight line.

I guided her away from the others. She still wore the gown and make-up from the show. I dabbed at a line of sweat under her nose.

"I ran into trouble in the dressing room," she said. "I'll tell you later."

I handed her a drink. "Big-time trouble?"

"Nothing I can't handle."

"That's my girl." I attempted to cheer her up.

"What's that new phallic symbol next to the TV?" she asked.

That got me a smile. "Remind you of anything?"

I made a big deal out of looking around her at the sculpture Max had delivered, a polished oak pole with a translucent globe on top, full of crabapples. We held onto each other and chuckled. Two lovers against the odds.

Things got sloppy later. Dotty bristled at the crude assessment a flamboyant young woman made about the interior of Dick's nightclub.

"And whom might you be?" Dotty demanded.

Miss Razzmatazz informed her that she was an associate of our decorator, big Max. Turning beet red, she apologized about her crude remarks. "I meant no malice."

Dotty counter-punched. "Your claiming my husband's club is an homage to Art Wrecko merely points out your ignorance."

One thing about Kilgallen, she'd defend the son of a bitch.

Diehards stuck around. Rafael sat at my new white grand, playing softly. Dotty drowned his sounds by playing a record by Dinah Washington, and later she told me not for the first time to get rid of him.

"His visa has lapsed," I told her. "He's waiting to go back to Chile." I kept repeating his bullshit like it was gospel. "He's heir to a winery fortune."

Dotty wasn't buying. When Rafael ceased playing to look our way, she kissed me open-mouthed, and I went along with it until she broke loose.

"Has he been staying over?"

Would she ever give up? "Using the spare bedroom 'til he's leveled out."

"Take me in there."

"There's still a few guests."

"I don't care."

I'd grown to admire this kind of behavior in her. It was as if she wanted to make a game out of being daring, wanted to see how far she could push it. I liked that, but it scared me.

"I don't know."

"And when we get in there," she said, "leave the door ajar. And whatever you do, Johnnie, don't hold back."

We staggered into the spare bedroom. Rafael's cologne tinted the air. I left the door almost all the way open and moved on Dotty like a horny teenager.

"Come on," she said. "Get completely undressed." She stripped fast, breathing hard. Past the door and the short hallway, the noises of the others beat like music. I reached for the glowing bed lamp.

"No, leave it on," she said.

The room now must have appeared to others as half lighted, half open. I felt that it was half closed up in another way, with barely a chance for escape.

12

Dorothy

The Christmas season was Dorothy's favorite time of year, especially this one, the last of the decade. She arrived at the Waldorf Astoria that night feeling like a movie star. With its cut-glass chandeliers and Erte-inspired décor, the Waldorf made any occasion seem like a holiday. Tinsel and elaborate garlands added to its allure tonight, and the mood of celebration was contagious. Two more weeks until New Year's and the party she had been planning.

She walked briskly behind the maître d', past the college boys in Brooks Brothers suits trying to impress their dates, through the seasoned New Yorkers, toward what Clarice called Celebrity Central. Beyond the waiters' station, she waved to John and Jacqueline Kennedy, who were taking a respite from the campaign trail. Farther along, she caught sight of Tennessee Williams and a friend deep in drink and conversation. Her territory, she thought, and took the space in. This was her beat.

Of course glances lingered as she passed. She never would have dared to wear such a revealing dress before she had known Johnnie. A double rope of pearls softened the deep neckline of her dress, a trick she had learned from Sophia Loren.

As she tried to focus through the swarm of faces, her momentum shifted. She reached out and tried to steady herself. The maître d' hadn't noticed. She took small, quick steps to keep up with him. The faces around her blurred. That damned anemia again. When was the last time she ate? She did her best to maintain a smile, thinking of Queen Elizabeth. No matter how many hours she had been standing or waving, the Queen always managed to make everyone feel acknowledged.

Then she saw him, Johnnie, dressed in a tux, glass held in mid-drink. He had ordered for both of them, the darling. The maître d' stood aside as she hurried to Johnnie. On his feet at once, he gave her a passionate kiss. She pulled away and felt herself blush.

"Damn, you're gorgeous," he said. "Your hair. What'd you have done?"

"I took a chance and had my stylist tease it."

"It's beautiful, you're beautiful. Sit down and let me look at you."

"Must be the ring." She flashed the rose quartz he'd brought her from Brazil and settled next to him. "It complements my black dress, don't you think?"

"It matches your nipples." He glanced down at her cleavage, then back up, gazing into her eyes, all mischief and sex appeal.

"Come now. It's not that low."

"But my mind is."

She heard a noise and turned to see a patient waiter at the table trying his best to look unobtrusive. "Well, hello," she said, and straightened the square neckline of her dress. And to Johnnie, "Care for some hors d'ouvres, darling?"

"Would I! But since we're in public, I'll settle for some food. Hell, I'll even go for a little grape tonight. You got to choose though."

They ordered and, when the waiter left, they huddled, heads close. He smelled of leather and citrus. The satin-trimmed tux smoothed out his angular body as if someone had gone over it with an iron.

From the side of their table, a voice shouted, "Smile."

Photographers. That was the one negative about the Waldorf. Johnnie turned like the pro he was, crossed his arms on the table, and took her left hand in his. She smiled into the lens and heard the click. Immortalized, she thought, the two of them, together.

His job over, the photographer slid back into the crowd, looking for other subjects. Johnnie leaned forward, his expression serious. His scrutiny gave her pause. She needed conversation, laughter.

"You must have gotten here early," she said.

"Couldn't stand the thought that you might have to wait."

"I got tied up making party plans."

He gave her a lingering kiss. And why not? No photographer would dare snap them embracing. Such irresponsible picture-taking happened only in British tabloids.

The wine arrived along with two shrimp cocktails. Johnnie lifted his glass. "To the sexiest woman in New York."

She clinked her glass to his. "And to the most handsome man who ever stepped out of a tux. The sooner, the better."

"Vixen." He moved closer.

"Wild man."

She loved the way they played in public, teasing each other with words and glances.

His citrusy scent tickled her nostrils. She felt breathless and silly, the way alcohol had once made her feel when she was new to it.

"Dorothy." He looked uncomfortable the way he sometimes did with her public displays, but she didn't care.

"What's the matter?"

"They're sending me to California."

"What?" He wouldn't desert her on New Year's Eve. He couldn't.

"Morrie insisted. I tried to tell you right off, but I didn't know how."

"That son of a bitch."

"Don't blame him. I'm a performer. This is what performers do. I'm lucky to have the gig."

"Lucky!" She took a swallow of cold wine. "Do you know how long I've been planning this party?"

"I'll call you the minute the show's over."

More wine arrived. A long swallow, she thought. Just cool off and get past the disappointment.

"You look pale," Johnnie said. "Why don't we order you a steak and send you home early for once?"

A minute ago he called her the most beautiful woman in town. Now he wanted to feed her before midnight and get rid of her. At that moment, an idea occurred to her.

"Is Rafael going to California with you?"

"Why would you ask that?" The hurt in his voice relieved her, but she couldn't be too careful.

"Well, he's living off you. He's practically your manservant."

"This is business," he said. "It's important to my career."

"And you'd perform on the moon if Morrie thought it was a good idea."

"He's my manager. I don't need another one."

"The same manager who got you into that stupid bowling business when he should have been worried about your recording career."

"Saul terminated the bowling deal before it cost me too much," he said. "Besides, that's my problem, not yours."

"Your lack of gratitude astounds me." She straightened in her chair and made an effort to speak clearly. "Do you want to sing *Cry* for the rest of your life? Then stick with Morrie. Spend your New Year's Eves in dives all over the country. Turn your back on everyone who loves you."

"I'm not turning my back on you," he said, his voice drained.

"You're doing just that, and you don't even know it." She fought tears. "The party's just a metaphor for what you're doing to me."

"Ah, c'mon, baby."

"Fuck this whole thing." The words stunned her like a slap across the face. Crude, unplanned, they couldn't have come from her.

"Dorothy." Shock etched his features.

Miss Kilgallen didn't swear in public. Miss Kilgallen didn't shout. The next thing she knew, she was twisting the radiant quartz ring from her finger. Amazed, she watched herself bounce it hard across the floor of holiday merrymakers, doing her best to smash it and all it meant to her, to both of them.

Johnnie

New Year's Eve Day, Garden of Allah. Again. I still couldn't get over that nasty spat last week with Dorothy, the way she had flung the ring I'd given her to the Waldorf's floor. Thanks to a busboy, she got it back and put it on her finger again. I gave the kid a twenty and told him that he'd saved my life.

"Fucking L.A.," I said to Morrie and tossed my bags onto the bed.

He and his cigar smoke followed me in. "Better than Frisco," he said. "There they got poetry readings, musicians playing jazz serums."

"Theorems."

"Same-o, same-o."

I plucked his cheek. "You're too much."

He collapsed on the divan. Half the flight's dinner menu speckled his tie. "Got you Errol Flynn's room again." He pronounced it *Earl*.

I scoped the place. By god, he'd done just that.

He pointed above the bed. "Last tenant painted a face over the still life. Portrait in oil of Papa Hemingway." He said *earl* again, this time for oil.

"It's New Year's Eve." I sighed. "And I don't know where we're playing tonight."

"The Old Earl Carrol Theatre." He finally got it right.

"One out of three," I told him. "Your Earls."

"Who?" He made a claw out of his stubby fingers and scratched his bald spot. "Anyways, the place is called the Moulin Rouge now. Frog décor top to bottom."

"I've seen the real thing in Paris."

"La de dah." He hoisted his ass out of a cushion. "I'll be back for you in two hours."

"I'll be ready."

He started to wave a fat hand, then let it drift, and he stood as if he'd forgotten his way. Afternoon light glistened in his magnified eyes.

"One thing I gotta give you, Johnnie," he said. "You're a pro."

I watched him fumble with the doorknob, began a thank you, but figured, no, it might confuse him.

Maybe it was him, or me, or the combination of the two of us, but the fun had turned to work. Low-paying work, a two-man chain gang.

After he left, I lit a Lucky and unpacked. I stripped and posed for inspection in front of the bathroom mirror. "You lean bastard," I told my image. "Still got your twenty-nine inch waist."

Under a blanket that smelled of bleach, I stared at the prism-like reflections on the ceiling from the swimming pool. No starlets wearing bikinis out there today. I struggled with dreams I didn't want, more half-dreams, then the phone rang. When I answered, my sister's voice sounded miles away.

"Elma," I shouted into the mouthpiece.

"I'm in Hollywood," she said, her voice muted. "With Mark Wakefield and his wife. We'll be in your audience tonight."

So Mark had tied the knot with his girlfriend. Gosh, I couldn't even recall her name. "Great. How's the folks?"

"Doing well," she said. "They loved the Christmas presents you sent." She paused. "So did I, Johnnie."

"Nineteen sixty will be our year." I said. "I'll make it home again soon."

After I hung up, I fell back on the bed with a current charging me. Voices and sounds roiled out there somewhere over the Pacific. I bolted from the bed, stood naked, and fought a strong desire to run to the sea and plunge into its foam. I heard lyrics about tasting my tears in the wild water, and somehow I managed to dig out my note pad and write them down. One day, who knew? Maybe I could write some real music.

■ ■ ■

Morrie drove along Sunset Boulevard in our rental. Less time than it took to smoke a Lucky, and we pulled in front of the theatre. Lord, it looked like the *Ted Mack Amateur Hour* out below the marquee, every wannabe star in town trying for the spotlight.

Safely inside, I barred the dressing room door. Everything was laid out as I'd asked, even the special polish I'd requested for my kangaroo shoes from Australia. I tried to make myself pretty. Adrenaline kicked in. I added two ounces of vodka, pounded the table with the pads of my fists, and scaled a voice exercise composed by Tarzan.

Only once did I allow myself to think about Dorothy's gala in New York. Then I stormed out the door, strode past a gauntlet of faces aglow with hate, wonder, and worship. In the on-deck circle, Babe Pascoe's drums rained on my tin ear. Morrie bobbed up looking like a balloon wearing goggles.

He cracked a smile. "Keep it mellow, kid."

"Tonight," I told him, "I'll rip it up with my bare hands."

Three hours later. No break. No notes or program lists. No mercy. I opened it wide, full throttle. Teased 'em. Kissed 'em. I hit their jive, Jack. I drowned my lonesomeness in their blood.

Then, after the sad midnight song, I wished them a Happy New Year. Exhausted musicians flashed me glances that said they'd remember this one. Everyone wanted to touch me. My name rushed on thousands of breaths. I cried on my sis's shoulder. I toasted the New Year with Mark Wakefield and his wife. I wrestled Morrie around in a bear hug 'til he laughed out loud.

Finally, I trudged back to my dressing room and suffered a coughing fit.

Alone, man. So fucking alone.

But not for long.

■ ■ ■

An hour later, the legendary stripper, my old friend Tempest Storm, rescued me from my forlorn dressing room. "Get your skinny ass away from that mirror," she squealed. "We're going to a party."

The bash was in progress at Chip O'Hara's home on Laurel Canyon Drive. Chip had worked as a PR man for me until he had his fill of New York winters. It wasn't snowing here. In fact, about twenty of us paddled around Chip's heated kidney-shaped pool. Phillip Matthews, another PR guy, was also there. Standing tall, with dark hair going bald, he appeared too decent a guy for a party like this. He came over, limping slightly, to where I was hanging onto the pool's short ladder. Then he greeted me and held out a glass.

"Gin?" I inquired.

"Club soda. I gave up the hard stuff after the accident." I remembered something about a car wreck but didn't warm to the idea of discussing the virtues of sobriety right then.

I slid back into the pool. On my left, Tempest Storm came up from under water. Sexiest stripper I'd ever seen. And don't ask me about strippers. On my right, Marcie, a young cohort of Tempest's, measured me under her wet lashes. Only thing anybody wore was the fog coming off the water. Holding hands, we dropped off the ladder. Tempest surfaced, throwing water from her long red hair. Her breasts rose like twin volcanic islands.

Poolside, we snuggled under beach towels, and Tempest and I laughed about old times in Detroit. Marcie shivered and stared at me with eyes so huge and clear I felt guilty about all the evil in the world.

"Remember the night I bailed you out of jail in Detroit?" Tempest asked me.

A vision came to me—her coming into The Flame, telling me she loved my act and wanted to take me out for a good time. An hour later, we were arrested chasing one another naked around the deck of some motel down the street.

"Yeah," I said. "You put up the bail, we hit the rest of the night broke, headed back to the jailhouse, and asked if they'd please keep us until morning."

That true story called for more drinks. We watched the nude revelers. I couldn't help noticing how Tempest and Marcie ogled the bare asses of the others. Two exotic dancers reversing their roles. My blood ran hot. Chip O'Hara was with some babe in the deep water. His on-and-off loverboy, an actor with violet eyes like Liz Taylor's, sat in a lounge chair not bothering to cover his erection. He kept looking my way, I guess because I'd not bothered to cover mine either.

Tempest told me that she and Marcie had caught a couple of my songs at the theater.

"You didn't go by the book," she said."Took my muzzle off."

Marcie squeezed the sides of my face so tightly that my lips popped out. She kissed them time after time until we traded tongues.

Every time she glanced up at me, I knew in her mind she thought she looked like Marilyn Monroe. More like Marilyn Maxwell, I wanted to tell her. Lovingly, because it would have been compliment enough.

Tempest allowed her towel to slide over her breasts. Boys and girls alike gasped.

"Don't lose your style, Johnnie," she said. "All we got is our style."

"You're gorgeous," I told her, and meant it.

"Remember." She poked a fingernail into my thigh. "You try to satisfy gray flannel, and you'll find black chinos are in."

"I promise to remember that," I said. Something told me it would become a resolution.

Tempest and Marcie left me alone with my vodka and a sore throat. I watched them go, Tempest's hair a wet mane down her back. I looked for Phillip Matthews and guessed Chip had rounded him up and taken him back to the corral where it was warm.

Marcie returned from inside, house lights defining her curves, spiked heels clicking on the stone deck. She wore tasseled pasties and a jeweled G-string, and seemed to be searching for sorrows of her own.

"Tempest was picked up by a friend," she said. "Another singer."

"Damn."

"You got no worries," she said, and glanced down at me. She still looked too young, but there was no way we'd get arrested here for chasing one another without our clothes on.

Dorothy

Even though she and Johnnie had mended their Waldorf confrontation with an evening of endless sex, she wasn't happy that while she was entertaining everyone from Noel Coward to Lucille Ball that New Year's Eve, he was drunk at a Hollywood party cavorting with a bunch of strippers.

A couple of months into the new decade, she realized that she would have to live with her health limitations, but she didn't have to let anyone know about them. Already this year, her nagging anemia had grown so intense that she had to be hospitalized for a night until her iron could be built up. Her doctors had told her to quit drinking, which was what they always said, regardless of the malady.

"You wouldn't expect them to say start drinking, now would you?" she told Dick.

"Well, it wouldn't hurt you to cut down," he said, "or at least eat more."

As distasteful as he had become, she felt sorry for him. The club wasn't doing well, and he was convinced if he opened another, focused on food this time, he'd have the income and the recognition he craved. She hoped he were right. The radio show's seventy thousand a year barely covered the children's private schooling. She and Dick couldn't save a dime, let alone repair the elevator or the leaky roof.

Although she'd acquiesced to her health limitations, she was more determined than ever to overcome the pitfalls in her career. That nasty mess about Nina Khrushchev's attire back in September hadn't helped. Five years before, readers would have loved her truthful take on the First Lady of Russia and her homemade slipcover dresses. Now the *Journal* had to hire four secretaries to answer the letters of outrage, and Bill Hearst himself admitted that they had overstepped the boundaries of tasteful reporting, an oxymoron if she ever heard one.

At least she and Johnnie were finally back to entertaining friends after her Sunday night show. This Sunday, he sounded like his old carefree self, possibly because Cornshucks was back in town. Dorothy could hear him at the piano when she came into the apartment, which was as packed as a New York elevator. Good. All she had to do was appear healthy, happy, and in love. How difficult could that be?

Morrie gave her a stiff nod, drink in hand. "Kid's singing up a storm," he said, making myopic eye contact. "The jobs in Hollywood got him going again, just not sure which direction."

Cornshucks slipped in between them, a referee in a blond wig, black spike-heeled boots and leather skirt to match. She held a martini in each hand and gave a deliberate bump of her hip in Morrie's direction as if knocking him out of the way. He actually seemed to bounce back into the crowd. She handed Dorothy one of the glasses.

"You dressing like a black woman tonight." Her enormous eyes squinted at the full-length ermine.

"Want to wear it, Shucks?" Dorothy asked.

She drew a finger to her pursed crimson lips. "Now, you know that little thing's gonna look like a bolero on me."

Dorothy set the martini on the entry table and slid out of the coat. "Shorter furs are in this year. Come on. You know you want to try it."

She smothered a smile. "You sure I won't look like Miz Khrushchev now?"

"How did you—?"

"I do read the papers now and then." She reached out and stroked the fur. "I can't resist this stuff. I'd wear Sabrina over there if she'd let me."

"I wouldn't advise it." Dorothy eyed the pensive Doberman staking out the dining room.

Cornshucks took the coat and smoothed it over her black leather skirt. "Just look at yourself," Dorothy said.

She strutted before the full-length windows. "Not too bad if I do say so. When I'm a big old star, I'm gonna have me one for every day of the week. Diamonds too, like the ones you wear."

Dorothy wondered if the woman had any idea how many nights of singing it would take to duplicate the jewels she wore on her fingers and earlobes tonight. No wonder she and Dick couldn't afford to repair the elevator. Money ruled the world, regardless of one's dreams.

"You can wear it tonight, if you like," she said. "It's very becoming."

"You sure you don't mind? You won't get cold?"

"Actually, it's a bit warm in here with all the people," Dorothy said, fighting a chill.

She took pleasure in watching Cornshucks preen in her wrap. Back when she was in school, girls would borrow each other's clothes, but she had never felt close enough to another girl to do it. Now she felt connected to the solid decency of this woman who wanted only a touch of stardom. She'd gone from being repelled by her to trusting her, and Dorothy knew Cornshucks felt it too.

The piano music in the next room grew louder. She needed to get in there. Babe Pascoe joined them with fresh drinks and began chiding her for losing more weight.

"Just a pound or two," she told the drummer. "It was a hectic holiday."

"Look like she lost it, and you found it." Cornshucks patted his stomach. "You get rid of that before we hit the Flame. I want my drummer looking pretty for all the folks in Detroit."

"You don't have to worry about that," he said. "Ever think you'd be opening there, Shucks?"

She nodded and flashed him a dreamy smile. "Sure did. But I didn't think it'd take this long."

"You and Johnnie will be there for the show, won't you?" Babe asked.

"Johnnie said he wouldn't miss it," Dorothy said. "Neither would I."

The piano music grew wilder, more distracting.

"What's Johnnie singing?" she asked Babe.

"He's doing his impressions." His face lit up. "He's too much. Ever see him do Billie Holiday?"

She nodded, remembering their first fight at the Copa, as she followed Babe and Cornshucks toward the increasingly raucous crowd congregated around the piano. "Oh yes. I've seen him do Billie."

But this was no *Sweet Lotus Blossom* with a Basie backup taking place at the white baby grand. This was raw cabaret. Johnnie had loosened his tie, in the reckless way he always did after his first song, and his once-crisp shirt lay resigned against his shoulders. He finished his song to applause and shouts, spotted her, and blew her a kiss, then launched into another impression, this time of Edith Piaf, complete with French accent.

Then it was back to Billie. His version of *Ain't Nobody's Business* would have brought down the house in any nightclub. Across the piano from her, Morrie glowered. For once, she agreed with him. Cornshucks and Babe snapped their fingers, and Rafael, wearing a blue shirt, threw back his head in apparent ecstasy. Everyone else clapped and laughed uproariously, half-drunk, like bumpkins watching a freak show.

Dorothy stood motionless, her cheeks hot, as if watching someone else superimposed on her man. His movements were overdone, hilarious, if you weren't the woman who loved him. Of course men had performed the song before. Jimmy Witherspoon and Ray Charles had recorded it. Johnnie was doing more than singing, though. Like a female impersonator, in that moment, he *was* Lady Day singing about her lover—her *man*. He didn't even change the word to *gal* the way Witherspoon and Charles did.

He finished to greater applause. Rafael had lurked behind the piano bench. Now he offered Johnnie a martini. Oblivious to him, Johnnie crossed the space between them, took Dorothy into his arms, and gave her a lingering kiss. Through his citrus aftershave, he smelled of sweat, an animal scent that she knew came from an excitement that had nothing to do with her.

"Thought you'd never get here," he said. "You were great tonight."

She knew this was the cue to say something about what she had just witnessed.

"I feel a little shaky," was all she could utter.

"Let me get you a drink," he said. "Stay here, baby. I'll be right back." He disappeared into the kitchen before she could stop him.

Cornshucks took her arm. "Come on, honey. You better sit down. Don't want you getting sick again."

"I'm fine," she said. "Really. It was just a dizzy spell."

"Hope you're happy." Morrie bobbed before her like an apparition. "How did you like that bit of fagotry?"

Cornshucks stepped forward and glared down at him. "Butt your ass out of here, you and your lousy timing."

"You're no better than she is," he retorted, face puffed around his glasses. "Damn broads don't care about his future. You forget I'm the son of a bitch who made him a star."

"What is it about short dudes that always make them such ass-holes?" Cornshucks asked. "Excepting Babe, that is, you all go around pissed off at the world, especially at any woman who gets the gump-tion to say what she thinks."

"Well, you just go on saying it, honey," he shouted. "You, Kilgallen here, that stripper. What's happening tonight is just going to get worse and worse, 'cause the kid don't listen to me anymore."

Still carrying his glass, he stalked past them out the door and slammed it behind him.

"Guess he told us." Dorothy tried to regain her dignity.

"Asshole." Still wearing the ermine, Cornshucks put her arm around Dorothy and walked her toward the kitchen as the room swept past them. "Ever tell you 'bout the time back at the Flame, Laverne Baker and I tried to teach Johnnie how to bow like Al Jolson, and Johnnie asked who the fuck's Al Jolson?"

"You told me." She hated the weak sound of her own voice. "Bow-ing to Al Jolson's one thing. Acting like Liberace is another."

Cornshucks moved so that their eyes met point blank. "One thing's for damned sure, honey. After one of Johnnie's shows, ain't nobody going to think they saw anyone but Johnnie Ray."

"No, certainly not." Yet Dorothy felt herself shudder.

"Come on," Cornshucks said, as if talking to a child. "Johnnie's got a mess of pizza pie in there. I'm going to get you some, and you're going to eat it, and everything's going to be fine."

"Good idea." She watched Johnnie come in balancing a tray of pizza slices. He looked like himself again—all angles, a man moving to his own jazz beat.

"You make yourself eat now, even if you don't want to," Cornshucks said.

"I'll try."

She felt empty, as if her plans for Johnnie had been taken from her. He was heading a different direction than she had hoped, a direction that would leave him only a footnote in an industry where he had the talent to be so much more.

Johnnie

Dorothy had been feeling better during the week, but I could tell she hadn't recovered from my little show on Sunday night. Now, almost a week later, she'd have to face *What's My Line?* again tomorrow night.

After an early dinner at some pasta joint in the Village, I brought her to the apartment, hoping she'd stay all night.

We entered my place, silent tonight because I had thrown out Rafael, at least for a while.

"Drink?" I asked.

"Drink and bed," she replied, "not necessarily in that order."

Later, we faced each other in our robes. Dorothy waved me over to the window, and we stared at a lavender sky filled with tiny Manhattan diamonds. My shanks trembled as I stretched. The lady looked frazzled too. Sometimes not even lovemaking could fix everything.

I'd been working on a theme since we lit our cigarettes. "I'm gonna ride this year out my way."

"Retiring?" she asked.

"Just want to show them the real Johnnie Ray. Right now I'm in limbo, between pop and jazz."

She sat on the bed and hugged her knees. "You'll accomplish more in jazz. Think how close you are to recording with Ellington."

"I can sing it all, Dotty." I waited for her to realize just how much I meant that. "When the smoke clears, it's still me."

"Are you quoting Tempest Storm again? That if you try satisfying gray flannel, you'll find black chinos are in?"

"Christ, will you leave her out of this? She's an old pal, nothing more."

"You've been telling everybody but me she was the one who helped you see the light."

"She got me thinking is all."

"I'll bet."

"But this is about what I think, not anybody else."

"Oh, it's about you now. What happened to *us*, Johnnie?"

I stepped toward the bed and softened my voice. "I got to perform the way God made me."

"Spare me the religion." Her eyes reflected the day's last light. "Is God's way that queer stuff you displayed at your grand piano last Sunday?"

"I was doing what I do best."

Silence. That word *queer* could do that. Especially when it was new to us. We hadn't used it. I stared at her dark hair, petrified hazel eyes, and circle of blood-red mouth. A nipple peered blackly from a crack in her robe.

Her teeth glinted. Still no sound.

"My popularity is going down, Dotty. I haven't been high on the charts for months."

"That's because you keep following Morrie's advice."

"I can fill any small room. I'll always be on top if I choose my venues."

"You better explain yourself," she said.

"I'm a cabaret singer, that's all. I can control a room, make it mine. Not the other way around."

"You'll do nothing but form a cult following the way you're going."

"Nobody stays on the very top forever," I said. "You have to decide who you can impact and where. Morrie doesn't understand that. I thought you did."

"I do," she said. "There are jazz singers who have remained popular in smaller venues without demeaning their art."

The insult hurt. "Is that what you think of me?" I asked.

"Give me a chance," she said, "and I'll show you that with a big orchestra, you'll hold onto the large audiences. They're still there for you, Johnnie." She rose and dropped her robe. "I should shower."

Usually, I'd shower with her, but I kept hearing the echo of her remark about demeaning my art.

"Think I'll finish my drink," I said. "When you're ready, I'll call you a cab."

I walked back to the window. The diamonds in the sky didn't look as bright as they had before.

Johnnie

A month later, in spite of our arguments about where my career was headed, Dotty accomplished the impossible. She followed her rainbow and obtained a full-out session with Duke Ellington. When she told me, I truly had no idea if I could pull it off. His legendary singers had sung that blues-jazz beat for years. Then Billy Taylor's words came to me. *"You are a reach, Johnnie Ray."*

"I'll get in shape," I told Dotty.

She hugged me. "Can I come along for this one?"

"Absolutely," I said. "I'm going to need all of the help I can get."

Springtime birdies chirped on the sidewalk as Babe pulled up in front of the Cathedral Studio on 30th. I got out of the passenger's side and held the rear door open for Dotty and Clarice. Dotty grabbed my elbow, her fingers surprisingly strong. Babe ran ahead and opened the studio door.

Duke Ellington greeted us graciously. His first lieutenant and writer, perfectionist Billy Strayhorn, scowled from a corner where he was marking up charts with colored pens. My throat tightened into a dry knot, my good ear buzzed, and my hand shook. I stifled a cough.

"Ready?" Duke stood waiting, those baggy eyes a complete picture of cool.

I smiled and fiddled with the mic and music stand.

"Okay if I move closer to the percussion?" I asked in a voice so unlike mine I felt my body had been invaded.

"So you can see Duke better?" Strayhorn's tone sounded so anxious I wanted to draw back my question.

"So he can feel the drums on this side of the stage," Babe Pascoe intervened on my behalf. Then he surrendered me to Ellington's two, yeah count 'em, two drummers. My request caused twenty-two musicians to give my hearing aid a second look.

The band flexed its muscles. Behind the glass, my team gave me the thumbs-up. The red light went on. Wham! That Ellington sound, man. I pretended like I'd been shot and was dying from the sound of his music. Then I dove into the sea of Ellington, an expanse of deep water without lifeguards.

First out of the chute was *The Lonely Ones*. I got it down and came in just when I should have. The tune free-flowed. It said goodbye, came around again, leaped, and found its way down another time, then another. I raised my hands and took a step back. Everyone watched. Duke hit a sustained chord. No man could match that sound.

"Gentlemen," I said, "at some point, even Errol Flynn has to climb off."

They all laughed, and I felt bad about making a joke at the one-time stud's expense. After that, everyone relaxed, and the session progressed smoothly. This band was so powerful that I waited like a good boy for the chance to jump in. Soon, drenched in sweat, I slumped a tad; it was more from trying to contain myself than from exertion. Between takes, Strayhorn showed me where he wanted me to go on the charts.

"I'm confused," I admitted, "but enthused."

He tried hard to encourage me. Everybody wanted to help. At times I felt amazed at how well I seemed to fit, but my hearing wouldn't let me be sure. Other times, I found myself about to fall into the drum kit trying to pick up the beat.

◾ ◾ ◾

After the session ended, and we drove away, Babe caught my eye in his rearview and winked. Maybe I had pulled it off. Clarice had moved up front with him, and I could tell she was impressed, a rarity for her. Next to me, Dotty could hardly contain herself.

"The big sax man told me you were a well, Johnnie, a deep well, and that you had hit a gusher."

She meant the baritone sax man. I felt my heart leap. "That's quite a compliment coming from him."

Outside, light pastels broke out in patches among the skeletal avenues.

"*The Lonely Ones*," she uttered, low in the warm vehicle, "will be a classic. People a hundred years from now will be listening to you with Duke Ellington."

"Babe," I said, "Don't let this limo lose its way to P.J.'s. My tonsils need some tonic."

Dorothy

The session with Ellington would prove to the musical world what she already knew about Johnnie's talent. More important, it would prove it to Johnnie as well. Morrie could label her concerns interference or anything else he chose to. Her rebuttal would be in the music,

in the public's reaction to *The Lonely Ones*.

With Babe driving, they drifted from P.J. Clarke's to the Copa, toasting Johnnie's talent, her brilliance in recognizing it, and their love that could endure anything. A couple of times at the beginning of the evening, Babe cleared his throat as if to censor their public displays of affection, but he soon either gave up or grew used to it. Too full of the night and Johnnie's sweet voice, she didn't care what anybody thought.

He sang the chorus of *To Know You Is To Love You*, one of the best songs from the session, while he lifted her hair and brushed her cheek with his lips.

Somewhere, at the Copa or one of the clubs later, Babe moaned and put up his hands.

"I give up. I can't drink with you pros."

"Don't go," she tried to say. It came out, "Don't grow," which threw all three of them into fits of hysteria.

"One more round then," Babe replied, "and I'm really going to split."

Was it then he left? She and Johnnie staggered off into the cold night and held onto each other for dear life. Everything went off course. They lost their balance, and she tumbled. Pain shot through her leg. She needed rest. Yes, just for a moment. Safe here for just a while on this hard sidewalk, she'd be able to sleep.

"Dorothy, damn it," someone shouted. "Johnnie. What the fuck?"

She forced her eyes open and saw the face that went with the voice. Babe. Somehow he had found them, and now he was shaking Johnnie.

"Oh, Babe," she said. "I thought you left." The cold closed in, the darkness. She trembled and turned to Johnnie, on his feet now, helping her up, his expression confused.

"We fell," he said. "You remember, don't you, Dotty? We just fell. What time is it?"

"Time to get you out of here," Babe broke in. He all but dragged them into the backseat of his car. Dorothy felt her stomach roll as they took off.

Johnnie pulled her to him, and she curled against him, trying to get warm. If she could tape her ankle and get something to eat, she'd be fine.

Johnnie's scent was harsh and metallic.

"You need a shower," she said.

"Yeah, more than that. I'm really sick, honey."

He covered his mouth with both hands. In the time they'd been together, she'd never seen him vomit. She didn't know what to do to help him.

"Want Babe to stop the car?" she asked. "Maybe we can find a service station, a rest room."

His answer was unintelligible, his voice muffled through his hands. She lifted her head and tried to focus in the dark.

He removed his hands from his face and held them before him, his fingers black with blood.

"Oh, God, Dotty," he said. "I think I'm bleeding."

Blood poured from his nostrils, down his face, his shirt.

"Babe," she shouted. "Take us to the emergency room. Johnny's hemorrhaging."

Johnnie

After the session with Ellington, I remembered only pieces of the night, all ripped beyond real life.

Babe Pascoe tried to keep up, but he gave up around midnight. He said at four in the morning, he got the call. A player he knew had found us, had stumbled upon us, actually. We had passed out in some piss-frozen doorway on 52nd. Night people had picked us clean—our coats, Dotty's pearls and purse, my wallet. Evidently the vultures had been shooed away from our carcasses before they got Dotty's rings.

Babe must have gone through hell. He'd thrown us into his Fairlane. I had gone into convulsions and vomited blood. By the time he got us to Sinai, Dotty had come around but was hysterical. Babe lifted me on his shoulders, grabbed her hand, and we spilled through the emergency doors, all of us soaked with my blood.

According to my doctors, I had suffered delirium tremens for nearly forty-eight hours. They let me know, in no uncertain terms, that my liver was turning to stone. Another bout with the booze, and like a flattened prizefighter, I wouldn't get off the canvas.

Then they gave me the bad news.

X-rays proved I had a nice little case of tuberculosis. They kept me down for days. At times I felt the straps and buckles. The nights lasted forever. Visions of a godforsaken world. Hallucinatory phantoms—Sinatra, Jimmy Witherspoon, Billie Holiday, Vic Damone— all their voices screaming like city sirens. Duke Ellington chanted a countdown, a metronome. *One. Two. One two three four. Wham.*

Around my fourth day in the sweaty sheets, real people gathered above me.

Dotty, looking strung-out, dashed to and from my bedside, and I saw her get eighty-sixed by the nurses. Cornshucks, tears on her cheeks, said in my good ear, "The doctors, they best not be fucking with you, JR."

Did I see the beautiful Ava Gardner, or was I dreaming? Was that Yul Brynner with a gang from Broadway, smiling like cheerleaders. I beseeched them all for just one more chance. One final gig. *A tour de force* finale in a cabaret room.

"I got to get up," I shouted to the walls, all that white nothingness.

When I woke in the afternoon, Morrie sat at my bedside holding flowers.

"I know you like carnations, Johnnie," he said.

I remembered Carol Channing bringing by the arrangement for me that morning, but I let it go.

"I came to get you out of here."

What a dreamer. I raised a hand and tried to say *okay* with my thumb and finger.

"We got you some new dates," he said. "Ed Sullivan wants you again. Overall a great summer calendar. Venues, kid, you won't believe."

I smiled with love for the guy, the way he tried to pour some good news over me. And I wondered if I'd ever make it out of this place still breathing.

Dorothy

The others came and went. Morrie, after finding out his star would probably live, made a hasty departure, clearly intent on using Johnnie's latest tragedy to propel him into a new recording deal.

"It's for the kid's good," he told Dorothy when she called him on it. "More than you're doing sitting here red-eyed day and night."

On the third night, while Ava Gardner was visiting Johnnie, Cornshucks came alone with a thermos of coffee and joined Dorothy in the waiting room.

She glanced at Johnnie's open door. "How is he doing?"

"Sleeping most of the day. Ava's in there right now." Dorothy glanced up to check the time. "Clocks," she said. "I hate them."

Cornshucks poured black coffee into Dorothy's cup. "The only way you're going to keep track of time, honey."

"Who needs to be reminded how long they've been sitting in this dreadful place?"

"I don't know." Cornshucks looked at the untouched sandwich she had brought at noon. "Sure you can't get some food down?"

"Maybe later." Dorothy took a sip of the coffee. "You know, you'd better make it as a singer, Cornshucks, because you'll never make it as a bartender."

"Straight Maxwell House, honey. Just trying to keep you out of trouble in case that old nurse checks to see if it's spiked."

"The bitch better not try it," Dorothy said. "She was the one who kept me out of his room the night we brought him in."

"Just doing her job. Johnnie was pretty sick."

"He still is. I think he might have recognized me today, though." She smoothed out her black-and-white sheath dress. The hat she'd put on with it had taken up permanent residence on the stack of magazines beside the sofa.

"How do I look?" she asked.

"Beautiful."

She saw the lie in Cornshucks' eyes.

"I want to look good for him."

"Hi, girls." Dorothy jumped up at the sound of the husky voice. Ava Gardner stood just a few feet from them, her hair wild, her body wrapped in a red, silky fabric.

"Hello." Dorothy strained her voice for a semblance of formality. "Have you met Ava, Cornshucks?"

"Oh, yes," Cornshucks replied. "Is Johnnie awake?"

"Not yet." Ava tossed her dark bramble of hair. "And if he can't wake for me, you better know he's sick."

"We know that all right," Cornshucks said. "He's been here for days."

"I know." Ava's voice softened. "I've been worried sick about the son of a bitch."

"He's going to be all right now," Dorothy said. "I'll tell him you were here."

Ava smiled and stretched to full height in the clingy dress. "He'll know," she said.

"Bitch," Cornshucks muttered after she'd left. "Who's writing her material now that she's dumped Sinatra again?"

"Probably no one, and that's the problem. I guess she and Johnnie were really close at one time."

Cornshucks scowled. "Word is Sinatra beat her up first night she met Johnnie, so she used him to get even with Frankie."

"A woman using Johnnie? That'll be the day."

"So, maybe they used each other." Cornshucks drained her cup and stood. "Johnnie never was gone on Ava like he's gone on you."

"I hope you're right." She hugged Cornshucks. "I need to go in now."

A hospital-white curtain partially surrounded the bed. Dorothy smelled smoke. Ava, she thought. She'd have the nerve to light a cigarette in Johnnie's room, despite his diagnosis of tuberculosis. Johnnie lay on his back, eyes closed in the filtered light.

"Darling. I'm here."

His eyes opened into a squint. "Dotty, man. I thought I saw you. Couldn't tell. They got me so doped up."

"I've been here the whole time. I wouldn't leave you."

"I don't feel so bad." He reached out for her hand. "Considering."

"You don't look so bad, considering."

"Feel better if I had a drink," he said, the familiar grin lighting his face.

"Maybe some water for now, Johnnie, like a good patient."

She spotted two glasses on the stainless steel table. Next to them, a saucer held a crushed Kool cigarette. Crimson lipstick coated the filter. *Bitch.* Cornshucks was right about Ava.

Dorothy poured him a glass of water from the small plastic pitcher. "I could go find you some ice."

He swallowed some water and grinned. "An ounce of Smirnoff would do wonders for me."

"You are looking better, Mr. Ray."

He propped himself up on his pillows, gown open at the neck.

"I'm feeling okay, Miss Kilgallen."

"Just wanted to be sure. I don't know if you are aware of my little tussle with your nurse the other night."

His glanced at the door. "Saw you getting eighty-sixed. Thought I dreamed it. Dreamed a lot about you, baby."

She sat carefully on the bed next to him. "I hope they were good dreams."

"They were dynamite." He drew her fingers down his thigh.

"Oh, Johnnie."

"Such sweet dreams. Must have had you a hundred different ways. Wish you could have been here for it."

"I'm here now."

"Oh, baby."

Her hand moved on its own now, fingers stroking him through the thick thermal blanket. Poor judgment, she knew. They'd have to stop. They would in a minute. But first, just a kiss. Only a tiny bitter medication taste lingered on his tongue. "Oh, Johnnie, it's been so long."He pulled her into another kiss and pressed his palms into her back as she covered the length of him.

"God, you feel good."

Barely able to breathe, she whispered, "What if someone comes in?"

"Fuck 'em."

"Say it again."

"Fuck 'em."

She reached down and pulled up her skirt. "This damn garter belt."

"Take it off. Take everything off."

"Darling, we can't." But already her mind raced ahead of her body. Yes, she could take them all off—the garter belt, panties, her shoes. She managed to raise one of her legs so that she was half-straddling him. Her breath came so fast she nearly lost her balance. He tried to take off the hospital gown and cried out.

"Don't," she said and slipped out of his arms. "You stay right where you are and let me take care of this."

"We're crazy, you know that?"

"I know." She pulled the curtain the rest of the way around them. "There now, darling." Before she could make another move, Dorothy heard the curtain being yanked back open, and a firm hand grabbed her shoulder.

"Out," the nurse demanded.

Dorothy shrieked and tried to gather her clothes around her.

Johnnie pushed the nurse's arm away. "Give us a minute, will you?"

"I want her out of here right now." The woman glared at Dorothy, "You're not allowed in this hospital again, not ever."

"Do you know who I am?" Dorothy said and tried to regain her composure.

"I know *what* you are. Now, out."

She should have been embarrassed, but the entire scene struck her as comical. Clinging to Johnnie, she felt herself smile. "Looks like your baby got eighty-sixed again," she said.

Johnnie

Out of the hospital, I stood on solid ground and set my jaw like my hardscrabble ancestors. I refused to lose sight of my goals. It wasn't easy. Columbia rushed me through a recording date with Mitch Miller. Even the Beard yawned his way from song to song. I tried to give it some jazz.

"Can't make chicken à la king out of chicken shit," I said when we were done. My complaints rained on ears as deaf as mine. Columbia stuttered when I asked about the target market for this tripe.

"Got you booked in Vegas," Morrie said like he'd found a cure-all.

"Maybe I can take on Sinatra's Rat Pack all by my lonesome."

"Well, Tempest Storm is out there. Get her to nurse you and maybe scramble your brains." I noticed actual affection beaming behind his specs.

"Look." I grabbed onto his slumping shoulders. "I'll go to the desert, but I want some say in my destiny."

He sucked on his dead cigar. "Make enough money, and destiny will take care of itself."

I thought of what Dotty might say. "Singing the same old hits doesn't always work."

Morrie shook off my grip. "It doesn't work in the red either, kid."

So, I did five weeks at the Desert Inn, building my health and courage. The audience went nuts. If I closed my eyes, I could imagine I was on top again. I did the heartbreak stuff and felt it to my soul.

"How can love like ours be ended? It's the talk of the town."

When I came to that last line, all I could think about was Dotty.

I called her that night. "I wasn't bad," I told her. "The crowd seems to like me. When I came to the end of *The Talk of The Town*, I missed you more than ever."

"You should be on bigger stages," she said.

"This offers an intimacy. I feel I'm performing for people who've loved my work since I broke out."

"Ma and Pa Kettle," she said.

"They pay for tickets with American currency, and I don't come cheap out here."

"Oh, well." She sounded tired. Her voice had a heavy, breathy echo. "Try to make it back by Thanksgiving."

Later that night, after my gig, I met up with Tempest Storm.

"Find the ones who love you, Johnnie," she said. "You'll fill any house if you don't try to be all things to all people."

"I'll just be me."

"You do and you'll beat the odds."

In the desert night breeze, we rode in her convertible, top down, streets soaked in neon. I knew that Dorothy wouldn't approve my taking advice from a stripper, but like Tempest, I had few options. For now, I was held captive in this town, where good luck and second chances waited behind every door, and the doors never closed.

Dorothy

Despite their time apart, she and Johnnie were more committed than ever. November brought with it the excitement of John F. Kennedy's victory over Richard Nixon. Optimism filled the air, and the country felt young and hopeful.

When she told Johnnie she had been invited to Sinatra's pre-inauguration party for John Kennedy, he said, "I don't like the idea of you dealing with the Rat Pack alone. Want me to go with you?"

For a moment, she considered his offer. "No, it wouldn't work," she finally told him. "Too many people, too many cameras."

Instead, she invited Clarice to the party. They could both take advantage of the photographers. Regardless of how much she loathed Sinatra, she wouldn't dare miss his gala if only for its news value. The hundred-dollar-a-plate event he and his Rat Pack gang hosted would help ease JFK's campaign debt. It would take its toll though by publicizing Kennedy's not so public friendship with the King Rat—a friendship whose days were already numbered if old Joe Kennedy had his way.

A blizzard ground Washington activities to a halt the week of the event. Trolley cars were derailed, automobiles stalled. Various accidents claimed the lives of forty-seven people. When she departed on January 18, the day of the festivities, the *Journal-American* photographed her boarding a train at Pennsylvania Station, which looked better in print than it did in reality. Once they arrived, she and Clarice rode in one of the chauffeur-driven Rolls-Royces reserved for the dignitaries.

They arrived at the Mayfair Hotel in time for her to change into her brocade gown and coat. Most of the other guests weren't that lucky. Bette Davis lost her luggage and had to perform in street clothes.

"Wear my coat," Dorothy insisted as they stood in the massive armory.

"That's cute of you," Bette said, "but there's no use pretending I'm anything that I'm not."

Onstage, Ethel Merman belted out *Everything's Coming Up Roses*.

"She's in street clothes, too." Bette pointed out.

"But she's a Republican," Dorothy said.

Rat Packer Sammy Davis, Jr. hadn't made it, insulted, it was rumored, by Joe Kennedy's objection to Sammy's interracial marriage to the very blond Mae Britt. Dean Martin also bowed out, which didn't surprise Dorothy. If Bobby Kennedy as Attorney General did indeed target organized crime, Sinatra and the Rat Pack would be guilty by association. Martin had quietly begun divesting himself of his Las Vegas gambling interests. Showing up here would lose rather than gain him points with the new administration.

In spite of the absences resulting from the weather and other causes, traffic was as clogged indoors as it was out that night. Dorothy and Clarice sipped champagne in a long reception line. The air vibrated with anticipation, those high, apple-pie-in-the-sky hopes Sinatra was singing about.

"Feel it?" she asked Clarice.

"Oh yes." Clarice had let her hair grow, and she wore it straight down her back in a European bohemian style. "It has all the electricity of an opening show. Are you worried about running into you-know-who?"

"Heavens, no." Dorothy took a sip of champagne. "He wouldn't dare pull anything at his own party."

"I don't know." Clarice lowered her voice. "He's done some terrible things in the past."

"Not even he will try anything here. He wants this to go smoothly so that he'll stay in JFK's good graces. He already has Jackie and the old man against him."

"But that bastard has called you every name in the book."

"True. Johnnie says the same, but I'm the least of Sinatra's worries tonight."

Frank surely had the sense to conduct himself in a respectable manner. Besides he had been close to her once, and this was a time of new beginnings. A time of high hopes.

He finished the song, and she and Clarice joined in the applause.

By the time she encountered him, the champagne had calmed her. Clarice stepped away to talk to a sculptor she knew, and Dorothy was momentarily alone when she spotted Sinatra heading her direction.

He stood in his tux, smoking a cigarette, Peter Lawford nearby as the two moved through the crowd. Lawford once headed Sinatra's enemy list because of a rumored dalliance with Ava Gardner. After JFK, his brother-in-law, began campaigning for the presidency, Lawford had weaseled his way back into Sinatra's good graces.

Lawford saw her first, and his face stiffened, mask-like, ready for the worst. His lips moved, saying something under his breath.

Sinatra stopped. Their eyes met across the room for a second. Neither of them stirred. Dorothy tried to smile.

Sinatra's icy stare hardened, then his features relaxed. He handed his cigarette to Lawford and strode across the room, arms out. "Dotty Kilgallen. How the hell are you?"

She took his hands and allowed him to hug her briefly. "Very well, thank you. Such a lovely event."

"Yeah. Bummer about the storm. Didn't keep anyone away though, did it?"

"Apparently not."

"We packed the place," he said.

"Indeed you did."

"Well, enjoy the night."

"I intend to."

"And take care of yourself, Dotty."

"You too, Frank."

Her smile came easily now as she stared into the blue indifference of his eyes. It was dialogue from a bad movie, but it didn't matter. At least he knew enough to behave for one night.

As he walked, away, she let out a sigh. Peter Lawford approached, still carrying the cigarette. He looked uncertain, as if trying to decide whether to smoke it or to continue following Sinatra.

"Good evening," he said, in the overdone British voice that always made her want to imitate it. "Enjoying the evening?"

"Quite."

"It's a marvelous night for everyone."

"That it is," she said. "Frank looks wonderful."

"Indeed he does," he said, his tone condescending. "Nice to see you two chatting."

"Equally nice to see *you* and Frank getting along so well, Peter."

He colored slightly and gestured with the cigarette. "That was different. Frank and I worked out our misunderstanding."

"Well, based on his behavior tonight," she said. "Perhaps we've worked out our misunderstanding as well."

Lawford watched a long ash fall to the floor. "Don't kid yourself."

"What do you mean?"

"Frank hasn't forgotten everything you wrote about him," he said. "There's only one reason he was civil to you tonight, and that's Ava."

"Ava? What about her?"

"She's the only one who can put a muzzle on Frankie," he said.

Dorothy fought to control herself, to keep this scum from seeing the shock and humiliation she felt. "I guess it worked."

"For one night," he said pleasantly. "That was the agreement. Funny thing. Frankie can't figure out why Ava gives a damn about how he treats you."

"Neither can I," she said with a shrug. "Nice seeing you, Peter."

"Same here." He glanced at the cigarette once more and frowned. Then he dropped it before her and crushed it into the floor with his shoe.

Clarice appeared from the crowd.

"I watched your exchange with Sinatra," she whispered. "It looks like you won that round."

"No, I didn't." Dorothy felt frozen in place. "Ava won it."

Johnnie

Morrie went easy on me over the holidays. I looked like a relapse ready to happen. Dotty said she'd tried to call me from a pay phone. I told her I never got the call, and we agreed to meet at the Stork Club for an early dinner. I jumped into a taxi. The cabbie worked his way through the circling snow and snapped his fingers to Charlie Parker's sax.

I hadn't seen Dotty since before Sinatra's party for Kennedy. Inside the club, I checked my coat, passed the captain's station, and spotted her sitting along the Cub Room's banquettes. Instinctively, I glanced at the dance floor, the empty orchestra stage.

"This place," I said, sliding next to her, "is dying." I met the stiff-necked glances of a few bold refugees from the storm. "Tubesville."

"It's early," she replied, her expression hard.

I kissed her.

"I thought we might talk," she said.

Sherman Billingsly, the owner of the Stork Club, cruised by, throwing kisses at his loyal patrons.

"So, let's talk. I got my ear on, and I can lend it to you if you want."

"Not funny," she snapped. "I'm still hoping you'll tell me why you felt it necessary to conspire with Ava Gardner while supposedly recovering in the hospital."

Uh-oh, I warned myself. Dotty had boarded that train again. "When Ava came to see me, I was too foggy to conspire."

"You managed to clear up your head long enough to get me in trouble with the nurses."

"You were the one on top."

"Spare me."

"Jesus, can't you smile?" I returned Billingsly's wave and gave him both palms up, like *Where are the drinks?*

Dotty scowled. "Don't encourage that hoodlum."

"Thought you liked him."

"That old rum-runner? He's nothing but a lackey for Walter Winchell."

"Winchell's washed up," I said. "Talk nice about the dead."

"Quit changing the subject."

She was dressed in a maroon suit, the first time I'd seen her in anything close to red. I moved a table flower so I could follow the plunge of her collar. "You can't still be pissed about what happened at Sinatra's bash."

A waiter brought us drinks and showed his dentures. "Compliments of Mr. Billingsly."

I tossed a five dollar bill onto his tray. "Tell the old bootlegger *gracias*."

She lifted her glass and glowered at me over its rim. "I was humiliated to find out how you plotted with Ava behind my back."

"I was just trying to help," I said.

"Please."

"You were going into an enemy's camp, JFK or no JFK."

"So you and one of your lovers—"

I cut her off. "Christ, Dotty. Ava and I were briefly friends, nothing more."

"Ava is briefly friends with many men," she said. "But she doesn't do for them what she did for you."

"Bend Frank a little?" I laughed, but it didn't work. "Ava does that just for kicks."

We drank and then ordered another. I took in the room and saw a few people waiting to be seated. They looked cold and sad. So did the stork with top hat and cane painted on the foyer wall.

"Come with me," I said. "We'll go see Babe and the Shucker over at Tabby's. They're working on her act."

"I must eat."

"Fine, we'll go after."

"Can't. I have a full day tomorrow, a full week. I have things to do, or have you forgotten?"

Right then I felt the funky reaches of The Flame. "Then I think I'll go to Detroit City with Babe and the Shucker."

She kept her face down. We had talked about going together. "You sure you feel well enough for that?" she finally said.

"I feel okay. You could always come with me if you think you can break free from your schedule."

"Guess we have conflicting dates." She fingered her bare throat as if she'd lost a favorite charm. "That seems to be happening more and more."

Johnnie

A blizzard raged outside, but Tabby's was glowing when I strolled in. Cornshucks's voice ruled the joint as she put a cap on her first set with *People Get Ready.* She burned the song to embers. With the audience, I got on board that long train to Jordan.

At the end of the hymn, Babe Pascoe leapt from his drums to the mic, announced they needed five, and broke from the stand holding the Shucker's arm. He caught my elbow, and the three of us waded through all the frenzy to a table in back. Piano man and bass stopped at the bar and mopped their glistening brows. A girl with Orphan Annie hair rushed us drinks.

I raised mine in a toast. "Better warn Detroit you're coming with work like that."

Babe smacked a hand on a stack of his charts. "My Bible."

I grinned at Cornshucks. "Didn't know you could read music."

"I do it by Braille." She'd squeezed into a shimmering gold sheath. Her sweat smelled like rich perfume and upturned earth. She shot her drink in one easy motion. "Lord of mercy," she said, and big-eyed the glass.

"Stinger," said Babe. "Brandy and crème de menthe."

I tossed mine down. It felt hot when it hit bottom. Maybe I'd discovered something that might save me.

"You going to Detroit with us?" Babe's shirt lay wet against his muscles and his paunch. "We take off day after tomorrow in the Fairlane."

I faked amazement that he planned to go by auto. He could out-drive Jack Kerouac's buddy in that book *On the Road*.

"I'll fly," I said. "Meet you there."

"No, you got to go with us." Babe folded his hand like a vise over my wrist. "We'll shoot up to Scranton, pick up my sister, head for Rochester, then pick up Rose Helen's brother. Hell, we'll be at Niagara Falls by dinnertime."

"Rose Helen?"

Cornshucks stood and pulled at the bunches in her dress. "That's me."

"Niagara Falls," Babe repeated with furious joy. He got up and gave the sign to the other two musicians at the bar. Cornshucks wobbled on her spikes. Tabby's window sign projected a garish display across her backside.

The drinkers at the bar started to recognize me like *Who's the clown with the Johnnie Ray hearing aid?* I savored the warmth in my gut from the stinger. Been a while since I'd felt that mellow.

"What's at Niagara Falls? "I asked.

Up ahead, Cornshucks beamed. "Church," she said. "Babe and I are getting married."

"Married? Where the hell was I when all this took place?" I reached out, embraced them, and started singing *"Let's Go Get That Church."*

And, by God, I heard someone say, "Look, there goes the real Johnnie Ray."

Dorothy

Johnnie had actually gone to Detroit without her. At least Cornshucks and Babe would keep an eye on him. No one wanted a repeat of that terrible night they rushed him to the hospital.

She didn't feel the picture of health that morning either. She stood at the mirror in her bedroom and steadied her hands long enough to check her makeup. No one would mistake her for Sophia today with these puffy eyes. Thank God this was radio and not TV.

She couldn't screw up this morning, and she couldn't let Dick screw up either. They'd been more unstable than usual, as much her fault as his. Any professional who read her column would know she didn't remember much of the inauguration. After that dreadful scene with Lawford at Sinatra's party, she had collapsed, and Clarice had taken her to her room.

Even now, when she tried to visualize the inauguration, she saw only Robert Frost's hair, silver in the glare of the snow. Only from someone else's column did she learn that he had read his poem, "*The Gift Outright.*"

She swallowed a valium without water, as if the lack of ritual would make the act less important. It was just a pillsky, as Johnnie would say, and she needed it to face the microphone this morning.

Dick and the engineer waited in the dining room. Behind the engineer stood a large, crew-cut man in a dark suit.

"Hello, darling," Dick said and looked from her to the stranger. "We have a guest joining us this morning."

"So I see." She moved closer, and he kissed her cheek.

"Mr. Marshall, my wife Dorothy."

The stranger stepped from behind the engineer, and she realized that he was just a kid in a good suit. Yet he moved with purpose as if he was in charge, and his handshake was firm.

"Vince Marshall, Miss Kilgallen. I'm with the station."

"Another engineer?" she asked, knowing better.

"No. With management."

"They're promoting them young these days," she said.

"I've had the position for some time. This is just a policy change."

"What type of policy, Mr. Marshall?" she asked. " What exactly is your reason for being here?"

"Same as yours, in a way. Just want to be sure the show is a success."

"I'd hardly say we have the same function. I am the show, my husband and I, that is."

"Dorothy," Dick interrupted, his face already shiny with sweat.

"No, she's right," the kid said. "Without you, there is no show."

"And without you?" she asked, and felt the valium smooth the demand into a polite inquiry.

"Without me, there is no you," he said.

"I beg your pardon?" She glanced across the room, past his shoulder, at Dick, for support. The engineer bent over the controls and tended to invisible dials. Dick stared back at her with a blank expression.

"That's just one way of putting it," Marshall replied, his tone as calm as hers. "As I was telling your husband, I'm here to be sure you're both comfortable going on the air."

"Comfortable or capable?"

"Perhaps that's too strong. The station is concerned about your tardiness and, to be blunt, your condition on some of the shows."

"There is not a thing wrong with my condition. We've been doing the show since 1945."

"That's true," he said. "I'm just here to be sure we stay on course."

"And this comes from station management?"

"Top management, Miss Kilgallen."

"We'll see about that."

Julian arrived with a coffee server. She noted with relief that he'd known to omit the ice bucket this morning. In its place, a silver bowl of fruit joined the microphones on the gleaming table. No champagne. No crystal carafe of vodka.

"Coffee, ma'am?" Julian asked already extending a cup.

"Please." She took it from him and sat beside Dick. "Ask our visitor if he'd like some coffee," she said, as if Marshall were not just a few feet from her.

"Mrs. Kollmar wonders if you'd care for some coffee," Julian said, taking the cue.

The kid blinked then narrowed his eyes as he figured out the snub. "Coffee will be fine," he said. "It could be a long morning."

"Since he probably skipped breakfast, perhaps he'd like some fruit," she said, and gestured toward the bowl in the middle of the table.

"No thanks," the kid said.

Marshall had been right. It was a long morning. He sat at the dining room table next to the engineer, taking every refill Julian offered.

Thanks to the valium, she relaxed, and Dick continued his hearty display of enthusiasm although, as he did more and more frequently, he put most of the burden of the show on her.

"Tell me your favorite moment of the inauguration," he insisted, once the Juicy Gem commercial was out of the way.

"Robert Frost's poem," she said brightly, aware that Marshall was watching her.

"What did you like about it, darling?"

"The sincerity, I think. It didn't contain the imagery of, say, *Birches*, or *The Road Not Taken*. It was more intellectual than emotional, but exactly right for the occasion. Frost himself was majestic standing out there in the snow."

Take that to the top management, Mr. Marshall, she thought.

"I wish I could have seen him in person," Dick said.

She looked up quickly and saw only a bland smile on his face. He had meant it as a dig, the bastard, right here in front of the station henchman.

"So do I, dear," she said.

"But one of us needed to stay home with the children."

"The Rat Pack Party was divine," she said in an attempt to change the subject. "In spite of the blizzard, everyone came through. Bette Davis and Ethel Merman performed in street clothes."

"And what did you perform in, darling?"

Her head jerked involuntarily toward him. She caught the false smile again. "Luckily, I had a brocade gown with a matching coat. Which I offered to Bette Davis, but she is just so gracious. She could have worn a gunny sack, and no one would have noticed. But enough about me, dear. Tell me what you did while I was gone."

Let him discover how it felt to be put on the spot.

"Well, the other night, I raided the refrigerator," he said. "You weren't here, and the children were back at school."

"And what did you find?" she asked.

"Some wonderful chicken. It has an entirely different taste, you know, eaten ice cold while you're standing with the refrigerator door open."

Immediately she regretted their phony civility. They had played right into the kid's hands.

Marshall stayed for the entire show.

"Show our visitor out," she told Julian.

"I'll be back tomorrow," Marshall said.

She accompanied him to the door. By the time she returned to the dining room, Dick already had the vodka bottle out.

"Pour me one," she told him. "Now this is a cozy situation. How can we be expected to do a show with this spy breathing down our necks? And why the hell didn't you ask him to leave?"

"Wouldn't do any good." He tipped the carafe and let the vodka cascade into her glass. "They're out to get us. They think we can't do it anymore."

"And no wonder, when you show up reeking and goad me right in front of him. And now he's coming back tomorrow, Dick."

He settled back at the table where the microphone had been. "You blame my goading for that?"

"Well, it didn't help to imply that I dumped you at home so that I could attend the inauguration alone."

"It was said in good fun, Dorothy."

"It was not." Her voice rose above the valium. "You're constantly baiting me. It's not good radio, and incidentally, it's not good for our marriage either."

"Don't you talk about what's good for our marriage." His voice boomed out. Its sheer ferocity frightened her. "Not after the way you've publicly humiliated me."

"I could say the same thing to you," she finally ventured. "You have been far from the ideal husband."

He glowered, his face so purple that she feared for his health. She couldn't let him lose control now. "Let's stick together," she said. "We have to if we're going to hang onto the radio show. I'm on thin ice with *What's My Line?* too. I can't keep throwing away my career."

"Is that all you care about? My nightclub is going down the tubes, and all you talk about are these fucking shows."

"If your club does indeed go down the tubes, those shows may be our only means of support."

He gripped the edge of the table. "I've have had it up to here with you, Dorothy. I really have."

She started to retort that she'd had it with him, too, but something in his voice stopped her. The wrong word, and he could snap, maybe even hurt her. Had it gotten so bad that she actually thought her husband might cause her harm?

"And speaking of reeking," he said. "You might try laying off the booze for a night or two."

"As you know, I haven't been well." She reached for the bowl of fruit and held up an apple. Its waxy surface reflected the gleam of the chandelier. "Please, Dick. Let's discuss this later. That man upset us both terribly today. I need to eat now. I feel absolutely faint."

To make her point, she bit into the apple. It filled her mouth with a juice so sweet she felt it could heal all of her ills, even the ache in her heart.

Johnnie

Sun-up on Wednesday, Babe Pascoe helped me fit my bag on top of the others in the trunk. He started scraping ice off the blue Fairlane's windows as the engine pumped plumes of ghostly exhaust. Cornshucks popped out of the passenger side in furry pelts. She shook up a bottle of cola and sprayed the windshield. The wipers slung amber crystals into the early light.

"Coca Cola," she shouted at Babe. "Keeps the windshield from freezing up."

He grinned at her and got behind the wheel.

The car's interior felt warm, and I arranged my bones in the back seat. We moved off, Babe cursing because we were departing later than planned.

Cornshucks gave his shoulder a teammate's pat and raised the spent cola bottle.

"Got more of this in the trunk," she said. "Want to stop somewhere and get some rum to add to it?"

Babe laughed. "Save that for our wedding night."

The city slid past us, the buildings monstrous vessels on a frozen sea. Babe and Cornshucks bantered like mismatched lovers. Same as Dorothy and me, I thought, as the day's first sun poured into my lap.

We dashed through the Holland Tunnel, Babe honking the horn for good luck. Effortlessly, he tooled the Ford over the Jersey Turnpike. The weather looked to be breaking, some blue showing in the sky. Cornshucks hummed a bar. Babe grunted in time and swatted the wheel. Lyrics swarmed in my head, and soon we had us a tune.

When we paused for breath, Babe indicated his stack of music on the seat beside me. "Score that mother on those sheets back there."

I wrote down our new song, got ideas, and wrote some more. We commenced singing again. Cornshucks' voice covered mine like molasses. It struck me again why she was in such demand for back-up vocals. Babe winked in the rearview mirror. When we turned the volume down, he told me to sleep. "Sixty miles of snowdrift along here."

"Too charged," I said. "This country is like back home."

Undulating hills drifted back to quaint farms. Stark orchards marched in fields of white.

Cornshucks turned and caught me in a smile. "You a virgin to this kind of travel?"

Her message was obvious. "Been mostly first-cabin for me," I admitted, and didn't go into the early years.

We picked up Babe's sister at her brownstone apartment in Scranton. Introduced as just Lillian, she looked like a string bean compared to Babe. Paler, too, with straight, dishwater-blond hair. Much older than he, she had a school-teacher manner about her and was happy to point out to me and anyone who cared to listen, that she and Babe came from a long line of Irish Catholics. She didn't say the word, *white*, but I felt it in her voice. Her husband, I soon learned, had been killed over in Korea, and the woman seemed angry. She sat stiff as concrete next to me as we took off once more.

"Lil, relax," Babe said. "It's been five years since I seen you."

Her eyes were riveted on the back of Cornshucks' wig.

"Lil's husband Jack was in the same outfit as me," Babe said, softly as he drove. "We were all from Hell's Kitchen. Now most of us have moved on."

"Moved on," Lil said. "Yeah, Jack moved on, all right."

Babe sighed, and Cornshucks sucked her teeth.

"I was 4-F," I put in meekly. "My ear."

"What's wrong with your ear?" Lil asked. That got a small laugh from the two lovebirds.

Next I knew, we'd stopped at a trucker's café. I must have slept for over an hour. Last road sign I'd seen had said Binghamton.

We ate burgers and drank thick shakes. I felt sixteen. Our booth had one of the jukebox selector things. I flipped through it, saw my two albatrosses, *Cry* and *Little White Cloud*. Then, I put in a quarter and played Tony Bennett, Nat King Cole, and Kay Starr. I noticed Lillian held her gaze mostly on Cornshucks.

"What do you think of Martin Luther King?" she asked.

Cornshucks slurped her shake through two straws, licked her lips, and gave Lillian a full count of deadpan.

"Shit city." Babe sighed.

Lillian seemed undaunted. "Reason I ask is the man preaches nonviolence, and just a year ago, a colored guy tried to rape me not a block from my home." She glared at Babe. "I wrote you about it."

"You said a black man propositioned you, Sis."

"Said he close to raped me, is what I said."

The naugahide booth squeaked as Cornshucks shifted her weight. "I know the feeling," she said. To my surprise, she reached across the table and took the widow's hand. "Black and white sonsabitches have done the same to me." She nodded in my direction. "Including that freckled fool sitting next to you."

That drew a smile or two. I lit a cigarette and blew smoke away from the table. I noticed Cornshucks didn't release Lillian's hand. The engagement ring on the Shucker's finger gleamed in contrast to Lillian's wedding band, so thin from wear it was near invisible.

Suddenly, I longed for Dorothy. Nat King Cole spread *Mona Lisa* throughout the café. We slowly made our way out of the booth. I spied Babe punching the numbers for my two songs on the jukebox as we passed it.

"Still had some plays," he said. "Can you believe a place where they still have five for two bits?"

On the highway, the women snoozed in back while I co-piloted with Babe. Snow swirled in the headlamps as the sky darkened. Babe refused my offer to drive and found some faint jazz on the radio.

"Listen," he said. "Sounds like Symphony Sid, spinning records in his glass cage. Hi-Hat Club late at night. Remember?"

"Sounds like Diz," I said and matched the horn to Dizzy Gillespie.

"Howard McGee," whispered Cornshucks into my hearing aid from the rear.

And of course she was right.

Then we hit the lights of Rochester, gemstones in the cold nightfall. We discovered Cornshucks's brother in front of a flophouse downtown, dressed in a suit short on leg and shoulder room for his young, athletic body.

Cornshucks embraced him, and the three of us filed into the back seat, with Lillian joining her brother up front.

"Off again," Babe informed us. "One hundred miles to Canada."

"They love you there, Johnnie," Cornshucks added.

Lillian shot her a patronizing expression. "With this quintet, we'll need all the love we can get."

I settled back and listened to Cornshucks chat with her brother. His name, Carlton Banks, rang a bell with me.

"Don't I know you from somewhere?" I asked.

"I play some guitar," he said, "but mainly I play ball. I'm waiting for the Yankees to start spring training in Florida."

I wondered what the Shucker was thinking and peeked at her face. She kissed the kid and held him to her furs like a lioness would her cub. "This boy's gonna be a New York Yankee."

"Playing major league baseball does beat most club dates I ever made," I conceded.

"Damn straight," Cornshucks said, and rocked Carlton until he groaned.

A couple of hours later, Babe instinctively picked the right exits, ramps, and tolls, and eventually we rumbled onto Niagara Falls Boulevard.

Lillian muttered so we all heard, "Just another street on the ass end of New York."

Sadly, I believed her to be more right than wrong.

We crossed a customs bridge to the Ontario side of the Falls and located the motel where Babe had made his reservations. Like Cornshucks said, it sported a neon rainbow on its sign just like the one in the movie *Niagara*, starring Marilyn Monroe.

"Do you know Marilyn?" Lillian asked.

"We're old friends," I said. The Shucker gave me a long, skeptical look, and I added, "Dorothy and I had dinner with Marilyn and her ex-husband, Arthur Miller, right before they split up. He's a nice guy for a writer."

"Did you know Clark Gable?" She began to warm up. "Did Marilyn really cause his heart attack by being late all the time when they were filming *The Misfits?*"

It occurred to me that the prim little widow was star struck, one of those people who kept *Confidential* magazine hidden under the *Saturday Evening Post*. What she hadn't figured out yet was that her new sister-in-law was the real thing.

"Don't believe everything you read," I told her. And to Babe, "I think the office is right up here."

The motel clerk didn't hassle us but frowned when we notified him that Mr. Pascoe and Rose Helen were getting married the next day. We peered through fogged windows at an odd little structure that, to our horror, was the wedding chapel.

"That's the one in your brochure?" Babe asked. "It looks different."

"The other picture was taken on a bright day," the clerk said. "How do you want to handle payment for the rooms?"

"I got it," I said and took the key for one single.

After some rest and freshening up, we found a restaurant and devoured our dinners like wolves while onlookers pointed at us with their forks.

Back at the motel, we joined a gathering on the wooden deck and watched the American side of the falls become illuminated with colored lights. The steady sonata of water petrified us under a frozen circle formed by our breaths.

After a time, I found myself standing apart from the others with Cornshucks.

"Crazy, ain't we?" She folded her arms as if waiting for my reply.

"Lunatics," I agreed.

"How are you feeling?"

This girl was jumping into a mixed-blood marriage, and she was worried about me. "Stronger every day," I bragged.

"Try hard, Johnnie. Stay off the booze and the pills. You're too valuable."

"Worry 'bout yourself, dear."

Her chuckle joined the cadence of the falls. "What's to worry?"

I could have given her a list, but I didn't.

She turned to me. "Getting married tomorrow. Going to Detroit City with a deaf fool, his career on the line. Carting a white widow lady who thinks I'm Sheena of the Jungle for a sister-in-law, and the only brother I can locate out of six."

She looked off into the distance, the Falls spectacular up ahead.

Carlton Banks was silhouetted against the view. Her eyes glistened as she watched him.

"This is his third, fourth shot at the Yankees," she said.

I put my arm around her.

"And he be a clunker on guitar," she said with sorrow.

Her shoulder felt like a small boulder under my grasp.

"Look at him," she commanded.

"Looks like he's waiting," I said.

"He is," she said, "but he don't know for what."

Dorothy

Two days passed before she heard from Johnnie, and the call only made her wish that she'd agreed to go with him. The happiness in his voice cut through the static that might or might not have been the sound of the Falls.

She didn't bother him with the dismal news on her front—the constant pressure of the kid from the radio station, the TV show, Dick's dour state.

"Just come home to me," she said. "As fast as you can."

"I will, baby. You know, I look at the Shucker, what she's willing to risk, and I think maybe there's hope for everybody."

"I know."

"For you and me, I mean. Like maybe there's hope for us."

"I feel there is, Johnnie."

"We'll talk when I get home, okay?"

"Yes," she said. "We can talk then." They were dreaming big, but she liked talking to him this way. It gave her hope.

"You better behave yourself while I'm gone."

"You too."

"You know I will, baby. All I want is what's waiting for me at home."

"You sure about that? No old pals from your Flame days?"

"No way."

"No Ava?"

"Baby, please." He sang a line from *Ain't Misbehavin.* "One thing's for sure, Miss Kilgallen. You don't have to worry about me. I got a woman waiting for me hotter than anything in Detroit City."

"That," she said. "just might be the truth."

"I know it is," he said. "Wish I were there right now. Know what I'd do?"

"What?" she whispered. "Tell me."

They spoke like that, in whispered eroticism, until he ran out of quarters, and they reluctantly said goodbye.

After the phone call, Dorothy sat in her darkened room wrapped in the warmth of his words. Outside, a storm raged through the city, not an omen, she hoped, for Dicks' grand opening that night.

"Paris in the Sky" was his last hope, *their* last hope, if the radio show didn't improve. They'd lost their grip on the audience, and even at her best, when she'd had as much sleep as her body would accept, she sounded brittle. Dick came across even worse. As much as she fought station management, she feared the day would come when they would cut back or maybe even cancel the show. Losing *What's My Line?* would publicly humiliate her, but their financial survival depended on *Breakfast With Dorothy and Dick*. She had to prepare.

She'd scheduled two buses to deliver their friends to New Jersey for the grand opening, and she had made up her mind to play the smiling hostess to the utmost. She rose slowly, still feeling close to Johnnie. Cornshucks' wedding gave her hope, as well, not just for Johnnie and her, but for Dick. He was still a young man, too young to give up. He deserved his dreams.

She dressed in a long white dress she'd worn when she'd had cocktails with Marilyn Monroe and Yves Montand. As she stood before the mirror, she heard Dick's knock at the door.

"Come in," she said.

He entered the room, handed her the glass of champagne, and sat on the bed, the bottle in one hand. "I know you don't keep clocks in here. Just wanted to be sure you know what time it is."

"I wouldn't be late for your grand opening." She lifted her glass. "To Paris in the Sky. Long may it flourish."

"Longer than The Left Bank, I hope," he said.

"Don't give up on it yet."

"I have no choice." He seemed to brighten. "I'm fortunate this new opportunity presented itself. I have a good chance."

"Especially with your knowledge of music. Your taste is impeccable."

"Why thank you, my dear." His voice deepened at the compliment. His features seemed more defined, sculpted with the aristocratic boyishness that had once attracted women of all ages.

"I mean it. I think you're wise to manage the talent, not just employ it. Lee Evans is a great start."

"The RCA contract is almost in the bag for him," he said. "There's a chance of some TV, *The Gershwin Years*, they're calling it."

Dorothy sat next to him on the bed and held out her glass for a refill. "You know," she said. "Mike Wallace has been after me for an interview for ages."

He frowned. "Absolutely not. You don't need the publicity. He'll open all those old wounds, hound you about Sinatra."

"I like Wallace," she said. "I just had no reason to put myself through that before, but now I think I would."

"Why?"

"For Paris in the Sky. I'll agree to do the show if they'll include footage of the club, maybe even have Evans appear on the show."

He peered at her steadily over the rim of his lifted glass. "You'd do that?"

"I will do it. Mike Wallace doesn't scare me."

"No. I'll bet he doesn't." He smiled, showing teeth still shockingly white. "Wallace is the one who'd better watch out for you." He poured more bubbles into his glass and offered her the rest of the bottle. "I must say, darling, you're looking lovely tonight."

"Thank you, Dick. I've only worn this dress once, that night with Marilyn and Yves Montand."

"The actor with the long fingers and the French accent? Marilyn was foolish to walk away from her marriage because of him."

"You know how she is. She always falls for her leading men, and he's very charming. She's just a little girl looking for someone to take care of her."

"She had someone to take care of her, and look what she did to him." He patted her leg and rose from the bed. "Not smart to leave what you have just because something else looks better. She'll be sorry."

"Maybe she'll find happiness," she said. "I hope so. Now let's go open ourselves a nightclub. Paris When it Sizzles."

"Paris in the Sky," he corrected, swinging the empty bottle. "Let's go."

Although the love she once felt for him had long departed, she felt a mutual bond connecting them. For this evening at least, they'd be a team. They'd open another nightclub. She'd do the Mike Wallace show, too. Regardless of how far apart they had grown, she would help Dick reach his dream.

He walked down the hall, humming like a man whose luck had changed. And all because of a woman named Cornshucks he'd probably never meet.

Johnnie

The wedding day broke yellow with the sun. We walked under the Falls in rented rain gear and laughed in childish wonder. Just before noon, we dressed as sharp as we could and gathered in the small chapel. Cornshucks had poured herself into a pink hourglass suit and shoved her feet into a pair of four-inch heels. Looking splendid, she glanced out from under a floppy white hat with a pinkish veil. She smiled and held the flowers I'd ordered. Babe looked elegant in a tux that I'd bought for him over in Italy a few years before.

An assortment of curious witnesses meandered about. Lillian seemed more relaxed in a rose-colored polyester suit. Carlton strummed the wedding march on a rented guitar. The rites were performed by a wild-eyed preacher, half-drunk in preparation for his own Armageddon.

Cheers rose when Babe hugged his bride. Carlton played *At Last*, Cornshucks' favorite, and one she'd always said I should record. I wailed it above the Falls and thought Etta James might give me an A for effort. I threw it up there so it was all by itself for the Shucker, high and mighty for her to share with Babe.

We toasted with paper cups of champagne. Cornshucks and I hammed it up a bit for the assemblage. Preacher Man almost kissed me when I handed him three twenties.

Finally Babe laid down the word. "Let's blow," he said. "Five-hour drive to Detroit City. We got a gig tomorrow night."

"Meet in one hour," Cornshucks shouted.

"Should take off sooner," Babe warned and looked at his Timex.

"Any sooner, and you in trouble, Drummer Man."

Seeing how happy they were made me miss Dotty even more. I wanted her to see how in these simple surroundings, two people could find such great joy.

Dorothy

That Saturday, Clarice insisted they attend the cocktail party Joe DiMaggio was holding for Marilyn's new film, *The Misfits*. "You need to see your old friends," she had told Dorothy. "You're keeping to yourself too much." Since Dorothy had inadvertently stood her up on two occasions recently, she agreed.

It had been a dreadful week. Marshall, the young executive from the radio station, had her under constant scrutiny, and this morning had actually picked up a glass of water from the bar and sniffed it. She retaliated by lifting the Juicy Gem bottle and asking, "Are you thirsty this morning?"

She and Clarice arrived after nine and were greeted at the door by Joe himself, a picture of quiet reserve in a light suit only he could wear. If anyone could turn Marilyn around, he could.

She was having a difficult time, more lost than ever since Clark Gable's death in November. The heart attack had struck the day after they'd finished filming, and Marilyn clearly blamed herself. She had been so fragile the last time they met that Dorothy couldn't bring herself to print the rumors about her behavior on the set or about the pills that were reportedly flown in from her Beverly Hills doctors. It was unsubstantiated gossip, after all.

Dorothy hoped her attendance would show her support for Marilyn, but her reporter brain also smelled a possible reconciliation between Marilyn and Joe DiMaggio. He certainly acted in charge as he saw to their wraps and ushered them through the hundred or more guests that moved like slow traffic through the rooms of the penthouse.

"Marilyn will be so happy you're here," he said, and squeezed Dorothy's arm.

"How is she doing," she asked, and hit the *is* to convey to him that she knew more than she was reporting.

"Better," he said, his tone careful as if he were choosing his words. "She considers you a friend, you know. There are no other reporters here."

"I appreciate that," she murmured.

"Have some champagne, and I'll get her." He indicated a waiter with a napkin-wrapped magnum.

"Sounds good," she said.

The champagne went down in a rush of icy bubbles.

"Lovely," she told Clarice.

"Expensive," she replied.

Clarice had let her hair go dark again, and with it, taken on an air of aloofness to everyone but Dorothy, as if a change in hair color required a personality adjustment as well. Articles in the art magazines described her as sophisticated, but in reality, success had made her more comfortable with herself, and she no longer cared what others thought of her.

"Well, I think Marilyn's taste is impeccable," Dorothy said.

"I hear she had taste for little else on the set."

"Perhaps you should write your own column." Dorothy immediately regretted the remark and lowered her voice. "The poor girl's had her share of problems lately."

At that moment, Marilyn arrived and softly eased up to them. From head to toe, she was beige, blond, and ivory. The monochromatic tiered dress that enclosed her was made up of varying shades of off-white, and her short curls complemented the rest of her attire. The only color she wore was a slash of scarlet on her lips.

Everything about her was slightly yet charmingly askew, from the hairdo to the tilted champagne glass to the way she cocked her head to study them.

"Dorothy. Thank you for coming."

They embraced briefly. In spite of her curves, Marilyn felt brittle, like a stick figure the least amount of pressure could splinter apart.

Dorothy gently let her go and introduced her to Clarice.

"We've met," Marilyn said. "My former husband, Mr. Miller, took me to your gallery a couple of times."

"I was sorry to hear about you and Arthur," Dorothy said. "I've been thinking about you."

"He is a wonderful man and a great writer." She spoke in a sing-song, memorized tone, and Dorothy knew that she would ultimately see that statement in print.

"I can't wait to see the film," Clarice put in. "Hard to believe it's Clark's last."

Marilyn's glass froze midway to her lips. Her eyes grew larger.

"Clark was a dear man." Dorothy tried to soften the impact of Clarice's words.

"I kept him waiting," Marilyn said. "Kept him waiting for hours and hours on that film."

"He wasn't well, dear." Dorothy said. "It would have happened regardless of which picture he was working on."

"You think so?" She looked up wistfully from her glass. A soft curl fell over her arched brow. This was her appeal, the combination of sexuality and vulnerability, and even when she tried, there was nothing planned about it.

"Yes," Dorothy said. "For that reason, I've refrained from printing anything about the problems with the film in my column."

"Oh, I know. Thanks a lot for that. It's been hard enough, losing my marriage, losing Clark." Her voice trailed off. "Here I am getting divorced and releasing a picture, both in the same month. Johnnie will get a kick out of that."

"He's in Detroit," Dorothy said. "He sends his love."

A tender smile wiped the sadness from her face. "He's such a dear heart. Why aren't you with him?"

"I have too much business here right now. I've even consented to an interview with Mike Wallace."

"Mike Wallace," Clarice butted in. "You can't be serious."

"I think he's nice," Marilyn said.

"Mike Wallace?" Dorothy asked.

"Him, too, but most of all Johnnie. He doesn't have any meanness in him at all. You two are the sweetest couple. I wish—"

Dorothy leaned closer, trying to hear the last words she spoke, but Marilyn only smiled apologetically and held her empty glass between them.

Joe soon joined them and led Marilyn away into the crowd.

"What do you think will happen to her?" Clarice asked in a hushed voice.

"I don't know," Dorothy said. "Joe's a strong man. Maybe he can do something."

"Yes," Clarice replied. "Maybe he can."

After Marilyn's departure, there seemed little reason to remain at the party. They finished their champagne and left. Insisting that it was too early to go home, Clarice suggested they stop at the Drake. Dorothy acquiesced but dreaded it, half-expecting a lecture. She'd caught the disapproving frown on Clarice's face when she'd mentioned the Wallace interview and didn't feel like dealing with her overprotective friend tonight.

The Drake's dim, opulent interior soothed her. The booths on the other side of the room looked like shadowy caves. They gave the place a clandestine ambiance all good drinking bars had. And like it or not, this was going to be a drinking bar tonight. The champagne, like Marilyn, had provided momentary enjoyment but little solace. If anything, Dorothy felt more depressed than she had earlier after her confrontation with Marshall. She ordered her martini extra dry and straight up. It slid down like liquid ice.

"We've got to discuss this Mike Wallace interview," Clarice said without preamble.

She lit a cigarette she didn't really want. "I'm not worried," she said. "What can he do to me?"

"Don't you know?"

"You mean the Sinatra stuff? I'm a big girl. Nothing he has said will bother me."

Clarice sat stiff as a doll. "Oh really?"

"And if you're thinking of the Rat Pack party, it wasn't Sinatra who upset me. It was Lawford and what he said about Ava and Johnnie."

"I'm well aware of that." Clarice lifted her drink.

"Besides, I wasn't at all well."

"Your anemia."

"Yes. And Dick needs my help right now, Clarice. This interview will draw attention to Paris in the Sky."

Leaning across the table, drink in hand, Clarice looked like an Erte painting, an Art Deco lady. "If you cared about Dick, you wouldn't consider doing the show."

"How can you say that? He needs the business."

"But you don't need Mike Wallace tearing you apart." She patted her dark hair. "Dick seems to be depending on you more than ever. When are you going to stop putting up with the way he treats you?"

"He and I both do fine independently," she said. "And when the chips are down, we stick together as we vowed to all those years back."

"I know it's none of my business," Clarice began, then sighed before Dorothy could agree. "I'm afraid he'll hear one too many rumors about you and Johnnie and just blow."

Dorothy felt a gnawing dread. Perhaps just vodka on an empty stomach. Perhaps Clarice's honesty had hit too close to home. Dorothy crushed out her unfinished cigarette.

"Rumors are my job, dear, or haven't you noticed? And if I listened to everything that was whispered about Dick, I couldn't show my face in public."

"You're stronger than he is," Clarice said. "You can take it."

"And he can't?"

Before she could answer, an elderly couple approached the table and asked for her autograph, a request that Dorothy found especially touching at the moment. She signed her name on a cocktail napkin, and they thanked her repeatedly then disappeared into the shadows.

"You see," she said to Clarice. "I am a public figure, and I have to live with what people say about me, good and bad."

"Just don't let Mike Wallace have a field day with your life."

"Dick wants me to go. He knows I'm doing it to help him."

"That may be what Dick wanted at first," Clarice said. "It isn't what he wants now."

"And how do you know what my husband wants?"

She looked down into her drink. "I'm not supposed to tell you."

Dorothy sighed and lit another cigarette. So that's what this whole meeting had been about. "Go ahead," she said. "What did Dick say to you?"

"Not to me, to Roland. They met last night. Dick was beside himself about you and Johnnie."

She thought back. Yes, perhaps he had been chilly for the past few days. They hadn't really had a conversation since she agreed to do the Wallace interview.

"If those rumors were going to bother him, he would have divorced me years ago," she said.

"He tried to ignore them, especially with the other things he's heard about Johnnie."

"That he's gay? Come on, Clarice. You've seen us together."

"I didn't say I believed it," she said. "At first, you were more careful. If you went out of town with him, you used me as your beard. Now, it's as if you don't care what Dick hears. You flaunt Johnnie, and you think no one's going to say anything."

"There is a certain courtesy in our profession," Dorothy said. "You don't see the media rushing to report on Jack Kennedy's private life."

"People still talk. Roland will kill me if he finds out I told you this. Dick said he heard that a nurse walked in on you and Johnnie when he was in the hospital. It's not the kind of thing you want repeated about you, Dorothy."

Being a journalist had taught her that there was a time to talk, a time to listen, and a time to leave. She wouldn't have any trouble hailing a cab at this hour. Dorothy swallowed the last of the vodka.

"I don't care what you believe." She gathered her bag and her wrap. "I'm going to do the Mike Wallace interview and get Dick what he really needs, which in case you haven't noticed, is a source of income. The next time we meet perhaps we can discuss something more interesting than my sex life." Exhausted and annoyed, she started to slide out of the booth.

"Wait." Clarice grabbed her arm. "It's not your sex life I'm worried about. It's your husband. I tell you, Dorothy, he's not going to take much more."

"I appreciate your concern," she said and pulled away. "I really do." And she left before she could hear another dreadful word.

She knew that sooner or later she'd have to reevaluate her friendship with Clarice. She didn't need friends to judge her and try to make her feel guilty. Hypocrite. She'd probably trade a lifetime of Roland for a moment like the one she and Johnnie shared in that hospital bed.

■ ■ ■

Dorothy gauged Dick's behavior for the next couple of days. Yes, he was definitely upset about something, probably the salacious hospital story. She almost wished he'd come out and ask her instead of drinking, brooding, and berating Julian for imaginary infractions. Surely she could convince him the stories weren't true. He'd be the first to agree that she wasn't capable of such wanton behavior.

"Do you still want me to do the Wallace interview?" she asked that Wednesday as they waited for Marshall to arrive. She had a dreadful hangover, and Dick didn't look much better.

"Why wouldn't I?" he said. "I thought you wanted to help me."

"I do, darling. I just wanted to be sure you wouldn't be bothered by anything Wallace said."

He took a swallow of coffee. His cup shook as he returned it to the saucer. "He's not going to say anything worse than I've already heard, you can be sure of that. I just hope you generate some customers."

So much for Clarice's concern. Dick, as always, cared about Dick. He might have been shocked by the hospital story, but he'd probably dismissed it and was counting on her support with his new business venture.

"I'm sure I will," she said. "I'll certainly give it my best effort."

"Good. I'm depending on you."

His eyes darted from her to the coffee to Julian, and he feigned nonchalance. She couldn't take the drumming fingers, the clatter of china when he lifted and replaced his cup. Finally she rose from the table, lit a cigarette, and demanded of no one, "Where is Marshall anyway?"

At that moment, the doorbell chimed.

"Right there," Dick said in a chiding voice. But his eyes remained dark and distant, as if he couldn't trust himself to look at her too closely.

■　■　■

The Voice of Broadway: *Wedding news from Niagara Falls. Talented R&B singer on the rise, Rose Helen Banks, who performs as Little Miss Cornshucks, wed Johnnie Ray's drummer Babe Pascoe last Saturday. Best man was the Atomic Ray himself, who will be on hand when Miss Cornshucks opens next week at Mr. Ray's musical alma mater, The Flame Showbar in Detroit. Congratulations to this dynamic duet.*

Johnnie

I woke up to a hard, shiny Friday and stared at the ceiling. I had been in bed since Babe had dropped me off sometime yesterday. Took me a moment, but I remembered this was the Statler Hilton, so I called room service for bacon and eggs.

A sudden languorous desire nudged me. I wanted to hear Dorothy's voice, more sex talk, like my call to her from Canada. Dick Kollmar picked up the phone, and I followed the old universal rule for when a man answers. I hung up on the son of a bitch.

Then I called Morrie. As usual, he wasn't around, so I conveyed my message carefully to his secretary.

Her voice sounded new. "Didn't catch your name, sir."

I spelled it out for her, then told her in detail what I wanted her to tell Morrie.

"Oh, Mr. Ray," she said. "Give me your number, and I'll have him call you."

"I'm in Detroit," I said. "Tell him to dig up all that cash he's been burying in his backyard."

"Got it," she said.

"Good, very good. What's your name?"

"Heather."

"That's beautiful. Your voice is beautiful, too."

"Thanks. Your voice sounds—" she hesitated. "Like it does on your records."

"That bad?" I asked, and she giggled.

■ ■ ■

Rested and squeaky clean, I bundled up, went out, and walked the streets near the hotel. A flower shop lured me in. The florist was confident that his Manhattan contact could match my choice and make the delivery that evening.

"Anything else I can help you with?" he asked.

"A white orchid corsage," I said, "delivered to The Flame by seven o'clock."

I scrawled my mushy cards, paid the guy, and inhaled the shop's fragrant smells. Outside the windows, the bright sky had dulled, and thin snow fell sparsely.

Feeling uncommonly limber, I flagged a taxi, boarded it, and gave the cabbie my destination. At the corner of Garfield and Canfield, I couldn't hide my elation. "There it is," I said. "The place looks as evil as ever."

The cabbie checked my tip and smiled. "It's been here all the time, just waiting for you, Mr. Ray."

"It's like returning to my old high school." I blinked at the pink neon bubbles rising into the cold night, the crimson tongue of electric flame. People devoted to the ceremony of nighttime strutted and preened with decorous bravado under a brilliant marquee that displayed Miss Cornshucks' opening. *The Flame Showbar*, it announced. A place jammed with promises, all of them worthless lies that roared in your ears the morning after.

I strode into the joint like an ex-champion prizefighter. The attention I expected didn't bowl me over, just occasional nods and hip gestures from figures more anonymous than familiar.

A bartender who looked sixteen asked me to name my poison. I boldly hissed, "Stinger," instead of staying with beer. Word traveled the bar that Johnnie Ray had walked in. Old sports gathered around. Young strangers stretched their necks. Red lips smiled, and you could smell the blood in the air. I played it with my best boyish look and let a hank of my pompadour drop over my right eye.

A man held my hand a count too long. I allowed my innocent demeanor to stiffen. "Don't be keeping that hand from its drink," I said in a stage voice.

The man matched my height, heavier but carried himself like a dancer. He hadn't shed his topcoat. His face under a short-brimmed fedora appeared finely sculpted and as white as his silk scarf. His age was hidden in the perfection of his features. Maybe forty, I thought.

He dropped my hand and stepped back. My vision narrowed, and I viewed him as if he were at the end of a tunnel or a path lined with trees. Funny, but I saw him this way, his hand still poised like he expected me to reach for it and join him in some kind of ritual or contest.

"What's your game?" I asked him.

His lips parted as if to answer, but he was bumped away by my fans. He retreated and tipped a hand to his brow. For a moment, I felt trapped in the wake of his energy, kind of like the space around me had turned cold with danger. Thin martini music was winding down. Two rhythm and blues musicians held their saxophones and waited in anticipation to play for Miss Cornshucks. I joined them near the bandstand, slapped their hands, and watched them seize the stage like victors.

Then I spotted the Shucker.

She wore the corsage I'd sent her in a nest of multi-colored hair, some of it actually hers. Standing with her brand new husband, she grasped his hand in both of hers. A fire burned in her eyes, brighter than the neon outside. Her darkness showed through her white gown.

I kissed her cheek. "You're too much."

"Bought this dress today," she said, and ran a hand down her flank. "Think it's too see-through?"

Shyly I turned away. "Nah."

"Thanks for the orchid. I love you, baby." She moved off for a last-minute chat with the piano man.

I grabbed Babe's arm. "Is this gang ready for her?"

"Shit no. She balked during rehearsal."

"Don't sound like her."

We watched her near the stage, and Babe swore under his breath. "Her kid brother boosted her money last night and split the scene."

"Carlton?" I swallowed a knot. I could feel Mr. White Scarf's intense gaze on me from across the tables. His lips parted as if mouthing a silent message.

"Yeah," Babe said. "Carlton."

"That motherfucker."

"That's what my sis said."

"Don't let it drag you down."

He shrugged his thick shoulders, ran his fingers through his matinee black hair, and turned for his stool on stage behind his drums. "I've seen you go on, Johnnie," he said, "and perform with worse troubles."

From a table reserved for the Flame's elite, I viewed the stage, Babe's beat jolting Cornshucks alive, the rest of the band coming in. Before I braced myself, the Shucker reached those sacred, stained-glass notes some women hoard deep where nobody can find them. She opened now with *Why Don't You Do Right?* miming terrible anger at Babe.

He cowered and drummed a pratfall.

Hands on hips, she let him have it. No frills, just honest-to-God song. How I admired her. I promised myself to take heed and search for more honesty in my own voice.

Faces around me glowed. She spread a kind of unreal glare— indigo as she flattened notes, brassy as she raised them to glory.

Across from me, Quincy Jones beamed at her. Next to him, his first mate, Joe Reisman, shook his head as if he'd lost any comment.

Thrilled to the gills, I re-ordered drinks. A sleek black woman I remembered from the old days halted behind my chair. Cool, dry fingers gingerly covered my eyes. "Guess who?"

I pulled her hand to my mouth and kissed her soft palm. "Only one lady with your charms, Annette," I said.

Cornshucks, in mid-note, watched from above. The ways I could get into trouble tonight blurred in front of me like a flicked deck of cards. I felt Annette's breasts brushing my neck and scalp. I closed my eyes and listened to the band.

Her breath was hot in my naked ear. "You're looking fine, J.R."

"Fine as wine," I said, trying for suave. On stage, Babe signaled for a break.

Annette said something that sounded like a warning about imminent evil, but it was half lost to my deaf ear in the applause for Cornshucks, then she stole away. In the far quadrant of my gaze, Mr. White Scarf lowered his eyes as if he'd caught Annette and me misbehaving.

Quincy Jones waved a no-no finger from a nearby table. Did he mean no-no Annette, or no-no to my drinking?

I sat down at his table. As usual, he looked impeccably cool.

"Stay within bounds tonight, Johnnie," he said.

"You think I'm out of line?"

"Just concerned, that's all."

"That's Morrie Blaine's job."

"He still pull your strings?" he asked.

"When I let him."

Quincy drew a horizontal line with that finger. "Decide which side of the fence you're on, Johnnie. Then hold to it."

I sulked. Was I always the bad boy, the Weird Kid who couldn't find his way? I knew Quincy had been planning to produce an album for me.

"I know what side of the fence I'm on," I told him. Then I tried my most convincing smile. "Fuck Morrie Blaine and his road back to the Top Forty."

Quincy's handsome face assessed mine. "If you mean that, meet with Joe Reisman and me later tonight after hours at the Brass Rail."

"Solid." And I meant it. "I'll be there."

Babe and Cornshucks joined the table and soaked up our accolades for their first set. The Shucker drained a club soda, took a drag on my cigarette, and scowled at my stinger.

"Only my second," I lied.

"My ass." Furrows creased her wet brow. "I promised Dorothy I'd watch over you."

Nothing to say to that. I lit another smoke. "Your show is the most."

Her tough attitude melted. "Sing one with me, baby."

I played shy. "Nah."

"Join me in *People Get Ready*," she said. "For old times' sake."

I glanced over at Annette, who hadn't exactly disappeared.

"You ain't going there, Johnnie," Cornshucks said. "Now get off your ass and follow me."

By closing time, I'd managed to get shit-faced. I'd sung with Cornshucks, I remembered that. The joint had come apart, and I'd played it cool, letting her have the spotlight. Babe told me after how hot he was on us recording together.

Way later, I found myself under the Brass Rail's marquee with a few other gritty characters, all of us holding onto the night by our fingernails. I sort of swooned, passed out on my feet. Then I snapped out of it and realized I'd come here to meet Quincy Jones.

I wasn't gonna make it. Best I waved down a taxi and get my skinny ass back to the Statler Hilton.

Another lapse. Man, those stingers. My face had gone stiff, my hands numb. Musical aftershocks rocked my tin ear. This was one of those drunks that could make you fear tomorrow. I heard a taxi beep down on Garfield and waved like some forgotten survivor.

"Gotcha." Strong hands under my arms kept me upright. "You're doing fine, Johnnie."

Standing straight, I feared my bladder would burst. "Got to piss," I announced to this overlord behind me.

"The alley."

Footsteps joined mine, and I felt those strong hands again, balancing me.

"Here." The voice sounded muffled in the deep blackness.

I opened the wings of my coat, held them back with my elbows, assumed a wide stance, and unzipped.

"Might be drunk," I said, "but I know better'n to piss on my shoes."

Urine splattered. Acrid steam rose from brick. Another stream suddenly splashed alongside mine. I chuckled at a goofy thought—two buddies after a high school beer bust.

Just dribbles now, and I shuddered in the cold air.

"Shake it more than once," my pissing partner said, "and you're playing with it." His words were so close they percolated against my cheek.

I rocked back on my heels, threw out a hand, and stumbled against the icy brick wall. "I'm wasted."

"Let me help you. I said let me give you a hand."

"No."

"Steady," he whispered.

"You're hurting me."

"Bullshit. You're getting hard."

His grip tightened. Thin light, maybe moonlight, showed me his white scarf.

His other hand caught my fingers and jerked them onto him.

"No." I was trembling bad. My knees buckled. My teeth chattered.

He forced me down on my knees. Our shadows followed us against the wall. Light finally struck us from down the alley.

"Help." I'd found my breath and began to yell into the beam of light.

He threw me down, my face against the alley's freezing concrete, my ass in the air. Above me, the white scarf hung down and covered my eyes for a moment. Then I saw him. He'd removed his hat, and his short, blond hair glowed in a flash as the light moved over us. He stood there all zipped up, composed, the expression on his face triumphant.

He's *mob*, I murmured to those few sober cells in my brain. Or *law*. Or something more dangerous than both.

Another voice approached with the light. "You in trouble, Zellnik?"

"Nothing I can't handle."

The light blinded me. "Help me," I pleaded.

"Who we got?" The other man loomed above me, a monster in his winter police uniform.

"Johnnie Ray, the singer. The queer tried to grab my shlong while I was taking a leak."

The big cop huffed an oath. "He tried that?"

"Not for long."

"What now, Zell?" the cop asked. "It's three in the fucking morning."

Their voices sounded like waves slapping at my hearing aid.

"Read him his rights."

"Shit, Zell. He ain't going nowhere."

"Do it. Then cuff him and take him to your car." The voice took on a quality of force. "This whole move on the motherfucker isn't about you or me."

"No?"

"No." The voice found its secret level again. "It's about something more complicated, something higher up."

Dorothy

The black room held enough of the day's light to allow her to read. With the newspaper on her lap, she leaned back on the sofa. Reading her own column filled her with an optimistic pleasure. As Johnnie had said, if Cornshucks and Babe could defy the obstacles to their happiness by getting married, there was hope for all of them. Johnnie had been right to go with them, and she was happy he had. Somehow he and she would overcome their own obstacles. She would do the Wallace show and help Dick succeed. Then maybe she and Johnnie could find some happiness together.

She stood and stared out the window at the silver reflections cast through the drizzle. She needed a little rainy day music, something Johnnie would croon to her if he were here.

"Ma'am?"

She whirled from the window. Julian stood in the doorway, his wooden form poised as if he were standing for a full-figure portrait. Although he would be the last person to judge, she didn't want him to know how often she came here to drink and brood after the radio show.

"I was just taking a rest," she said. "That officious boy from the station is driving me crazy."

"Miss Cornshucks is on the phone for you, ma'am."

"That's wonderful. She probably read what I wrote in the column about her wedding. Thank you, Julian."

She dashed past him on the way to take the call and thought that he seemed more reserved than usual. That damned kid from the station was probably getting to him as well.

"Cornshucks," she said when she picked up the phone. "How does it feel to be a Mrs.?"

"We got trouble." Her voice scraped out the words. "He wanted me to call you right away."

As she stood clutching the phone, she saw that Julian had followed her in. He waited at the door, holding the vodka bottle. Dorothy began to tremble.

"Tell me," she said and motioned to him with her empty glass. "What's happened?"

Dorothy

The charge was accosting and soliciting. The words played over again in her mind as Dorothy drove to Johnnie's apartment. Dick had tried to stop her when she'd briefly explained where she was going and why.

"But the club," he'd said. "Why are you deserting me now when I need you? What will people say?"

His questions could wait. Johnnie needed her. She could see the headlines now. *Johnnie Ray Accused on Morals Charge. Vice Squad Police Nab Singer.* Johnnie accosting an undercover officer after meeting with the great Quincy Jones? It was absurd. Dorothy couldn't get to Detroit in time for the summary arraignment that morning, but she'd be waiting for him when he returned to the apartment.

When she entered the flat, it looked like a sanctuary of crystal, velvet, and leather. Sabrina greeted her, then settled next to her on the elegant salmon-colored sofa where she and Johnnie had entertained their friends, shared private conversations, and made love. Dorothy pressed her fingers into her aching forehead. How could this have happened?

Sabrina stirred even before Dorothy heard the rattle of the door. "Johnnie?"

The door opened. He stepped inside, deposited his suitcase on the floor, quieted Sabrina, and stared at her from across the room. He looked freshly shaven and pale in a navy suit, the tie still knotted tightly.

He reached out to her. "I hoped you'd be here."

"Johnnie." She walked across the room to his outstretched arms.

He held her away from him. "You know what could happen, don't you? If I'm found guilty, they'll yank my cabaret card. I'll never work in New York again."

"But they won't," she said. "I have contacts. I'll call the presiding judge myself. By God, I'll be your character witness."

"You mean it, don't you?"

"Of course. We've got to fight, Johnnie."

"You're something else, little girl," he said. "You come in here loaded for bear, ready to risk everything to save me. Most women I know would be demanding to know what happened. You don't even ask me if I'm guilty or not."

"I don't have to." She felt the certainty that had flooded through her when Cornshucks had told her the charges. "I know you didn't do what they say you did." He put his arm around her and drew her next to him on the sofa. "That cop set me up," he said. "Waited 'til after closing. Got me in the alley. First I thought it was because of the black thing."

"Prejudice," she said.

"Yeah, they think I'm too close to the blacks. Mob and the law both. Someone's put my name on an enemies list."

"Those sons of bitches. They would do that, wouldn't they?"

"In a heartbeat." He paused. "I need a drink, baby."

"Me, too." She located the vodka bottle and poured their drinks tall with lots of ice. That would get them through these first dreadful hours.

He took a swallow, then put his glass on the table. "That's my first since all this started. Kind of lost my taste for it."

"Had you been drinking?" she asked. "When it happened, I mean?"

He nodded. "Way too much. Cornshucks was a sensation at the Flame. She couldn't possibly keep her eye on me there. Certainly not when I went to the Brass Rail to meet up with Quincy again. I got blasted, and this man just came up out of nowhere, same guy who'd been eyeing me in the Flame. He followed me when I went to take a leak and grabbed me." He cringed as if he'd drawn up the memory. "Real rough stuff. Lucky for me, a uniform came along wanting to know what was up. So my guy, this son of a bitch in an overcoat and scarf, tells him, 'This isn't about you or me. It's about something higher up.'"

The vodka set her mind working. "That proves he was out to frame you, Johnnie."

"Cold motherfucker will tell his own version in court."

"Let him. The truth will come out."

"Not the whole truth." He reached for the tumbler again and rattled the ice. "Know who's out to get me?"

She shook her head. "You have no real enemies."

"I have one," he said, and looked straight at her. "Who owns Detroit? Who has mob connections there? Who said I'd better never set foot in that town again?"

"Sinatra." Her skin crawled. "But why?" She paused. "Not Ava?"

"He's obsessed with her," he said, "just like you wrote in that article about him. When she asked him to go easy on you at the inauguration, he agreed, but it pissed him off. He's been after me a long time, babe."

She swallowed more of her drink and felt its heat spread through her as her anger grew. "So it's back to Sinatra again."

"I can't prove it, but it's what I think."

"We'll win, Johnnie. We're going to beat this thing."

He smiled slowly. "You really think we've got a chance?"

"We do because you're innocent."

"Innocent people don't always win."

"This one will," she said. "I'm your secret weapon."

That got another smile out of him, but he still wasn't the old Johnnie. What happened had robbed him of his spirit. It had left him guarded and doubting.

"You do believe me, don't you?" she asked.

"I believe you'll do everything you can to help me," he said.

"We'll dance on Sinatra's grave, just watch."

"I kind of doubt that one," he said. "The bastard made his point. I'm never going back to Detroit City again."

"Of course you will," she said, "once this has blown over. You love the place."

"No." He moved closer now, and she could see the flat conviction in his eyes. "I'll never go back to Detroit City, not as long as I live."

⬛ ⬛ ⬛

She wasted no time making good on her promise. The chance that Sinatra might be behind it just pushed her harder. Her colleagues dealt with Johnnie's arrest the way they dealt with any unpleasant subject: they simply ignored it. Johnnie's friends offered support. Marilyn Monroe phoned late one night after the news was out.

"Tell Johnnie I don't believe a word of it," she said in a soft whisper. "I know what it's like when everyone's out to get you."

New Yorkers like Clarice and Roland voiced support but kept their distance, not just at social events but at Dick's club as well. As Dick struggled to attract a tony clientele to Paris in the Sky, she worked at putting pressure on the presiding judge, calling in favors owed her by power-wielding officials.

"You've got to stop this," Dick said one night shortly before Johnnie's trial in March. "Everyone's talking about it."

"They've talked before. Remember the Dr. Sam Sheppard case? I'm a news reporter, not a Walter Winchell."

They sat in the dining room after dressing for different destinations that night—his, the club, and hers, drinks with Johnnie's attorney. She knew he'd expected her to go with him.

"How can I hope to attract the right crowd when my wife's out defending some queer on a morals charge?"

"That's enough." She got up and poured a quick drink from the bar and didn't offer him any. "Watch your name-calling. People have said as much about you behind your back."

He sat, unmoving. "You'd do it, wouldn't you? You'd destroy my business, our family, me. You'd destroy it all for him, wouldn't you?"

His theatrics were the last thing she needed tonight. She tossed back the last of the drink and waited for it to kick in and lift her past this ugly scene. "Leave the family out of it, Dick."

"That's what you've done. You've left the family out, all right, paid to send your kids away so you have more time for God knows what with him."

"You haven't been the ideal parent yourself." She glanced at the gruesome bell jar and its clock within. "I'm late," she said, and brushed past him. "Don't like to keep attorneys waiting."

He grabbed her arm. "You'd better not be his character witness," he said.

She tried to pull away but couldn't. The fury in his eyes frightened her. "Let me go, Dick," she said.

He released her, and she hurried for the door. "I mean it," he said. "No wife of mine is going to stand up for that bastard."

If Johnnie's lawyers thought it would help, she'd be his character witness in spite of Dick's threats. Yes, Dick was right. She'd risk anything to save Johnnie.

■ ■ ■

Icy winds cut through Detroit the day of the trial. At least last night's rain had ceased, but the steps to the courthouse were wet and slippery. She sat in front, but the jammed courtroom made her claustrophobic. She eased her hand into her purse and felt around until she found the tissue-wrapped valium tablet. She swallowed it without water, then folded her trembling hands in her lap as the trial got underway.

Already the effects of her influence were visible. The jury was made up entirely of middle-aged women, motherly types who would think of Johnnie as a son.

Johnnie looked the part, dressed in a suit, watching with a serious expression, as his attorney argued passionately for at least an hour and a half. It was a simple case of enticement, he said, a long-time vendetta this person and others had against Mr. Ray. Dorothy felt tears in her eyes, looked around the courtroom, and realized that she was not alone.

Then it was Johnnie's turn. Please let him be all right.

His hair lay sleek against his head, and he looked like a little boy who'd just gotten ready for church. At Cornshucks' insistence, he hadn't joined in the drinking the night before, which probably contributed to the clear blue of his eyes. No one could convict this man.

He answered the questions politely.

"How did you meet Lieutenant Zellnik?"

"He asked for my autograph."

"Inside the bar?"

Johnnie nodded politely. "It was inside. I gave it to him, and he invited me for a nightcap."

Dorothy began to relax. Anyone could see his innocence, especially these women on the jury.

The prosecution began vigorously. As Johnnie's attorney had predicted, the prosecutor brought up Johnnie's prior conviction in 1951. Dorothy listened intently as he answered. They'd discussed it before when they were first falling in love. If only he could tell the story now as he had told it to her.

"I was an unknown kid back then. Penniless," he said. "My appointed attorney told me the only thing I could do was plead guilty, so I did."

He was believable, Dorothy thought, encouraged.

The judge's instructions to the jury were careful. "Remember," he cautioned, "police officers must not assist or encourage acts against the law."

He was doing his best to help, to give her the favor she'd requested within the boundaries of his job. She looked up, found Johnnie's gaze, and smiled her encouragement. Then she looked down into her lap and did something she hadn't done for a long time. She prayed. *Dear God, let the verdict be fast. Let it be right. Let Johnnie go free.*

Johnnie

From the Detroit City prisoner's box, I got a glimpse of Dotty. She looked hard Irish, the way she raised her clenched fist in encouragement, then dropped her eyes as if she was counting off her Hail Marys.

I'd had a bad moment earlier this morning outside the jammed courthouse, my entire body going into this kind of spasm that sent my legs into a Saint Vitas dance. I'd had the sensation before on stage. Maybe Elvis stole it from me, or maybe he too was cursed with the malady. Who knew? Hoping I could control myself, I waited for the jury to come back with the verdict. They were all women, these jurors, and that would work in my favor. They'd been giving me magnanimous winks and half-hidden smiles from the trial's get-go.

They filed in. I figured it had been about an hour since they retired. My attorneys told me anything under six hours was okay in a case like this against Detroit's finest.

The judge asked the foreman, an older woman I'd named Granny for Dotty's amusement, to read the verdict.

Granny took what seemed an hour to adjust her eyeglasses. "Not guilty."

My legs went south. I began herking and jerking so bad I faked a full-out faint so I could hit the floor and stretch out my trembling bones.

"He's fainted," screamed someone, probably Granny. She helped my attorneys plant me back into my chair and fanned my face with her purse.

"Praise the Lord," I said, really meaning it.

Then Dotty embraced me, and I felt like I'd won my life back.

I walked with Dotty toward my freedom. The way the crowd descended the granite stairs with us reminded me of how many times I had been swarmed in the past by adoring fans. Right when I was being congratulated and slapped on the back by people I'd never seen before, I caught the terrible dead-on stare of Lieutenant Zellnik. A well-wisher tilted me so I was lined up right in front of the dick.

He was hatless but wore the white scarf. His hair shone like brass in the war-torn light of the afternoon. "We'll see you again in this town, Johnnie," he said.

I allowed a moment to pass. "The fuck you will."

Dorothy

The Voice of Broadway: *In all the hubbub over Peter O'Toole as Lawrence of Arabia, don't miss* To Kill a Mockingbird, *based on Harper Lee's poignant novel. I hear Gregory Peck is a sure Oscar nominee in this one.*

Congratulations to the year's perfect box-office couple, Doris Day and Rock Hudson, for their hilarious performances in Lover Come Back.

Congratulations are also due to Walter Cronkite, who is succeeding Douglas Edwards as anchorman of the CBS Evening News. Look out, Huntley-Brinkley.

Dorothy finally appeared on *The Mike Wallace Interview*, although she no longer believed any interview she did could help Dick or Paris in the Sky.

As she expected, Wallace asked about her feud with Sinatra and his public attacks on her.

After a pause, she spoke the answer she'd planned. "Some men turn into little boys when they don't get their way," she said, "and little boys can get vicious when their egos are damaged."

The story spread at once. Frank Sinatra had been negatively reviewed by Dorothy Kilgallen for his gangster-like posturing, and he still hadn't gotten over it. That's what they said any time he attempted to degrade or insult her. Dick didn't understand why she'd want to start a new round with Sinatra, but Johnnie cheered her victory.

"Mark Twain said not to fight with someone who has more ink than you," she said. "Today it's more TV time."

August brought with it muggy days and oppressive nights. She and Johnnie had plans to attend a book-launching party on Saturday. Early that evening she dined with Phil Matthews, a public relations man Bennett Cerf had recommended. Phil had been part of Johnnie's party crowd in California until he'd almost lost his leg in an automobile accident.

At the Stork Club, they chatted about John Glenn's space orbit and made small talk as she summoned her nerve. Tall and a bit stooped, Phil was Johnnie's age, but he looked older. If she were guessing his line, she'd take in the narrow forehead, thinning hair and quiet demeanor and say studio musician, college professor, anything but a public relations man. That sense of decency he conveyed was the secret of his success in a materialistic business.

She suspected that he had a quiet, unspoken interest in Johnnie, but he was too much of a gentleman to step out of line, especially since he didn't have the excuse of alcohol.

"Do you miss drinking?" she asked as they looked over the menus, he with a glass of club soda, she with her vodka tonic.

He looked down at his right leg, which rested stiffly in the chair. "Not the way I miss getting around without pain."

"One would hardly notice," she said.

"Thanks, but you're being polite. Besides, I notice. It hurts all the time."

"Poor boy. You're just lucky to be alive." She looked at her own empty glass and decided to forego another out of respect for him. "I want to talk to you about Johnnie."

"No one can make him quit drinking until he decides to," Phil said.

"It's not his drinking that concerns me," she said, annoyed. "I'm talking about his career. He needs to get rid of that opportunist Morrie. Someone has to better navigate his career, and I believe you're the perfect candidate."

"The business is bubblegum right now," he said. "Do you see Johnnie singing *Surfin' Safari* or *Palisades Park*?"

"Of course not. But look at Ray Charles. Look at Miss Cornshucks."

"Rose Helen," he corrected her with a smile.

"That's right. On the Top Forty, no less. Johnnie has been Number One. There must be a way we can climb back up."

"I agree," he said. "He can still nail down a song like no one else."

"We just have to get him to break it off with Morrie once and for all."

"Morrie's the same as the booze," Phil said. "Johnnie has to make the decision himself."

After dinner, she drank a grasshopper while Phil worked on his third cup of coffee and seemed to avoid anything but small talk.

Finally, she looked directly at him. "Phil," she said. "If I can convince Johnnie to get rid of Morrie once and for all, will you be his manager?"

His scrutiny was as intense as hers. "You'd want that?"

"Yes," she said. "I know it's the last chance for Johnnie. Would you do it?"

He reached out, took her hand, and held it in both of his. "You're quite a lady. You know that?"

A dozen responses spun through her mind, a hundred second thoughts. But she'd already made the decision. "Does that mean you'll do it?"

"It means I'll think about it," he said.

After Dorothy had left Phil, she and Johnnie attended a party for Helen Gurley Brown's new book, *Sex and the Single Girl*. She could write a year of columns just about the guest list, everyone from politicians to film stars to one or two mistresses of powerful married men.

Johnnie stayed quiet as they made their way through the crowd.

"How was dinner with Phillip?" he finally asked.

"Lovely. I trust him, Johnnie. Let's talk more about it later."

"It being my career?" he asked.

"I said later." She noticed a dark-haired man watching her from a group by the bar. He had arrived with friends of the Vice President. "Who is that man?" she asked. "He looks familiar."

"Never saw him before." Johnnie put down his glass. "I'm not feeling the greatest. You mind if I split and crash early tonight?"

"I shouldn't have dragged you to this," she said. "I know how you hate these things."

She watched him leave and decided their conversation about Phil could wait. He still hadn't recovered from his hospital stay, not to mention, the humiliation of the trial.

The man she had noticed earlier crossed the room and joined her. Dark suit, dark hair, dark eyes. He held two glasses.

"Looks like you could use a fresh one," he said.

He appeared about the same age as Johnnie yet lacked his boyishness.

"Have we met?" she asked.

"I've tried to catch your eye a couple of times, but you're always moving too fast."

She took the drink from him. "I'm not moving now. Are you going to make me guess your name as well as your line?"

"Sean Walters," he said. "I watch you every Sunday. You're even more attractive in person."

She knew she was blushing. "And you must be in the business of flattery."

"Not even close," he said. "You can do better than that."

"Well," she said. "You have friends in high places. You blend into a crowd, and you don't miss a thing that's going on around you."

"Right so far."

"I'd guess your line is something in the government, something covert, an agency identified by three initials."

He grinned. "Such agencies require vows of silence."

"That leaves you speechless then."

"Not so speechless that I won't call you sometime," he drawled. "If you don't mind."

"I'd have to think about that one." She wasn't sure how far she wanted to take this flirtation.

"You never know. I might provide useful. My job gives me access to considerable information."

Dorothy looked around and realized that he had isolated her from the rest of the crowd. "Why would you want to help me?" she asked.

"Because some stories need to told, and you're a fine reporter," he said. "Besides, I like you."

Before she could respond, he moved gracefully back into the crowd.

▓ ▓ ▓

Dorothy awoke that morning to the sound of hammering far away. Workmen so early? Oh, God, her head.

She must be late for the radio show again. No. She remembered that today was Sunday, and they had decided to record it.

"Mrs. Kollmar?" The pounding grew louder. No, not workmen. It was right outside, on her bedroom door. "Mrs. Kollmar. Can you hear me, ma'am?"

"Coming, Julian." She had little voice. Must have given most of it away in meaningless conversations last night. "Coming." She threw the door open, then stopped when she saw the look on Julian's face.

"What is it?" she demanded.

"Your editor's on the phone ma'am. I told him you were sleeping, but he said to wake you up. Marilyn Monroe, ma'am. She's gone. They're saying she killed herself last night."

"Marilyn?" She could barely get the name out. Her eyes filled with tears. "No."

"Your editor said he needs to talk to you now. He wants you to write the story."

Dorothy steadied herself against the door frame. "Tell him I'll call right back."

▓ ▓ ▓

"Somebody should have taken care of that poor girl," she told Johnnie at his apartment that night. "She still hadn't gotten over Jack Kennedy's assassination, and her affair with his brother was driving her over the edge."

"You're not going to print that, are you?" Johnnie asked.

"I don't print my suspicions," she told him.

In a way, she did, though. She just omitted Bobby Kennedy's name. She owed some mention of the truth to her readers, and she definitely owed it to Marilyn.

"*Sleep well, sweet girl,*" she wrote in her column. "*You have left more of a legacy than most, if all you ever left was a handful of photographs of one of the loveliest women who ever walked the earth.*"

How could someone she knew in that superficial way celebrities know each other matter this much to her? She knew only that Marilyn's death took something from her own life, and that she was less for it.

Johnnie

Reaction to my arrest was mixed. Some said I was poison, but that bunch always reacted that way to the very mention of my name. Others weren't rattled. A few actually saw it for the setup it was. Now I knew who was in my corner and who was not.

Phillip Matthews was for sure.

Dorothy proved her loyalty again.

Saul, bless him, had been keeping me in cash. Those white envelopes from his firm kept piling up with my other unopened mail. I'd have to deal with my financial statements sooner or later. Not even I could fool myself into believing I continued to rake in a million a year.

Morrie kept his distance. He still owed me expenses for last month.

Babe and Cornshucks? What could I say? They'd taken flack for standing by me. How could I ever repay them?

And Marilyn Monroe had always been loyal to me for reasons I didn't deserve. Her death hit me hard. We'd been buddies through some tough times, and I couldn't imagine her anything but full of life.

The newspapers were doing their best to beat me up. They'd plastered me all over page one when I'd been busted. Now, after we'd proved entrapment, and I'd been acquitted, the rags wanted to bury me on the back page. And the scandal sheets were deaf to my claims of a frame-up. The scavengers didn't want any part of my story about the mob and Sinatra.

A month after my trial, Morrie popped up to my pad and burst in without knocking. Raphael was prancing around bare-assed. Morrie didn't see him at first, then caught him in his specs.

"God almighty."

I cinched my terrycloth robe, walked to the bar, and fired up a menthol with my Zippo. "Over here, Morrie," I said. "Follow the flame."

Raphael was loaded. He grabbed two magazines and interpreted a fan dance. Sabrina chased him off stage.

Morrie raised his hands. "I can't take this."

"Quit breaking and entering," I said, "and you won't have to."

"Visiting my client is a crime?"

"It's a crime holding my money for weeks."

"If you want money, Johnnie, you got to work for it."

I made a short movie out of pouring vodka from a cut-glass decanter into a glass. He stood next to my phallic totem sculpture with his hands on his hips like skimming from my funds was honorable work.

"What do you want, Morrie?"

His scrunched-up face began to flush. "First, lay off all this police vendetta shit."

"You weren't there," I said. "That sadist came close to killing me."

"And lay off the mob."

Something Dorothy had told me came to mind. "They're homophobic."

"Homo what?"

"They hate blacks too."

"What else is new?" Morrie collapsed on the sofa. He squinted as if he heard the call of bad news. "Columbia is dropping us."

I chugged my drink, and chills raced up my arm. "Nothing lost there."

"Only the Beard, and all your hits he played a part in."

"Fuck them and Mitch Miller. Get another label."

"Already have. Decca gave us an option I want you to approve."

I did my best to take this news of working for a new label with joy, but the way Morrie's face looked, like his own words tasted sour to him, terrified me. The more he went on praising this new opportunity, the more I wanted to bolt.

"There's got to be a catch here somewhere," I said. "I can tell you're holding back."

"We got no choices, Johnnie. Besides, you look sick. Your gut is all pooched out."

"Get me some work, see that I get paid, and I'll unpooch it," I said, and prayed to God he'd leave.

He grunted like Methuselah, took what seemed an hour to light a stogie, and struggled out of the pink sofa. "We record next month for the new label."

"Peachy."

"I thought you wanted work."

"I do."

"Can you make an engagement after the recording date?"

"You book it, and I'll be there." I wanted another drink, but the way my hands shook, I was afraid I'd break the bottle.

Morrie started to clean his glasses with his tie. "We got five nights at Angelo's in Omaha."

"Nebraska?"

"Last time I looked at a map."

"Jesus." I'd heard him right. He was sending me to Nowheres-ville.

"It's a hotspot."

"What's the deal?" I asked.

"One dollar cover."

I heard that right too.

Praying hard that my legs didn't go, I clenched my teeth and sucked in my stomach. Off stage, Raphael sounded like he was retching, or Sabrina had learned a new way to howl.

"Like I say, man," I replied, "I'll be there."

Johnnie

By spring of '63, I felt like a pariah in the business. I chided Morrie on the phone. "If we can't score on the charts now, cousin, we never will."

He gave me eighteen reasons why I couldn't catch the top rung, starting of course with my morals charge.

I countered him with reasons why I could. My competition included the singing voices of Bobby Vinton, Walter Brennan, and Richard Chamberlain. "Morrie, even Dr. Kildaire beat me to the Top Forty."

Decca had buried my singles before they'd released them, and I had nothing much lined up in the way of venues.

Later that day with evening closing in, I ended up crying into my beer with Dotty in the deep shade of Tabby's back booth.

"Why don't you call Phil Matthews?" she suggested. "PR is his thing, and he's always been willing to offer his expertise."

"You think?" Neither of us had ever touched on the fact that Phillip was gay.

She must have read my mind. "You could trade him for any one of your hangers-on, and you'd be ahead."

"He *is* smart." I felt the idea strike me in a lot of ways. I cast a look into the deep part of her eyes. I wanted to inform her that my hangers-on had already jumped ship, or had sunk off shore. I placed my hand on top of hers and hoped her eyes would brighten, but they did not.

"Hold the fort," I said and got up. I'd reserved this booth near the pisser for a reason. My bladder. Man, I'd be in rubber diapers soon. Last night Raphael had put a waterproof mattress cover on my bed.

Returning, I studied the back of Dorothy's head, her dark hair, her slim neck above her gauzy summer dress. So young from this angle, so tender. I touched her bare shoulder, then slid back into the booth across from her, feeling like I might be losing her—to whom, I didn't know. Up close, she appeared fragile, too fine a species to be sitting with me.

Hoping to lift her mood, I suggested a quiz game she'd invented. "Give me a song fragment," I asked her, "and remember your rule. No fewer than two words, no more than four."

"What shall we bet?" She leaned forward in her seat and rubbed her palms together.

"A blow job."

Her lips twisted into that pixie smile. "No clear winner in that wager."

"Okay. Winner buys another round before we split."

"You operator." A vertical wrinkle divided her forehead as she concentrated. "Okay, here goes. *Whose broad.*"

"Whose broad?"

"Did I stutter?"

"That's from a song?"

"One down, nine to go."

"South Pacific?"

She mimicked John Daly turning over a prop card. "Not even close."

"Nothing Like A Dame?"

"You're so chauvinistic. You'll never get it. Give up?"

"Yeah. You and your damned parlor games."

She hummed a key, began singing in perfect pitch. "Whose broad stripes and bright stars..."

"Not the *National Anthem*?"

"Yep."

And there it was, that smug bit of lonely loveliness that killed me when she'd taken off that blindfold after the first game we'd played a hundred years ago.

I brought my beer napkin up to blot my eyes. She fished in her purse and handed me a tissue that smelled of lavender. Past her, the waning light stroked listless figures at the bar.

"I've got tickets for tonight," she said.

"I didn't know."

"*Swan Lake*'s opening. Nureyev and Fonteyn."

I pictured us being ushered into choice seats, the covert glances over blue noses.

"They'll be lying in wait out there, baby."

"I'll be ready," she said. "I bought a new gown. Gossamer. You'd think Gatsby picked it out for me."

"New guy in your life?"

"Great Gatsby."

"Oh, that Gatsby." I was grinning with her now. "I'll wear white head to toe," I said, "a picture of chastity."

"I'll hire a limo and ask friends to join us," she said. "Maybe hit a supper club after."

"Deeper into enemy territory."

"We'll go to one where I'm on the license."

"No way, Dotty."

"To The Left Bank," she said. "Dick will be across the river in Jersey at Paris In The Sky."

"I don't know," I muttered again, but I was starting to like the idea.

■ ■ ■

Our party danced into The Left Bank, each of us doing a version of Rudolph's or Margot's ballet movements. My legs reacted to an unknown puppeteer, and my bladder threatened to burst. I'd enjoyed the ballet, but it seemed to go on forever. The theater was hot, and there was no booze in the limo because Dorothy had put Roland in charge of transportation.

Between the Left Bank's modernistic bar and the restroom, I did a double take. There stood Dick Kollmar holding court with a sparse crowd not a dozen steps away.

I located Dotty and pulled her aside. "Thought the bastard was across the river."

She stopped cold and blinked like she was seeing something in her husband's image that she'd forgotten.

Kollmar raised his drink to her. Two women drifted away from him like weary sirens. He shrugged his wide shoulders. His eyes were black holes in the surreal light. I felt like a matador with bad kidneys.

"Excuse me, Dotty," I said. "Got to run to the men's room."

She relaxed her grip on my arm. "Don't be gone long, Johnnie."

I used Kollmar's cheap-ass, trough-style urinal. Roland came in while I was washing my hands.

"Grand ballet, wasn't it?" He glanced at the urinal. "I meant *Swan Lake*, not the ballet that we all did when we entered this club."

Strangely, the fucker could grow on you. Before I could answer him, he broke into a laugh. "I guess we all want to be in show business." He cleared his throat, and I automatically gave him my attention.

"Yeah, Roland? What is it?"

"The charges you had to face in Detroit," he said. "I never really believed any of it."

"I'm glad you're on my side," I told him. "Now let's go have a drink."

I found Dotty alone at the rearmost table, Clarice at the door.

"The others have elected to go to your apartment," Dotty said.

Clarice intercepted Roland, and they took off, both waving. In the dimness, I counted a dozen patrons finishing dinner or just listening to the piano near the bar. Kollmar had positioned himself behind the counter and kidded the bartender in front of the two drifting women, a few diehards, and a cocktail waitress. I joined Dotty at the table she'd picked out.

She grabbed my hand and placed it on her gauzy bodice. I started to take it away when a waiter walked by and again when the cocktail girl brought us drinks.

"No," Dotty said to me. "Don't remove your hand."

The girl played it cool. "Two vodka martinis with olives and onions, Miss Kilgallen."

When the girl had gone, and we'd dipped into our drinks, Dotty placed her fingers on my hand again. "You feel cold, Mr. Ray."

"Too cold."

"Let me take it," she said, moving my hand under the table, "to someplace warm."

At least one table heard this. I know others could tell what we were doing. Dotty seemed oblivious to everybody as she leaned across and placed her lips against mine.

I broke the kiss and asked, "Why?"

"It's time," she said.

We were breathing open-mouthed, and my legs had gone weak when we took a minute to finish our drinks. And as I broke loose to visit the john again, Dorothy smiled like a woman with a mission.

"Hurry back," she said.

Dorothy

They hung onto each other as they stumbled into the elevator. Against his ear, Dorothy sang a line from *Walk Like A Man*.

"Four Seasons," Johnnie said, naming the group, as if he were on a television game show. "Now they got guys that sing like girls, and no one thinks anything of it."

As the elevator door slid closed, Dorothy pressed herself against him. "I took off my panties at the club," she said.

"In the ladies room?"

"At the table. I just slid out of them while you were talking to Roland. Want to see?"

She picked them from her purse and dangled them in front of him. As the door opened, the indifferent frame of Julian greeted them from the other side.

"Hi there, Julian," Johnnie said, and hastened past him.

"Have a nice evening, Mr. Ray, ma'am," he said.

"Wait for me," she said, and caught up with Johnnie. "Julian is blind to what we're doing." She handed him her panties. "For you, darling."

He took them like a bouquet and sniffed. "Ah, my favorite flavor."

"That made you smile," she said. "Why so nervous back at the club?"

"Just didn't like the look on your old man's face."

The black room was truly black tonight. She lit candles. He poured drinks, slid next to her on the leather sofa, and pulled a brown plaid throw over their laps.

"I didn't think Dick would be there," she said. "But he doesn't give me an itinerary when he leaves the house in the morning. Besides, I don't care anymore."

"You mean that?" He moved close to her and slid his hand up her skirt, past the tops of her stockings, to her inner thigh.

"Oh, Johnnie. Do that again."

"Here?" He stroked her softly.

"We have to wait," she said and pushed his hand away. "I have a surprise for you."

"What kind of surprise?"

"I bought one of those new Polaroid cameras. Thought we might take some photos."

"You did not."

"Did too. I hid it in the closet. Come on. Let me pose on the drum table for you."

"Right here?"

"Why not?"

"Where will you hide the pictures? What if someone finds them?"

"I don't care." Her body moved on its own now, making small strokes against him. "Kiss me," she said.

He slid his hands inside her skirt.

"Oh, Dotty." His hair had fallen over her face. Through it, she could see jagged candlelight and strange shadows. They lay body-against-body now, her buttocks almost entirely off the sofa. She wrapped her right leg around his hip, and they kissed repeatedly.

She heard the door click open and saw the splash of light from the hall.

"Get the fuck away from my wife."

Dick. Dorothy grabbed for her skirt as Johnnie tried to cover her with the throw.

"I said get the fuck away from her, you two-bit has-been."

Dick towered over them. Flickering shadows from the candles made him look like a distorted caricature of himself. She pulled her legs under her and drew back against the sofa.

"Look, man," Johnnie began, straightening his shirt.

"I'll kill you if I ever see you with my wife again."

Dorothy gasped and tried to find her voice. Dick waved his fist, and she didn't doubt for a moment that he could kill her and Johnnie right there and then.

Johnnie, she could tell, was holding tightly onto whatever composure he could muster. Robot-like, he reached for his drink. "Seeing me is up to Dotty," he said.

"It's up to me." Dick grabbed the glass from him and threw it against the wall.

It smashed into pieces before the fireplace. Dorothy screamed. "Dick, please."

"Shut up." He spun toward Johnnie. "I want you out of here, you fucking queer, out of my house, out of her life."

Johnnie slung his jacket over his shoulder and looked at Dorothy. She had waited for years for the time to be right. This was it.

She rose from the couch and went to him, trembling so hard that she could barely speak. "I want to go with you," she said, her voice a thin whisper. She knew he'd heard her, bad ear and all. Dick heard it as well. He seemed frozen in his rage. "Please take me with you, Johnnie," she said. "I don't want to be in this house anymore."

"Your children," Johnnie murmured.

"They'll understand."

"You'll lose the column, the TV show, everything you've worked for."

"I don't care." Her throat tightened. She felt the desperation in her voice. "Johnnie, please."

She looked at Dick, who appeared stunned by her words. They both turned to Johnnie.

"I'm sorry, Dotty," he said. "I gotta get out of here. There's no other way."

"No."

He waved a hand in the charged air. "You'll lose it all if I don't. I can't let it happen this way."

She began to sob, but he turned from her, stumbled through the door and into the hall. She wanted to run after him, but it would do no good. Nothing would do any good any more. Nothing.

Through her tears, she saw the glistening shards where Dick's glass had broken against the fireplace. She crossed the room, knelt before the fireplace, and picked up a large piece. Blood oozed out of her fingers, the palm of her hand. "I don't even feel it," she said. "I don't feel a thing."

"Dorothy." Dick came across the room like a wounded man. He picked up the wool throw and began forming it into an oversized bandage around her hand. "Come on," he said, and reached out for her. "Let's get you downstairs."

Johnnie

Back at my apartment, Raphael, dressed in a t-shirt and beret, bartended for a full house. Clarice and Roland had left, thinking, I'm sure, that without Dorothy, my pad was an asylum. Others had gone, but a cast of characters looking straight out of *Guys 'n' Dolls* kept milling about until I instructed Rafael to shoo them off into the night.

That proved to be a chore. One clown I didn't recognize answered a ringing phone, handed it to me, and mouthed Dorothy's name. I shook my head, and walked off toward my bedroom.

Raphael followed me inside and handed me a tall drink.

"You look shook," he said, watching my eyes. "Dorothy's called a bunch of times."

"I *am* shook." I held up my glass. "Give me something with this."

He left, came back with a pillsky. I washed it down and hoped for sweet dreams I knew wouldn't come. "Her husband will kill me if I stay in her life, Rafe," I said. "The motherfucker threatened me, man, really threatened me."

"Nothing is going to stop you, and you know it." He sat sadly on my bed.

"If I stay, she loses everything."

He said nothing to that.

"Her column, radio, TV, everything she's worked all her life for." I lowered my head in despair. "Her children."

"What'll I do if she keeps calling?"

"Tell her I love her, but it's over."

Raphael ran a hand along my arm. "Your beautiful white suit," he said. "It's a mess. Get out of it. I'll draw a hot tub."

"You understand. I don't trust myself to tell her."

"I understand," he said. "We all understand."

"Last time you took her call, did she say anything?"

"Not much, Johnnie. I'm not one of her favorites. She didn't say much."

"Not much?" His head was down, and I couldn't make out his answer. "Rafe, look at me. Not much?"

"That she'd kill herself," he said, and lifted his chin. "She said she'd kill herself if you didn't return her calls."

＊ ＊ ＊

The next day, I refused her call again. That said something about me, that I was scared shitless of Kollmar was what it said. That man had put the fear of God in me. I saw something in his eyes, man. Same as I saw in that detective's eyes the night in the alley outside The Flame.

The day after that, I received a letter from Dorothy, handwritten on stationery that carried her scent. Her words begged in a way I know had to be killing her. Sunday came, and I tuned in to *What's My Line?*, shaking all over so bad Raphael had to help me park in front of the RCA.

"She ain't on the panel," he said.

I moaned.

"Hold on," Raphael said. "They might tell us why."

The phone rang. I jumped up, stood petrified. Raphael answered it and handed it to me.

"Mr. Ray, this is Julian."

"Who? Please speak up. My hearing…"

"I'm Julian, the Kollmars's man."

Oh, my God. "Yes?"

"I'm not supposed to do this. Call you, I mean."

"Tell me," I said.

"Miss Kilgallen, they took her to Mt. Sinai just this afternoon."

Christ, I thought. My fault. "Did she—?"

"She was going downhill, not eating and not herself. When I couldn't rouse her, I called the doctor."

"Bless you, Julian."

"Well, I'll go on now."

"Where's Kollmar?"

"The mister was sleeping, but he's awake now, gone after the ambulance."

"Julian, can you call me when he comes back and goes to sleep?"

"Mr. Ray, she's in a guarded room."

"I'll get in somehow."

"Just answer her call, Mr. Ray, if she calls you. Just answer her call."

Dorothy's anemia had gotten the best of her. The doctor thought she would be okay with rest. With Rafael as my watchman, I managed to visit her in the hospital without the threat of Kollmar. The room was dark except for a soft night light. When I first stepped inside, she stirred, then motioned me closer to her bed.

"What time is it?" she asked.

That took the sap out of me, and I sat in the visitor's seat. "Of all people," I told her, "you're asking about numbers on a clock?"

"Johnnie," she whispered.

I had some bad thoughts of her not recovering, the way she lay so still, her eyes closed, the cloying scent of a dozen or so flower arrangements in the dim space. She made an effort to reach for me. "Johnnie," she said again.

I bent down and kissed her.

"I prayed you'd come tonight, Johnnie." She raised herself up, her face in a blue halo, ghostly.

"Take it easy," I said.

"I'm getting out of here day after tomorrow." Her voice rose with an inner timbre that I thought she had lost.

I pulled my chair closer and kissed her cheek. Rain struck the dark windows in gusts. "Maybe the sun will come out in New York just for you, baby."

"Maybe we'll be together in Washington, D.C.," she said. "Nice, quiet hotel suite."

She must have gotten an assignment before she'd become ill. "You're going back to work?"

"Nothing I can't handle. I'll do it all on the phone. We can picnic three days in satin sheets."

"Silk."

"Okay, champ. Silk."

Here we go again, I thought.

Dorothy

Dorothy returned home on a Monday night, still weak but determined to do the radio show the next morning. They told their friends that her anemia had taken a turn for the worse. Maybe that's what had happened. After Johnnie left her, she refused to eat and grew so weak she lost consciousness. At least she knew now that Johnnie really loved her. Their relationship would have to change, but they could still see each other.

Dick, who had been using guests on their radio show since she had been hospitalized, had sounded uninspired on the air.

She woke up shaky and cold that morning. She could never get warm these days. Her pink chenille bathrobe had seen better days, but at least it was cozy. No one downstairs would care. She'd worn it before to broadcast the show. She and Marshall, the station spy, had long established a relationship built on friendly sparring, and she knew he wouldn't mind what she wore as long as she showed up.

He and the engineer had already settled at the dining room table when she appeared.

"Look who's here." Marshall's colorless eyes widened with surprise, then he quickly glanced away.

"Do I look that disreputable?"

"Not at all, but I'm saving up to buy you a new robe."

"Think you can afford it?"

"At least a down payment," he said. "Glad you could join us today."

"Me, too."

Julian entered the room with a carafe of coffee. A smile broke through his solemn expression when he saw her. "Good morning, ma'am. Welcome back."

"We need to get going," the engineer said.

As Julian poured her cup, Dorothy squinted at the bell jar. Where was Dick? She glanced at Marshall, and they both turned toward Julian.

"I'll knock on his door again, ma'am," he said.

"Break it down if you have to," she said. "The show's starting in minutes."

She was already poised at the table over the microphone when Dick stumbled down the stairs in a bulky jacket that failed to cover his girth.

"Sorry," he said. "Thought we were pre-recording today."

"Sit," Dorothy said. Already, she felt weak. She needed someone to lead the show, and it wasn't going to be Dick.

"You're on," Marshall said.

Dick paused far too long between speeches, which gave the show a slow, drawn-out pace. Out of nowhere, he began speaking of endangered species; penguins, specifically.

Dorothy stared at Marshall, whose face had gone white. "Who needs penguins?" Dick said.

Marshall pounded the table. "Out," he whispered and stabbed a finger at Dick.

"Oh." Dorothy tried to carry it alone. "That reminds me of a marvelous party I attended last week. I've been meaning to tell you about it, dear." She stumbled over the words as Dick made his noisy departure.

She did her best with a running monologue during the rest of the remaining time, but the copy on the commercial she read was too long and the type too small. She looked up only once to see Marshall, his head in his hands.

"I'm sorry," she told him when it was finally over. "Maybe I came back to work too soon."

"At least you tried." He waved away Julian, who had returned with the coffee carafe. "Where's Kollmar?"

"He left the house, sir," Julian said.

"Okay," he replied. "We'll pre-record the show tomorrow."

Once the news would have thrilled her, but now it seemed ominous. "But you hate pre-recorded shows," she said.

"Yes, I do." He rose. "I have to think about our sponsors. They're paying good money for this."

"The station's still making money on us," she put in quickly. "Don't forget that."

He nodded. "I'm not forgetting anything, Miss Kilgallen, but we can't keep taking these kinds of risks."

She took his arm. "I'll talk to Dick, I promise. It's just that I've been ill, and he's had too much to manage properly." She couldn't even convince herself. The look in Marshall's eyes softened. What was he feeling? Remorse? Pity? Please, not pity.

"I have to talk to some people," he said. "Then I'll get back with you."

No arguments of hers, no promises, would change what happened now. "Fine," she said, and stepped back from him. "Thanks for your help."

"Thank you. Better get yourself a warmer robe. You look like you're going to blow away."

Dorothy forced a smile. "I'll be fine."

▩ ▩ ▩

The *New York Times* ran the announcement. The *Dorothy and Dick* program, which had been on the air since 1945, would not be back until further notice. Mr. Kollmar had been doing the radio show with guests since March 21, after his wife's hospitalization. Because of the pressures of business and personal concerns, the Kollmars decided to discontinue the show temporarily.

Dick blamed her, but Dorothy felt almost relieved. Now she had a chance to reclaim her journalism career and pursue investigative reporting on a fulltime basis. She had covered real news once, not just movie-star gossip and radio babble. *Breakfast With Dorothy and Dick* might be finished, but she wasn't. Somewhere she would uncover a scoop beyond the magnitude of Lindbergh, Sheppard, and the stories of her past. Without the weight of *Dorothy and Dick*, she would have the energy to pursue it.

Dorothy

That Thursday, she decided to risk Dick's venom and meet Johnnie for lunch at P.J. Clarke's. The loss of the radio show had reduced Dick to a barely coherent drunk, who depended on her even for pocket change. The explosive night that nearly destroyed Johnnie and her was Dick's last burst of strength. She no longer feared that he could do violence to her or Johnnie.

They were still together, although something inside her had changed that night in the black room. She had begged Johnnie to take her with him, and he had refused. Although she still loved him, she knew they would never be together. Her true love now was her career. She had to reclaim the journalistic respect she had lost over the years and prove herself a professional once more.

It hadn't been a good morning. Upon awakening, she had immediately regretted agreeing to meet Sean Walters later in the week. But he had access to information that might help her regain her career. Information about the CIA's supposed hiring of the Mafia to assassinate Fidel Castro in 1960. No point in kidding herself, though. Sean wanted to be more than a source. She still hadn't made up her mind what she wanted.

Holiday decorations sparkled across the city. She liked the festive atmosphere and wrapped herself in a maroon coat that smelled of wool and the perfume of happier times. She hadn't seen Johnnie for several weeks, and when she met him in front of P.J. Clarke's, his appearance stunned her. Scarecrow-thin, he looked bloated, and his once-golden skin had taken on a yellow cast.

"You look gorgeous," he said, before she could speak. A stiff wind struck them, and he brushed the hair from his forehead. "That coat's your color. Matches your you-know-whats."

"Thought you said the ring did." She lifted the rose quartz he'd given her.

"That too. Depends on how hot you are. How hot are you, Miss Kilgallen?"

He never changed. She took his arm. Once they sat with their drinks, she would find a tactful way to question him about his health, and she would insist that he see a doctor.

Blowin' in the Wind played on the jukebox, the voices of Peter, Paul and Mary a flawless blend of purity and conviction.

Johnnie made a face. "That folkie stuff is everywhere now. Grow my hair long, give me a guitar, and call me Dylan."

"It's just college kid stuff," she said. "As I said in print, if I had a hammer, I'd take it to that song and a few more just like it."

"At least Sinatra's having as hard a time making the charts as I am." He pulled out a patio chair and looked into the tavern. "What's going on in there anyway?"

P.J.'s, usually full of bodies in motion, was still. The people within stood as if in shock.

"Some game on the television?" She slid into the chair beneath the Michelob sign. "It's a little chilly, but let's sit out here anyway for old times' sake. Be an angel and get me something to drink."

"Dom Perignon," he said.

"You don't even like champagne."

"But you dig it, and we're celebrating your return to journalism." His features blurred momentarily then came into clear focus. The sparkle had left his eyes, replaced by a dull glaze. He looked even more gaunt than he had that time at Mt. Sinai.

"Why don't we try a mimosa?" she said. "It's early. We could use the orange juice."

"Be back in a flash." He kissed her quickly. "A mimosa for the lady, and a boilermaker for the tramp."

He didn't return from inside and she grew irritated. Women still approached him the minute he was out of her sight. The men she could handle. The women were a different story. He knew how jealous she could get. She tried to send him a mental message. *Don't make me have to go in there and get you.*

Still, no Jonnie.

She pulled back her chair and stood. At that moment, he appeared at the door.

"It's about time," she said. Then she noticed that he carried no drinks, and his face had drained pale.

The music had stopped, replaced by the muffled buzz of a television. "What is it?" she asked, and moved closer to him.

"President Kennedy," he said. "He's been shot."

■ ■ ■

Dorothy never had a chance to talk to Johnnie about his health. Instead she sat riveted, along with the rest of the nation, to replay after replay of the whole surrealistic drama, narrated in Walter Cronkite's hushed tones, as if repeating it all could make sense of the senseless.

Dorothy and Johnnie sat on his velvet sofa, which they had barely left since the assassination. Her children were flying home, and she would have to leave soon. In the meantime, this was no time to worry about appearances. John Kennedy was dead, murdered. It was time to weep and sit speechless beside someone she loved.

That night, as her driver headed toward home, she asked him to go around the East Side. On Fifth Avenue, actress Shelley Winters, who was exiting a restaurant with a group of friends, waved at her to stop. They embraced and shed more tears. "Pray with me at St. Patrick's," Shelley said.

"Of course," Dorothy said, and hugged her again.

Afterward, she stopped at the Stork Club, where Walter Winchell and others sat, then Jim Downey's, and finally back to P.J. Clarke's for one last stop. A sign reading "No Music" now covered the jukebox. The circle of disbelief was complete.

The weekend was a collage of images: The black convertible. The pink suit. The blood. Then, the ghastly image of Lee Harvey Oswald cringing and clutching his abdomen as a man in a drab suit and fedora —a man with a pistol —was wrestled to the floor.

"Jack Ruby." She repeated the newscaster's identification of the man who had just shot Oswald on live TV. "I think I know that man."

A new waitress placed a napkin on the bar in front of her. "You know that man, Ruby, Miss Kilgallen?"

"Not really," she said. No use telling just anyone that Jack Ruby, the man being mentioned as Oswald's killer, had sent roses to her *What's My Line?* dressing room many times over the years. She still remembered Ruby's flattering notes penciled so neatly on pastel stationary attached to every bouquet. A burning sensation deep inside made her long for the big stories she had covered during her brave younger years.

Johnnie

The last few days, I moved as if I'd been physically wounded from all the unreal shit on TV. I must have looked like a casualty when I began a string of appearances in Ontario. My total collapse occurred on stage in Windsor. This was the big fall, and it happened a stone's throw across a narrow strip of water from Detroit City, so close to the town that had done its best to destroy me.

I went down hard. A pile of tired, brittle bones.

During my descent, I realized how bad it was this time around. Before, I'd always felt too invincible to die. Not this time. This was the instant that slammed me into that dark space, all the way to a dimension in which I saw the start of my life, and now the finish. Like the whole movie had spooled out and couldn't be spliced, not even altered one frame.

It's over, I said to no one and everyone. *It's so fucking over.*

Death was a dream. I heard pure music. Sights were brilliant, cinematic marvels. There for me to see was a kind of perfection to everything. All became a fight for death rather than life.

From somewhere, a voice said, "No."

And it sounded like something I would say.

Another dream. I am being rocked gently as if strapped to a raft. No, it's not a sea; it's a road, and I am aboard a vehicle.

A solemn male voice speaks of an equinox. I beg someone, anyone, to prop my head up on a rectangle of frosted light. Someone shades my eyes with dark glasses, and I'm lifted carefully.

Ghostly landscape rolls by. I know it in reverse from the trip to Niagara with Babe and Cornshucks.

It spreads now in muted springtime, a hallucinatory marvel under a black sun.

"This is a point in time," I say.

No longer sure of time and place, I watched vague figures I knew had to be doctors, who ignored the chart they'd posted at the end of my bed.

"Too far gone."

I fought.

"Slow down, give it up."

I fought.

Heads shook gravely, side to side. Dead-still eyes observed. Hard-line mouths uttered epitaphs.

I fought harder.

Once, keeping my eyes closed so not to lose a dream, I said to no one, "Black sun."

"He talking some old blues," a man remarked.

Must have been a message from the big male nurse, all starchy white uniform over dark flesh.

"You'll have to speak up, nurse," I said without raising an eyelid.

Another voice landed heavily. "You know who you are?"

"I'm Johnnie Ray."

"You know *where* you are?"

I didn't answer. Somehow I was sure the question didn't come from a doctor or the starched nurse.

"You're in Montfiore."

"What?"

"Hospital in the Bronx."

I refused to open my eyes and looked instead at my dream. "I was in Canada."

"You died there," a vaguely familiar male voice said. "In more ways than one."

"When?"

"Weeks ago," he informed me. "You lost a Christmas, a new year, a birthday."

I offered this wise guy no reaction and retreated into my dream of ancient wonders, skies so old and blue, songs I wrote when I was a boy.

"Open your eyes," the voice demanded.

"Don't need to. I see it all anyway."

"Shmucko."

A bit of alarm jarred me. "Where's Dotty?"

"Away for a while."

"Can't hear you."

Rapid chuckle. "You know who this is?"

Suddenly I dared to believe that I did, and I felt somehow that I'd been reattached to the world. "Yeah, you hip son of a bitch."

"Really?"

Yeah, really," I said, my eyes still closed, as if I were on *What's My Line?* "You're Lenny Bruce."

"Heh, heh, heh. You may now remove your blindfold."

And there he was, his dark eyes piercing mine as if he'd found my very soul.

"As long as you're not going to die on me, Johnnie," he said, "I'm going to ask you for some help."

I could see how his soul must have been hurting more than mine. "Anything for you, man."

"Actually I need a favor from your lady."

"Dotty?"

"Yeah, am I wrong coming at her through you?"

I trusted myself. Not just to speak for her, but to speak for what I knew both she and I hoped was still alive. "No Lenny," I said. "You're not wrong, man."

▧ ▧ ▧

A couple of weeks later, I walked away from the hospital into the sun. It was cold, but March offered soft promises. Behind me, Phillip Matthews guided me with a hand on my back. Ahead, Dotty led the way with birdlike steps. Her form flexed as if she'd become frozen from her vigil. I chuckled. She and Phillip must have worn out their rosary beads.

At Phillip's Oldsmobile, Dotty turned and faced me. "I've asked Phil to stick close by you."

I managed to meet her eyes, so wet and bright they reflected every car in the lot. "Let's go home. We'll talk about it."

I scanned her, then Phillip. He seemed hunched, bearing the burden of grief.

"Dorothy wants me to move in and help you for a while," he mumbled.

He helped fold me into the passenger seat, shut the door, and cantered stiffly around the front of the car. I lowered my window and watched it pass in front of my lady's face. Painful melancholia grabbed my heart, then all time— past, present, future — seemed to flee, and I sat alone in the sudden emptiness.

I squeezed Dotty's hand through the window, released her gloved fingers, and the sedan carried me away.

Dorothy

Dorothy spent the early part of 1964 helping with Robert Kennedy's campaign for the Senate. In February, she traveled to Dallas. Although she had not been assigned to cover Jack Ruby's trial officially, she knew there was a story there and planned on filing her report.

She had lunch that Thursday with Ruby's two attorneys, Melvin Belli, the famous West Coast attorney, and Joe Tonahill. Joe showed her a ten-page letter he had written to J. Edgar Hoover, to each member of the Warren Commission, and to Attorney General Robert Kennedy. The letter requested all of the reports, minutes, and evidence in the possession of the Warren Commission. Hoover refused to cooperate. The assistant attorney general's staff turned over material gleaned from more than fifteen hundred Warren Commission witnesses. Information concerning Oswald's assassination of the President would not be available, Tonahill was told, because it did not appear to be relevant.

"How could information about Oswald not be relevant?" she asked. "Why hasn't anyone written about this?"

Tonahill shook his head. "You tell me."

She filed her first assassination exclusive on February 21.

"It appears that Washington knows or suspects something about Lee Harvey Oswald that it does not want Dallas and the rest of the world to know or suspect... Lee Harvey Oswald has passed on not only to his shuddery reward, but to the mysterious realm of 'classified' persons

whose whole story is known only to a few government agents... Why is Oswald being kept in the shadows, as dim a figure as they can make him, while the defense tries to rescue his alleged killer with the help of information from the FBI? Who was Oswald, anyway?"

The day her story appeared, Joe Tonahill summoned her to the defense table during the noon recess. Jack Ruby sat next to him, burly but exhausted looking, dark hair slicked straight back.

Tonahill was a huge man, pure Texas, and not much for small talk. "Mr. Ruby wants to talk to you," he said.

"Good," she replied. "I'd like to talk to him, too."

He made the introductions, then settled on the other side of the table.

Ruby continually rubbed his hands together, as if trying to wipe away his fear. One index finger ended abruptly, bitten off in a fight, she had heard.

"I'd like to compliment you on your composure," she said, in an attempt to relax him. "I always appreciated your letters regarding *What's My Line?"*

"You're the best one on that show." He gave her the nervous smile of someone who was used to having his every move watched. "Here I am. I should be in the hospital. That will never happen, though. Imagine, Miss Kilgallen, I set half these cowboys up in my clubs. Now they're trying to lynch me. This is a felony on my record. Do you know that's a first?"

"What do you mean?"

"Not one mark on my record like this," he said. "Once the trial's over, I might talk to you about it. You'd be amazed."

"What are your feelings about the trial?" she asked. "Are you anticipating questions about your club and those strippers you employ?"

"I don't put moves on the girls at The Carousel. Just because I'm their boss don't mean I'm not a gentleman."

Tonahill moved in his chair. The recess was almost over.

"Why did you do it?" she asked Ruby.

He narrowed his eyes as if the light pained him. "Not yet," he said. "Later. I should be wearing medals, the things I been through."

After she left the attorneys in the courtroom, she heard someone call her name. There in the hallway, stood Sean Walters. Instead of his usual dark suit, he wore an open-collared shirt and Levi's. They weren't supposed to meet until later, and she was taken aback by his presence.

"What are you doing here?" she asked.

"I thought I'd surprise you. How'd it go with Ruby?"

She had no intention of sharing that information. She had told him only that she was coming to Dallas to meet with the attorneys. "I'm supposed to be the one doing the interviewing," she said.

"Don't worry. I know how to keep a secret. Tonahill's an old friend of mine."

So the Southern boys' club was alive and well in Dallas. She regretted agreeing to meet with him. "It's been a long day," she said. "I'm bushed."

"I know a barbecue place that grills some mean ribs."

She began striding toward the outside doors. "It looks like it's getting dark out."

"Cocktail hour." He took her arm. "There's a bar across the street that serves tequila with lime and salt."

She hesitated.

"Dorothy," he said, "It's just a drink."

"Is it?" she asked.

He grinned at her in a way that made her recall the early recklessness she had felt with Johnnie. "That's up to you."

Johnnie

I sat on a park bench waiting for Dotty and realized it had been a month since I saw her off to Dallas. I wondered if things would still be the same between us. Then I spotted her coming across the green. She strode awkwardly, looking self-conscious in slacks and a baggy sweater.

I stood to greet her. She removed enormous sunglasses and kissed me on the lips. When we sat down, she wound the wool scarf I'd loosened around my neck.

"I'm not an invalid." I ran a glance over her. "Some kind of disguise?"

"Yes."

"Who you hiding from?"

"Start with Dick's cronies." Her eyes grew round and alarmed. "Go from there to just about anyone you wish to pick."

"Come on," I encouraged her. "They can't kill us."

She took a swipe at her windblown hair. "The hell they can't."

I knew she was thinking about Marilyn and Kennedy, maybe others.

An elderly man stopped at the bench. Practically bent in half, he regarded me out of the corner of one eye. "You're what's wrong with this country," he said, then nodding agreement to himself, he trucked away.

Watching his thin legs and slack ass in his worn pants, I started to laugh. Dorothy looked like she was about to cry and rummaged through her purse.

"Nothing for the pigeons," she said.

We sat in silence. A breeze came up, carrying small leaves and a hot dog wrapper.

"I testified yesterday for Lenny Bruce," she told me.

"Can you imagine him, coming into my hospital room?" I said. "I hope I was right about telling him you would help."

"I told the court he's a very moral man."

"You believe it?"

"I believe he didn't violate the New York Statute on Obscenity." She pulled at an eyelash and breathed deeply. "I was asked about motherfucker, shit, asshole, and plain old fuck."

"What happened to cocksucker?"

"I must have looked too innocent."

I thought of that night in Chicago after Lenny's show. "You are too innocent."

"I told them I'd heard the words before."

"Yeah?"

"From James Baldwin, from Tennessee Williams."

I lit two cigarettes and handed her one. She inhaled and stared ahead at two Frisbee players. She smiled at a woman pushing a baby stroller. I could tell by the way the woman returned her smile that she would carry her recognition of Dorothy Kilgallen with her. "Guess who I saw sitting in Central Park with some skinny dope fiend?" she'd tell a neighbor.

"You got claimed," I said.

"Wear pants and still I can't hide." She rubbed her cigarette ash out on the cement path. "Johnnie." She turned to study me. "I've got another exclusive interview with Jack Ruby. I leave again for Dallas tomorrow."

Suddenly I was aboard a glacier or riding those freezing Niagara Falls. Shadows from that alley behind The Flame fell darkly over me. My lady was leaving me for the dangerous world again.

"Is it cleared?"

She looked at me, puzzled.

"I mean with the FBI, the CIA, the government, fucking Hoover, Lyndon Johnson, whoever. Is it okay?"

I reached for her and held her in my scrawny arms. I couldn't stop shaking and trying to ask her questions. The battery pack I'd been wearing for my hearing had slipped down my spine, and I started to curse.

The old, stooped man had come back. Standing near a tree, he appeared to be spying on us. I held her tighter.

After a moment, I relaxed and squared my shoulders. "I got a gig myself coming up."

She pulled away. "It's too soon."

"At the Latin Quarter."

I could tell she was worried about how I'd stand up under the pressure. At the same time, she couldn't hide her excitement. "Headlining? How long?"

It hit me then, that she might be thinking of Sean Walters, the young guy she'd been seen with lately, the one Phillip had told me was involved with singer Phyllis McGuire and the mob. The song McGuire and her sisters made a hit ran through my mind, and like an idiot, I hummed a few bars of *Sincerely*.

The old man under the tree sent me the snake eye.

"About a week," I said, "with Johnny Puleo."

Dorothy's eyes dimmed. "The same Johnny Puleo who has the Harmonicats?"

"At least it's a gig."

"Morrie's choice?"

"The only choice."

Mustering all the brightness she could find, she rose. "You'll kill 'em."

"Yeah, yeah."

"What was the point of your humming that song just now?" she asked. "You owe me that." Then she shook her head as if to say, don't bother, and I realized that I'd never outrace her thoughts. "Sean is a friend and has been for a while. In a way, we are working together on the Kennedy thing, but that's as far as it goes."

"It could go much farther," I said, "if that mobster Sam Giancana shows up in the picture."

"That might just happen." She placed a gloved finger over my lips. "Must go. How did you get here?"

"Phillip."

"Come with me." She waved an arm into the wind. "I'm that-a-way."

"Gotta be here when he comes back." I studied my watch. "About twenty minutes."

And there it was. That small, sad resigned smile on her pale face. I wondered. Had I thrown in my hand too early? Would she still be willing to give up everything for me now?

"This Jack Ruby thing," I said. "Be careful."

"After that, I'm going to New Orleans. Johnnie, I think I'm onto something."

"Is there an end to it? Is it worth disturbing the water that's finally coming to a rest?"

"It's what I do."

We kissed goodbye.

She moved swiftly across the green, and I caught sight of the old man. Doubled over, he shifted his weight from foot to foot.

I got off the bench and waved one last time at Dotty's diminishing figure. Then I approached the old geezer slowly and gave him my Johnny Appleseed grin. "Restrooms aren't far away, Sarge," I told him. "Can I help you locate one?"

"I'll wet myself, Junior, if you can't."

I took his thin fingers in mine, assisted him along a path, then turned him loose. "Bear right at that fork in the road, and you can't miss it."

I didn't go any farther. Holding a man's hand near public facilities, no matter his age, wasn't something I should be doing.

The sun hid for a moment, then jumped out from among the treetops. Pigeons ran behind me as if I might have found something for them in my empty pockets. I saw Phillip standing up near the bench. Two boys, two girls, college types, passed by. One was singing a Beatles song. The others strummed imaginary guitars.

"I want to hold your hand," screamed the singer.

When I reached Phillip, I noticed the smile on his face. "Kids," he said.

"Kids who buy records." I smiled too, but it didn't come easy.

Dorothy

The case occupied her life in the same way Johnnie once had. She finally made arrangements through the judge for a private interview with Jack Ruby. Again Joe Tonahill acted as the go-between.

"Well," Tonahill said. "Guess you know you're the first newspaper person to see him alone."

He led her to a small office behind the judge's bench. The four sheriffs guards agreed to remain outside the room. At the noon recess, Ruby joined them. He already looked older, more helpless, like a man moving toward his inevitable end.

"Good to see you again," she said, as Tonahill departed and they took their seats at the dingy metal table. "I want to talk to you about what happened. I want to tell your story."

"Better think twice about that," Ruby said. "They're going to kill me is what's going to happen."

"Even if you're found guilty, you can appeal," she told him.

"It's bigger than me and Dallas, so big that I'll die before I ever get nailed for it."

"No one can get to you in here, can they?" she asked.

"My brain is turning to cancer, so you tell me."

His eyes wandered around the room, the only room, the attorneys had assured her, that wasn't bugged.

"Who wants to kill you?" she asked, purposely using a matter-of-fact tone.

"Who don't want me to talk?" he said. "Go figure. Your seeing me here is cancer. But you're a reporter. You gotta chance at the truth. What's going to happen to my family? Are they going to go after them after they eat my brain? Do you know the network, these people? The cancer cell labs?"

He was too rattled to make sense. An exclusive interview, and she couldn't get a comment worthy of print. If they'd only allowed her time enough to convince this man that he could trust her.

"I know that the whole truth has not been told. I've said so in print, and I'm going to say so in my book. The eyewitness who described Oswald to the police was too far away to see him. Who was behind it, Jack? The FBI? The mob?"

"They're the same, in the same network," he said. "Why do you think Hoover won't cooperate? This so-called Warren Report won't listen to the way it went. They march these witnesses out like ducks in a shooting gallery."

"Why did you kill Oswald?" She watched his eyes. "Tell me the truth."

He looked down at his open hands on the table. "Would you want Jackie Kennedy to have to go through a trial? Her little boy holding her hand, did you see that?" he said. "I used to love this country, no questions, but now they put cancer cells in my food, straight to my stomach, then to my brain, so no one will believe me." He raised his gaze to meet hers. "Eight to five, you'll never print this. You're scared too. Blue ribbons we ain't going to get, Miss Kilgallen. Christ, I thought they'd put my statue up in D-Town."

"D-Town? You mean Dallas?"

He shook his head. "Dago Town, Chicago, two, three blocks from the action."

"What action?"

"Where I used to run numbers when I was a kid." He looked off as if searching. "Just a little kid, Miss Kilgallen," he said in a soft voice. "A little kid, and I ran numbers for Al Capone."

"A Jewish boy in the Italian section." She tried to egg him on while keeping the frustration out of her voice.

"That surprise you?" He gave her a bitter look and chuckled. "You'd be amazed, the things we do to be made."

"What things, Jack?"

"What it means to have Mo's approval, his personal handshake."

Mo, she thought, as in Sam Giancana.

"Do you mean you shot Oswald in order to please the mob?" When he failed to answer, she directed her next question from a different angle. "Jack, was Oswald just a patsy the mob wanted killed before he could testify?"

A knock on the door was followed by Tonahill's lumbering return to the room. "It's time," he said.

Ruby leaned forward, his eyes tortured, pleading for her help. But still he hadn't answered her questions.

"But we've had only ten minutes," Dorothy said.

"Eight, to be exact," Ruby told her. "Keep in touch, Miss Kilgallen."

She caught him in a last glance. His hands covered his face. "In my head, behind my eyes, I see the killing of my brain," he mumbled. "Can you imagine that? They're using the Warren Report as a directory to kill us all."

After they led him away, she spoke with one of Belli's associates, a strictly business woman close to her age. "Who is 'Mo' to Jack Ruby?" she asked as a test as much as anything else.

"I'm not sure," the woman replied.

"Isn't it Sam Giancana's nickname?"

"I believe he's been called MoMo."

"Ruby told me I'd be amazed at the things a man would do to be made. What could he mean?"

"Being a made man, taking someone out," the woman said.

"Would Ruby do that? Would he shoot Oswald to move up in the mob?"

The woman gathered her folders and glanced at her watch. "I'm trying to find out why Ruby *wouldn't* do it," she said. "Sorry, I've got to meet with our client."

"I don't think he'd do it just for money," Dorothy said. "But he'd do it for fame, self-respect in his old neighborhood."

The woman smiled and shook her head. "Not bad, Miss Kilgallen," she said. "Not bad at all."

Dorothy left feeling victorious. With or without Jack Ruby, this was her story. Crazy or not, Ruby feared for his life. This only supported the reports she'd already heard about witnesses being threatened by the Dallas Police and the FBI.

Through another source, she gained possession of the police log covering the department's radio communications after the assassination. The police chief riding in the first car of the motorcade directed officers to get a man on top of the overpass. Yet the day after the assassination, he told reporters that the shots had come from the Texas School Depository, and that he'd radioed officers to surround that building.

The description the Dallas police radioed of Oswald was provided by a steam fitter. He was more than one hundred feet away from the sixth-floor window where the kill shots were reportedly fired.

Late one night after she had returned from Dallas, she solicited Dick's help in an experiment.

"What do I have to do?" he asked. He'd been hanging around a lot in hope of saving their marriage. Already he'd had too much to drink, but it didn't matter. She would be the clearheaded one.

On a sunny afternoon, she handed him a broom. "Go up to the fifth floor and lean out of one of the corner windows with this. Just don't fall. And don't shoot."

"Don't tempt me." He waved the broom, and she felt a chill, remembering the night she'd feared he would do just that.

She left the townhouse on East 68th Street, and paced approximately one hundred feet. If anyone were watching, they'd think she and Dick had devised a new parlor game. She looked up and squinted. No way could she discern Dick's features from this distance and this angle. Someone had lied.

* * *

The Warren Commission Report was scheduled for release in late September. Dorothy called in more favors and obtained one hundred and two pages early, much of them dealing with Jack Ruby's testimony. Of course she wouldn't reveal her source, Jerry Sartor, a former journalist and colleague, who had acted as a liaison between the Commission and the FBI.

Convincing her publisher to run it wasn't easy. This would be the first glimpse the public had of the Warren Report, probably the most anticipated document of the decade if not the century. Although it wasn't verbalized, she felt her publisher's reluctance to anger the administration. It was breaking news, she argued. She hadn't broken the law to obtain it. The newspaper couldn't afford to turn it down.

She argued her case until the publisher finally agreed. The excerpt, with sidebars of questions and speculations, would run in three parts, starting August 18.

"The administration won't be happy," Johnnie told her on the phone when she shared her good news with him. "Guess you won't be going to any parties at the White House."

"Lyndon's a bore," she said. "Who wants to go to his parties? It's J. Edgar Hoover who scares me."

The report stated that the steam fitter had been in an excellent position to observe the window from which Kennedy was allegedly assassinated. Her experiment with Dick had proven that it couldn't be true. The report was a sham.

Three days after her first excerpt appeared in print, Julian told her that two federal agents were waiting downstairs. She wasn't surprised.

After the introductions were made, she said, "Do come in and have some tea."

One talked. One took notes. Neither drank tea. The talker, sharp featured and well-dressed, had smooth, freshly shaved skin and stark, prematurely white hair. His overweight partner, eyes enlarged by rimless lenses, was around the same age but looked years older.

"Miss Kilgallen," the talker said. "How did this material come into your possession?"

"Well, it wasn't John Daly," she replied.

"I take it that's a joke?"

"An attempt at levity. John's the master of ceremonies on *What's My Line?* He's married to the daughter of Chief Justice Warren."

"I know that," the agent said. "Look, Miss Kilgallen—"

"Mrs. Kollmar to you."

"Is that what Johnnie Ray calls you?"

"What my friends call me is none of your business," she said.

"Everything about you is part of our business now, Miss Kilgallen, even your disrespect for President Johnson."

"You think I disrespect LBJ?"

"Perhaps you do. Perhaps you even find him boring. You don't like his parties. We're interested in all of it."

They had listened to her calls! Probably bugged the house. "I don't have anything else to say to you right now. You are aware that I'm writing a book?"

"*Murder One*," the talker said in a matter-of-fact tone. "Already four years late at Random House."

"But, as my editor Bennett Cerf says, worth the wait," she countered. "Be careful what you say. You may see yourself in print."

The note-taker looked up at this. The talker glanced at him, then back at her.

"There's no need to threaten," he said. "We simply want to know where you got the copy of the Warren Report excerpt. Are you going to tell us or not?"

Still shaken from the realization that her home phones were bugged, she replied, "You want me to name my source?"

"That's right."

"Sir," she said, and rose from the chair. "I'd rather die."

Johnnie

"You can't give up on yourself." Phillip Matthews massaged my shoulders.

I sniffed the air in the room. "Are you using Tiger Balm?"

"This is my last can," Phillip said. "I bought a hundred tins of the stuff a few years ago in Hong Kong."

"Well, you better line up another trip."

He slapped my bare ass. I could tell he wanted to boost my spirits by talking about my last gig. "Remember the Latin Quarter?" he asked.

Man, I remembered all my funerals. "Couple months after my final rites," I said.

"All the reviews agreed you stripped down to your soul."

"Yeah, right there in front of the Harmonicats."

"That's when I realized I'd never give up on you, Johnnie," he said. "That and later when you showed such fortitude in Vegas."

"Came into the Tropicana to jeers, performed to cheers, left 'em in tears."

"Dorothy wrote that," he said.

"She was there in spirit every night."

"I can believe that," Phillip said.

My bedroom had a moody feel to it, blue afternoon shadows, Sabrina thumping as she scratched her ear. No Raphael. Turned out he hadn't fibbed about his family's estate. He'd even offered to stay and share his inheritance.

"Sayonara," Phillip had said.

Of course getting rid of Rafael was Phillip's way of taming the apartment's wildness. In a way, it had worked, but I was still on the sauce. I tried not to flaunt it in front of him. "Got to keep my liver marinated," I quipped when he shook his finger at me. And when he insisted I pay attention to all of the financial reports from Saul Rosen, I said, "Later." I knew our boat was sinking, but I didn't want to see it in black and white.

On the edge of my bed, I reached for a towel from him and watched him turn to leave the room, his limp noticeable today.

"Hop over here, Phillip," I said. "Let me work on that leg."

"Some other time," he replied. "Things to do."

"Like what?"

"Like lining up our flight to L.A." He wiped his hands on a towel he'd stuck in his belt and appraised me with a level gaze as I pulled on a pair of jockey shorts. "I want to call a meeting before your West Coast dates."

"These dates. They amount to anything?"

"Truthfully, no. That's why the meeting. Morrie, Saul Rosen, you, and me."

"Morrie ain't going to like what we have to say."

"And you aren't going to like what Saul has to say."

It became apparent to me, as Phillip lumbered down the hall, that this would be one trip west that wouldn't be like old times.

Dotty worked heavy on my mind. I'd left a message for her at Tabby's, one of the places we used as an answering service. Lately we'd had trouble hooking up.

Later that evening I walked the floor alone, half drunk, fearing the night. The echo of a telephone ringing stopped me in my tracks. Thank the lord, Dotty was on the other end.   "Johnnie, I must see you." Her voice lacked its usual bell-toned gaiety. She spoke in a windy rush.

"When?" I asked. "I can never find you."

"I heard your Liberty recording with Timi Yuro."

"And?"

"She sounded like Dinah Washington on speed." Her small laugh sounded brash. "Matter of fact, so did you."

"That good, eh?"

No laughter, just the buzz on the line. "What's wrong, baby?"

"Johnnie, I've got to talk to you. You're the only one I feel safe with."

"Name the time and place."

"When I get back. I'm going to California to meet Mark Lane."

"The guy with the book on JFK's assassination?" I didn't feel good about this. Lane was already getting bad press about his conspiracy theories.

"Yes." She swallowed, and I heard the sound of ice against glass. "I'm making progress on my book, too, the Kennedy stuff."

I didn't know what to say to that. It made me shiver under my skin. I reached for my glass and found it empty when I tipped it up.

After a pause, she said, "Did you hear Malcolm X was shot down?"

I hadn't. In fact I wasn't sure who the cat was. "Maybe we can get together on the West Coast."

"You'll be out there, too?"

"We'll compare dates."

"Take me to the beach, first thing." Her voice started to drag like a record losing its spin.

Shit, I must have sounded the same to her. Longing for her, I tried for what I knew would never work. "Come up for a nightcap, baby."

"Can't. I just chased a goodbye."

A goodbye. Her pet name for Seconal.

"Be careful," I told her, and tried to beat the click of her hang-up.

In front of my long windows, I peered out at the night. Same lights, same moving line of traffic.

Same, only different without her.

Dorothy

Her head ached. The light from a blaze of candles hurt her eyes as she stared at the leather sofa and the too-silly drum table of the black room. Why was she here? Where was Johnnie? The phone rang. She grabbed it. "Johnnie?"

"Dorothy, it's me, Clarice."

"Be careful what you say."

"You sound terrible. Have you been ill?"

"Yes, ill." Those monitoring her phone wouldn't hear anything incriminating from Clarice. She wouldn't have to worry about that.

"I was just wondering. You missed our party for Sophia's new film last night."

The party. She'd forgotten. "Sorry. I'd written it down. This book has taken all of my time."

"I'm worried about you. It's as if you've disappeared into that project."

"It'll be over soon," she said, her voice halting.

"Roland, as usual, is concerned."

"About one party?" she said before she could stop herself.

"Parties, plural," Clarice replied. "People are talking, Dorothy. Some fear you're going off the deep end."

She closed her eyes and tried to lock out Clarice's voice. Everyone wanted something from her. The station had wanted too much. *What's My Line?* wanted too much. Her paper. Jack Ruby. Dick. The government.

"Clarice, I'm working on the biggest story of my life. It is a conspiracy, and everyone involved in it is dropping dead left and right."

"Do you really think Marilyn's death was part of it?"

"I do. My own life could be in danger." She realized they could be listening to every word she said. "I must go. I can't talk anymore."

"Very well. If you need anything—"

"Goodbye, Clarice. I'll talk to you later."

She hung up before Clarice could say another word. What was she going to do? She couldn't use her home phone and couldn't trust what she might inadvertently say. From now on, she'd rely on public phones. It was the only safe way.

The pearls around her neck felt as if they were choking her. She needed another drink. Halfway to the bar, she realized she was holding one.

A moment later, she saw a man at her door. It was Babe Pascoe.

"Goodness," she said, "I didn't recognize you in that suit, Babe. Where's Johnnie?"

"He's in California, remember? Sorry to give you such a start. Julian let me in. He was right here. I thought you saw us."

"Oh, that's right." She felt confused. Where were she and Babe supposed to be going?

He seemed to sense the confusion and answered the question for her. "Rose Helen is waiting downstairs. Remember? We have tickets for *Funny Girl*." He paused. "Don't have to go, though, if it's a hassle."

"No, I want to." Now, she remembered. She wanted to see Barbra Streisand, the young singer for whom everyone had such high expectations. And she needed to get out of here, away from the eavesdroppers on her phone.

"I'm ready."

"All right," he said. "Here, we'd better zip your dress, though."

That's what they were doing to her—making her absent-minded, forgetful. "You must think I'm terrible going around half-dressed."

Her fingers fumbled with the zipper. "Damn. Would you mind?"

"No sweat." He stepped behind her. "There you go."

"It's this story I'm working on," she said. "They're bugging my phones, Babe. I don't know who's on my side and who isn't."

"Well." He took her arm. "I'm on your side. You can count on that. And Rose Helen too, always."

"And Johnnie?"

"He's on your side too."

"I know." Counting the people who cared for her made her feel better. She took a deep breath. "I have a new source, Babe. He's tied into the government and knows a lot about what did and didn't happen in Dallas that day."

"Well, that sounds helpful. Ready to split?"

"Of course," she said, impatient with his solicitous manner. "What are you waiting for?"

He looked at her right hand so pointedly that she followed his gaze. She still held the tumbler as if it were part of her attire. "Oh, this," she said, and placed it on the drum table.

She nodded toward the phone and whispered as they left. "CIA. They listen to all of my conversations. Can't talk in here anymore. Not ever."

Johnnie

We hit L.A. a week before my first engagement. Morrie had booked me off Sunset in a club I'd never heard of. Hollywood, full of muscle, played a whole new game out here. Some real action popped up on the Strip again, kids everywhere on the street, marijuana in the night air.

Phillip drove as I gazed out the rental car's window, my eyes weary from jet lag.

"Lotta boo along here, Phillip," I said.

"Boo," Phillip repeated my word for pot and laughed. "Tomorrow is Halloween."

The sky was a lustrous dome ahead of the car. Phillip took his time. Cars honked along our procession.

"Where's the San Fernando Valley?" I asked him.

He jerked a thumb at the iridescent night. "Over the hill."

"My sister Elma remarried and came out here a couple of years ago," I told him. "I've got to see her."

"You will," Phillip said. "Tomorrow night at the Halloween party."

That threw me. "What?"

"I've rented Vic Damone's old place in West Hollywood, and I gave her the number."

In a trance, I felt the car turn off Sunset Strip. I heard Damone's sweet voice and indulged a memory of Dotty's small hand in mine as he crooned "An Affair to Remember."

"Are you going to be all right?" Phillip's strong fingers squeezed my shoulder.

"She might be here tomorrow," I said.

"Dotty?"

"Yeah."

"She will be," Phillip said. "I called her yesterday myself and gave her the address."

I couldn't believe it. "All this and Halloween too," I said. "Things are looking up."

■ ■ ■

The next day we met in Saul Rosen's place, typical Old Hollywood digs with lots of blond wood and beachy furniture. Saul and Morrie were waiting when Saul's secretary escorted Phillip and me into his private office. Like most women of a certain age, the secretary seemed a bit awed by me. These types, admittedly, had become a rare species.

The four of us sat around Saul's desk, lots of heliotrope and pastel in our attire. Cigar smoke hung above the desk, which meant Morrie had been there awhile. All started friendly at first, and I could tell that Morrie was thankful I hadn't died yet. Saul had always proven himself a straight shooter, so I was glad when he became serious.

"Johnnie, there's only one way to say this," he told me. "You're broke."

I looked at Morrie first as if to say *I expected this to be bad, but not broke bad.* Sunset and Vine clashed softly outside.

Saul must have read my mind. "Costs keep escalating. I've sent you warnings. You're like always one step ahead of the storm."

Phillip stood. "Johnnie's been getting smaller and smaller percentages."

"True," Saul agreed. He looked pale, a century old.

"Why didn't you cut back everyone else?" Phillip stared down Morrie. "Everybody but Johnnie keeps eating high on the hog."

Morrie waved his arms like he was trying to escape a straitjacket. "Damn it, I ain't taking the rap over here. Every time I want to discuss finances, Johnnie is smashed or laid up in a fucking hospital."

"No one but Johnnie could have survived his schedule." Phillip pointed at me. "He's been your meal ticket. It's time you treated him with respect."

Right then, don't ask what I'd have done for a drink. "How broke is broke?" I asked.

Saul didn't move a muscle.

I snapped my fingers. "You're telling me that I'm completely tapped out?"

Saul covered his face with vein-lined hands. "That's a correct assessment, thanks to the IRS."

"And just how bad are they on my ass?"

"I should be able to fend them off," Saul said, "but, Johnnie, they might lien your folks' farm. It's still in your name."

"Jesus, I can't let that happen."

Saul mumbled and dug through some papers. I started shaking but managed to get to my feet and lean across the desk. "Look at me, Saul."

A crack split his brow. Genuine sympathy shone in his eyes. Some fright, too.

"Okay." My voice trembled. "You've always been a friend to me, Saul, and I'm going to trust you with some requests."

Phillip placed a hand on my elbow.

"It's okay," I told him. Then to Saul, "I want you to fire everyone on the payroll except you and Phillip."

"Everyone." Saul repeated the word and looked smack at Morrie. "What about Mr. Blaine's contract?"

I turned so Morrie could see my face. "Mr. Blane's always said if it ever came to a point we weren't compatible, if the contract wasn't working, he'd tear it up." I almost choked, but I managed to keep my voice level. "So, fish it out of your files, and we'll make confetti out of the motherfucker."

■ ■ ■

Outside the office I caught up with Morrie. He seemed to have lost his car or was searching the streets for a ride.

"Can Phillip and I drop you anywhere?" Christ, I didn't know how to talk to him. Maybe I never had.

"No." He shaded his eyes. "Gladys is picking me up for lunch."

We stood on the corner. Memories swarmed like bees between us. I felt that I couldn't let loose of the guy but couldn't think of any gesture or speech that would give rise to anything worth all the times we'd shared.

"You know, Johnnie," he said, finally. "I was nothing but a song-plugger when I found you. A stupid, fucking song-plugger."

"Listen, Morrie."

"But I knew what I had."

"Ah, shit, pal."

"I've always known what I had with you. I saw things in you all the smart sonsabitches missed." He held out his hand. I shook it. "The trouble was, Johnnie, you must not have seen what you had, or you wouldn't have been so hell bent on throwing it away."

"I got some left, Morrie," I said. "I know I do."

His grip tightened. I swayed. He pulled me upright. "I know you do too, kid. Let's just hope someone else does."

We parted, and he gave me a bewildered grin as if saying good-bye wasn't in our language.

"Meeting the wife," he said. "Think that's her waiting up there at the wrong corner."

Like Gladys didn't know Hollywood and Vine. Like he could see that far to pick out his wife's car in all that traffic.

Johnnie

Vic Damone's place on St. Ive's Drive impressed me no end. Inside, I opened the sliding glass doors, and we got a view of all of L.A. A white piano sat on orange carpet in a perfect party room. Guests started arriving for our Halloween bash, tanned smoothies from Phillip's world, a few old ghosts from mine like my former PR guy Chip O'Hara and Marcie, the blond stripper Dorothy was so steamed about from that long-ago New Year's Eve swim party.

My sister Elma and her husband arrived. Seeing her lifted my spirits. We made plans for a reunion with the folks. I promised myself to save their farm from the IRS.

Phillip appeared fresh after a hard day. The guy was my rock. After the meeting at Saul's office, he called on half the booking agents in L.A. And now this party he had arranged.

Everyone entered in some kind of costume. Phillip wore a paisley mask to match his psychedelic Peter Max flared trousers. I'd put on a tangerine pirate shirt the same shade as the carpet and a hoop earring that clipped onto my so-called "good" ear.

Don't ask what costume Marcie had on. Mostly just her blond hair and some Playboy bunny ears.

We clinked glasses, told lies, and yuk-yuked. Then another couple flounced in. Man, here came Cornshucks and Babe Pascoe. Phillip watched my face beam. I figured this was more of his doing.

Babe pumped my hand. "We made it here from San Francisco in seven hours."

I grinned. "In your Fairlane?"

"What else?" He took a glass of wine off the caterer's tray. "Rose Helen and I are playing at the Johnny Otis Grand Revue later tonight."

Cornshucks looked slinky and radiant. She had ditched the wig and let her hair go natural.

"My, my," I said, and appraised her trim figure.

She made a full turn for me. "Just a shadow of my former self."

We jived a bit. I thought of Johnny Otis's revue and felt a pang, an old trouper's wish to be part of it.

The Shucker yanked me into the kitchen. "Johnnie, I got a show primed for the Latin Quarter late December. I mentioned it to Phillip on the phone."

"Wonderful," I said. "I'm happy for you."

She gripped my shoulder. "Listen, Bluebird —"

Took me a minute to realize she meant the pirate. "Bluebeard, if you're talking buccaneers."

"I'm talking cotton, fool." She flicked my earring with a scarlet fingernail. "Listen."

"I'm listening."

"I want your skinny ass up on that stage with me."

"If I'm in New York, I'll drop by to see your show. You know that."

"See my show? Shee-it. You in it, sharing my billing."

My knees felt that one. "Ah, Shucker, that's nice, but the last time I shared that stage was with the fucking Harmonicats."

"What's wrong with that?" Her grand smile sparkled. "You play a little blues harp yourself."

Later, when I knew I wouldn't break out in tears, I acted cool in conversation with her, Babe, and Phillip.

Alone with Babe, I told him how much I'd missed him. "No one can match your beat, man."

"There's drummers on every corner."

"There's drummers, and then there are musicians like you," I said. "By the way, how's married life?"

"Like Korea, 1951," he said with a grin.

First time I'd ever heard him make light of his war. "Is Viet Nam going to be another one of those?"

"Worse," he said.

"How's the Shucker's little brother?"

"Let's just say Carlton never made the Yankees." That tough Hell's Kitchen face softened under his road whiskers. "Best we run, Johnnie."

"I love you, Babe."

"Love you too, J.R." He put his rough cheek against mine. "We go back a ways, pal."

"Yep."

"Me and Rose Helen, we don't forget."

"I was out of it, but I know you came to see me in that Bronx hospital."

"Yeah." He pulled up his coat sleeve and checked his watch. "Phillip said Dorothy might drop by."

"Maybe, if she makes her connections."

"Give her our love."

"Will do."

"Last time I saw her, Johnnie, she didn't look good."

"She's trying to solve JFK's death all by herself," I said. "It's like she's fighting to salvage her career."

Cornshucks snuck up behind me. "Sometime we look for salvation in all the wrong places."

"You can bet I did," I said, but she and Babe had begun to take off, carrying their music and their wisdom with them.

Dotty showed up late. As we hugged, she felt like a current of electric energy in my arms. I fixed her up with a drink as other people started to greet her. When Christopher George and his wife started pulling me toward the piano, she smiled and whispered to me. "Break a leg, sweetheart."

A few diehards listened as I pounded the piano and sang *Walkin My Baby Back Home*, one of Dotty's favorites. The group warmed up, and I launched into one I'd performed at the London Palladium. "*Makes no difference how I carry on*," I sang. "*Just remember, please don't talk about me when I'm gone.*"

Thank God blond Marcie had split with some guy who looked like Johnny Weissmuller's younger brother. Dotty acted stiff but polite. It was plain she wanted to get me alone. We stole away to a small study and tossed back shots of vodka. She relaxed some and plopped in a leather chair looking high style in a black suit with pearls woven into her upswept hair.

"Who are you supposed to be?" she asked. "Errol Flynn?"

"I could be, if we go into a bedroom."

She smiled. "I checked into a Ramada Inn between Venice and Santa Monica." She slapped a hip. "Should have changed clothes."

The room felt stuffy, warm. The last thing we needed was another drink. I poured us more anyway. She drank and took a deep breath. Plainly, I could see that she was trying to hold herself together.

"I shouldn't be out like this," she said.

"Like what?" I asked.

My question had shot right by her.

"You promised to take me to the beach," she said.

■ ■ ■

I drove the rented Oldsmobile. Behind the wheel, I was no A.J. Foyt, but I managed to locate a fissured strip of asphalt so close to the moonlit beach and full of ocean smell that I relaxed. Even the metallic sound in my ears had ceased.

Dotty, though, appeared agitated. She jumped out of the car. I went after her, grabbed her arm, and we stepped onto the sand. The air hadn't lost all of its summer warmth. Fires burned farther down the beach, and Halloween screams broke faintly in the distance. Southward, a line of paint-worn structures faced the sea, and a pair of teen-agers seemed to be searching for love under the boardwalk lamps.

Dotty ran shoeless toward the waves. A phosphorescent glow brightened the pearls in her hair. I gave chase until our hands met. Cold froth broke against my knees. I tried to stand firm against the undertow, but I was too weak. We pulled one another in opposite directions.

"Dotty."

She resisted my hand. "No."

"It's sweeping us out."

We went under.

My pirate shirt billowed. I pushed it down and sought out her pale face in the black water. Sea water filled my mouth, and I felt its force. It yielded for a millisecond, and I broke the churning surface.

"Johnnie," Dotty screamed.

I flailed and hooked her slender neck in the crook of my arm. We rode the sea as it slid toward the beach. I feared that I'd splinter her neck as I stayed afloat on a crest. Then I loosened her as the current carried us ashore. My face against hers, I felt her ragged gasps. A cloud obscured the moon and made an equinox. After a time, I felt strong enough to urge her, and we crawled like wayward toddlers to dry sand.

"My God," I said, out of breath. "What the fuck are we doing?"

She shrugged, then shouted. "My pearls."

I touched the beads in her wet hair, and they cascaded into my palm. "Luck," I said.

"Of the Irish," she added.

At the Olds, I dug my wallet and keys out of my wet pants. I was about to open the car door when a police prowler grounded onto the strip and swung its spotlight on the two of us.

We froze. I wrapped an arm around Dotty's wet back. A tremor played her body like a tune, and I feared that she might break into pieces.

"Late to be taking a dip." The patrol cop had left his spotlight on and taken a stance in its beam.

"Officer." Somehow I found my voice. "You'll have to speak up. I'm Johnnie Ray, and my hearing aid is on the front seat."

He slowly moved toward the car's window. His larger-than-life size uniform gave me pause, and in a funny thought, I wondered if he was an imposter in a Halloween costume. The ominous patrol car emitted static and radio words that blew that thought. His leather squeaked as he put one hand on his holster and looked from me to the car's interior, then back at Dotty.

"What's your name, Miss?"

I heard her speak to him, but a chilling wind had broken free along the beach and wiped away her answer.

His question, aimed at me, stretched above the breeze. "Is this your car, Mr. Ray?"

"Rental." I got a good look at him. He appeared older than at first sight, his mug an outbreak of fine lines.

He moved his gaze for a second to the car again. "Open containers."

Now here came the fear. Dotty must have been terrified. "What?" she asked.

His uniform glinted as he shifted his weight. "Them itty bitty kind the airline gives out."

"Miss Kilgallen flew in today," I said. "She collects them."

"She collect them empty or full?"

"They've been empty for hours."

"Are you really Johnnie Ray?" he asked.

"Yes," I said, "but please don't ask me to cry."

He chuckled. "Know what I almost said when you told me who you are?"

Silence from me, and then I felt Dotty's hand pull away. "You almost said, 'Yeah, and I'm Little Richard,'" she said. "Right?" Her voice sounded hard on this desolate strip.

"Well, I'll be damned," the cop said. "I really was going to say that."

He gave a little smile and hustled to his car. Then he ignored his radio, eased into his seat, and pulled the prowler so close I could smell its interior.

"Where's home tonight, Mr. Ray?"

"Washington Street, not far," Dotty answered.

"I'll see you get there, okay?"

"We're a little shaky, sir," I said. "It's been a long night."

"Oh?" He looked up and down the beach. "You folks got no call to be out here like this. Now ease that Olds on out."

"I'm a tad rusty behind the wheel, but I'll do my best."

"I know you will, Mr. Ray," he said. Then he barked at his radio and pulled out in a low screech.

Next to me, Dotty said something about having to pee, and I could tell the encounter with the cop had left her terrified.

That night, in the shower, I noticed her body's changes. The drum tightness was gone from her flesh, not as much rosiness. Small bruises. A large, mean one stained her arm above and below her right elbow.

She turned, and in her eyes, I saw that hard, cold hazel, more deep-set than I'd remembered.

"You examining me?" Before I answered, she moved away and turned off the water.

"You look great compared to me." And that was the truth.

She swept the shower curtain out of her way and nearly fell while stepping over the tub's edge. Then she flung a towel into my chest.

With my face buried in the towel, I mumbled how young she still looked. When we'd finally dried ourselves, our eyes met, and we stood naked in the foreign space. After swallowing Seconal tablets, we returned to the tangled bed.

"Here comes the killing hour," I said.

Her face turned stoic. I swore I could hear her body buzzing as if she'd plugged her soul into a socket.

"Still scared?" I asked, and remembered how convinced she'd been during our wet drive from the beach that we'd be intercepted and killed as fugitives.

She pulled a blanket up to her chin. "Think I'm paranoid? Every-one else does."

I didn't answer soon enough.

"Don't pretend you can't hear me."

"I always hear your voice, Dotty." It was true. For some reason, I was tuned in to her like no other sound.

"Johnnie, listen to me. I know more facts than any reporter about the assassination. And I'm the only one willing to publicly attack the Warren Report."

"I know that."

"The government is lying about where the shot came from. Don't you care?"

"Yes," I said. "But different theories—"

She cut me off. "When the back of a man's skull and brains are blown into a phoenix behind him, and nearly every witness agrees the kill shot came from ahead of the motorcade, should I clam up about what I know and merely report the next Broadway flop?"

Maybe I should have left it alone, but that little guy in the back of my head wanted me to reason with her. "What do you know?" I asked.

"I know Lee Harvey Oswald was a pawn. I know Jack Ruby killed him, and I know, in a matter of time, Ruby and others will be killed."

"Ruby? He's locked up." I got out of bed and stood rocking back and forth, feeling sick. I wished the pillskies would kick in.

She sat up, dark hair against a propped pillow. "Melvin Belli won't let the state kill him, but Ruby will be killed."

"By someone higher up?" I asked.

"You talked about someone higher up when you were framed in that Detroit alley, Johnnie."

"That happens out there amongst 'em," I said. "It might not mean anything."

"After Detroit, you talked about Sinatra plus the mob, plus the law."

I rubbed my face. My mouth was so dry I could hardly reply. "A triangle."

"Well, try the mob, the CIA, and the FBI," she said, moving her finger. "One, two, three."

"Got it," I replied like a slow student.

"When I return from New Orleans, I should know more. I'm meeting with a D.A. there who's investigating the conspiracy."

For a short moment, I believed she wanted me to go with her. I headed into the bathroom and returned with more water. We drank with trembling fingers and spilled half our portions on the bed.

"We're a triangle too," I said. "Isosceles. I remember that from school. Are you impressed?"

She nodded but didn't smile. "It means indestructible. Three equal angles. You, me, and Dick."

"No," I said. "You, me, our careers."

I felt miserable and sat on the bed. She leaned into my lap. "You've always been the one, Dotty. That's the only thing I know for sure."

"Oh, God," she said, and raised her mouth to kiss my lips.

Fever raged along my skin. "One, two, three, wham," I said. "Ellington's metronome." I walked from the bed to the window. The motel was California style, two stories wrapped around a pool. I gazed down at vehicles and heard their echoes as they raced for the Pacific.

"Come back," she called. "Hold me."

In the window's rectangle, my outline must have looked whittled too thin and brittle. I ran the one question I'd wanted answered all night over my tongue.

I tried it on her out loud. "You doing this investigation just to stay on top?"

"What would you do to stay on top?"

"I'd risk only so much."

"Me too. Now tell me, what would you do if you'd lost it and wanted to get back up there again?"

"Anything," I admitted, and felt a chill.

"There's your answer."

I started another question, then let it fade into the room's blue shadows.

"What were you going to ask?" she said.

"Nothing."

"Then say goodnight to me, Johnnie, before the goodbyes knock us out."

Dorothy

Everyone, even other reporters, was afraid of what she knew. No one wanted to talk about the fact that the Warren Report concealed the truth, for whatever reason, about the assassination. Even *Nightlife* backed off after inviting her as a guest. When she showed up with her file bulging with notes, she was greeted by a producer in her dressing room who asked her not to discuss the subject of her book.

"Too controversial," the producer said. "Don't even bring it up."

"Then why did you invite me?" she countered. "You know it was to discuss the conspiracy. What changed your mind?"

He shrugged. "This is television," he said, as if that should explain it all.

She lost interest in her *Voice of Broadway* column. Who cared if Elizabeth Taylor and Richard Burton reserved an extra hotel room just for Elizabeth's wardrobe? She could barely muster the malicious energy to report Ava Gardner's costly little tantrum at the Regency, involving spaghetti sauce and broken furniture. Tired of gossip and bored by show business, she needed time to work without interruption on *Murder One*.

November began with snow flurries. Her trip to California was a blur of furious action, full of panic and recklessness. When she and Johnnie spent the night together in Los Angeles, he didn't seem to realize how much she needed his support. Perhaps he had forgotten how many times she had been in his corner. More likely, he couldn't think about anything beyond his spiraling career.

On November 7, the snow stopped. Dorothy chose a black gown with bat-wing sleeves for *What's My Line?* The dress was cut so low that she needed more foundation to cover her décolleté than her face. In the dressing room, she sat before the mirror as Marie applied her false eyelashes piece by piece.

"Makes them appear more natural this way," Marie said. "The way the British models do. No more shaggy look for you."

Dorothy regarded her haggard appearance in the mirror. "Maybe I could use a little shaggy."

"Nonsense. You've got your sparkle back, you do. Must have been your trip to the West Coast."

Little did she know, Dorothy thought. "It was quite a trip."

Marie dusted a fluffy powder puff over her face, against her closed eyes. "More work on the JFK story?"

"Yes, very cloak and dagger."

"Tell me."

She couldn't, of course. She'd told all she dared to tell. Now it was time to go through it page by page, and gather her courage to fill in the gaps. "I'll not give up."

"You'll get to the bottom of it if anybody can."

She met Marie's dark eyes in the mirror. "If it's the last thing I do, I'm going to break this case."

"Well, you just be careful. Here." She pressed a tissue against Dorothy's lips. "You really do look beautiful, like a star yourself."

Dorothy's vision blurred. Why did she feel so close to tears? The woman was just being kind. She shouldn't have had that martini. She couldn't go before the camera a blubbering mess.

"There are those," she said, "who think I bear a resemblance to Sophia Loren."

Marie drew back and studied her reflection with an expression Dorothy couldn't begin to read. Slowly, she nodded. "I can see that."

"You can? You can really see it?"

"Oh my, yes," Marie bounced back. "There's certainly a resemblance, all right. The eyes, I think."

"I don't really see it myself." Dorothy had to bite her lip and look away to hold back the tears.

She ran into Bennett Cerf in the hall. He was a gentle, monochromatic man —suit, hair, glasses, voice all the same tone. He never pushed her, although she had owed him *Murder One* for more than four years now. Away from the show, he was her editor at Random House, but on the show, he treated her like a colleague. Two weeks ago, he had walked in to find her sobbing about her poor job of guesswork that night.

"It's just a game," he'd told her.

It wasn't a game to Alistair Parker, her producer, though. She'd show him tonight.

"I read the chapters you gave me last week," Bennett said. "I like them."

"Wait until you see the rest."

"The Kennedy part?"

She nodded. "I have a stack of files this thick." She showed him with her hands, then noticed they were shaking.

"You okay?" Bennett asked. "You're safe and all?"

She couldn't think about that right now. She needed only to keep a clear head for the show. "As safe as any reporter," she told him.

On the show, she was as quick as she'd ever been, besting Arlene, Bennett, and Tony Randall by identifying, with damn few clues, a woman who sold dynamite for a living.

"You're on tonight," Bennett whispered.

Joey Heatherton, blond and breathy, was the mystery guest, on her way to entertain troops in Viet Nam.

Then the Kool cigarettes commercial. Then another guest. At the end of the show, with just moments remaining, Dorothy identified a woman sports writer in record time.

"Good heavens," John Daly exclaimed.

Take that, Mr. Parker, Dorothy thought and flashed what she hoped was a gracious smile. The panel exchanged rapid goodbyes as the show wound up.

"Goodnight, Dorothy Kilgallen," Daly said.

"Goodnight," she replied.

In her dressing room, Marie handed her the phone.

"He insisted on waiting," she said, holding her hand over the mouthpiece.

"Johnnie?" she asked.

"No. It's Mr. Walters."

Dorothy took the phone. "Wonders never cease," she said. "Are you in town?"

"I just got in and caught the last of the show in my room. You were on fire."

She wished he wouldn't surprise her like this. She liked to plan her evenings down to the last detail. "I promised my producer we'd stop for a drink after the show."

"All right then," he said. "I'll wait for you downstairs at the bar."

* * *

At P.J. Clarke's, she had a drink with Alistair Parker, as they'd planned. He praised her successful evening on the show. At least this TV job seemed secure for now. She turned down his offer of a second cocktail.

"What's the hurry?" Parker asked.

"I've got a late date."

He winked. "Say hi to Johnnie."

If only he knew.

Next stop, The Regency.

She waved at the drummer, picked out a table deep within the bar, and ordered her usual vodka tonic. As she drank, she reconsidered the wisdom of this meeting. Her relationship with Sean had taken off fast, maybe too fast. Perhaps she was just being paranoid, but just then, she couldn't shake her uneasiness.

Johnnie. She needed to call him—right now, from a phone that J. Edgar Hoover himself couldn't eavesdrop on.

She found the pay phone she'd used so many times before and dialed the Hollywood number. Music mixed with his voice as he answered.

"Hi, Johnnie," she said. "This is Esther Williams."

He laughed into the phone. "Dotty, I don't believe it. I just finished watching you."

"Was I good?"

"The best. Are you okay, baby? You sound funny. Did you catch cold from your swim in the ocean?"

"It's the phone. I'm at the Regency. Can't use the ones at home. I told you they're bugged."

"If you say so."

"They are, Johnnie. This is not something I made up. I'm meeting someone tonight, the man who will fill in some gaps before I go to New Orleans."

"Can you trust him?"

Good question, one she hadn't been able to answer herself. "You're the only one I've ever trusted."

A click sounded on the phone.

"What's that?" she asked. "I'm calling from a pay phone. Is it on your end?"

"Nobody here," he said. "I'm spinning Cornshucks' latest record. Can you hear her?"

Cornshucks' LP played in the background. Dorothy could make out *At Last,* the Etta James hit. "Barely, but she sounds great."

"Top of the charts without compromising her sound or her soul. Can't imagine how that would feel. Dotty, you sound shaky."

"I am a little."

"I'm afraid you jumped into this conspiracy thing too deep. Are you really sure they're shadowing you?"

"Of course. I thought you'd see that. Johnnie, they can't bug this line, but they could be bugging yours."

"We'll talk about it when I'm out there." She could hear the finality in his tone. He seemed convinced that she had gone off the deep end.

"I need to see you again," she said. "I'll show you the notes for the book, the stuff no one's seen. This is bigger than you can imagine."

"I was planning on coming out for Thanksgiving, but I'll get there next week. We'll meet wherever you want and talk about it."

"All right," she said, although it wasn't. It just wasn't enough. "I love you, Johnnie Ray."

"I love you, Miss Kilgallen."

She couldn't remember how long she'd been holding the phone like that, with her forehead pressed against the wall. She glanced at her hand, wrapped tightly around her empty glass. Somehow the sight of her white knuckles spawned a vision of Jack Ruby's stub of a finger. On her own finger, the rose quartz ring glowed as if lit from within. *Tiny hands. Cute feet.* What had Johnnie said about her feet?

Someone gripped her arm from behind. She whirled around. Sean stood smiling in that familiar navy suit, an American flag pin in his lapel.

"Here you are," he said, his drawl soft and low. His dark hair and eyes were as far removed from Johnnie's features as if she had conjured them herself. Perhaps she had.

"You needn't grab me like that."

"You weren't at the table. I came looking. Let's have a drink and talk."

He helped her back to the corner table, where a martini and a new vodka and tonic stood. She couldn't remember ordering them and didn't know how long she'd been on the phone with Johnnie.

"He's flying out next week," she said and lifted her glass.

"Who's flying out?"

"Johnnie Ray. He doesn't believe me, about the phones and the FBI." Why was she going on like this? She couldn't seem to shut up. And what was wrong with her drink that made it so incredibly bitter?

"No one believes until they've been through it," he said. "You look lovely in that dress. Sexy."

The compliment felt impersonal, an observation made by a stranger, which, despite everything, this tall, quiet man really was.

"Better than two weeks ago. I was so terrible that I broke down and wept after the show. Bennett saved me."

"From what?"

Why had she gone into this? Well, she might as well be honest. "Humiliation."

"You should never feel humiliated, Dorothy. You have more right guesses than anyone else on the show."

"That's what my make-up woman says, but she's been with me from the start. How do you know?"

"I'm interested, that's all. You and your panel seem to be in pace with the movers and shakers." He took his turn at smiling. "You're a sophisticated bunch."

Dorothy tried to read his features, his deep brown eyes. "What's your real interest, Sean?"

"You, of course."

"We both know better than that. Why are you risking everything to help me with my investigation?"

"Risk is what I handle best."

"That doesn't answer my question."

"I'm doing this for the same reason you are. The truth needs to come out."

She reached for her glass but couldn't quite navigate. He helped lift it to her lips. That bitter taste again. It caught in her throat and burned her nostrils.

Music came from somewhere. *Hang On Sloopy*. The closest thing to a love song today, Cornshucks aside.

"He's flying out in a week," she said.

Sean's perfect brow furrowed. "Who's flying out?

"Johnnie Ray," she repeated. "He's the only one who understands."

More music. Beatles and Byrds and Rolling Stones. Loving feelings and yesterdays and turn, turn, turn. *Get Off Of My Cloud, Eight Days A Week, Mr. Tambourine Man*. Music pressed into her pores. She managed to lift her drink. Important to sit straight in the chair, to sit like a lady.

"We fell in a doorway once, Johnnie and I. Babe found us there. We'd been picked clean as chickens."

Had she said it aloud, or was it a stray thought drifting through her brain? No, she could see the shift of his eyes, the sympathetic nod.

"Those things happen, even to people like you."

"Johnnie nearly died. Babe took us to Sinai emergency." She chuckled as the next thought fluttered past. The curtain around the hospital bed, her skirt up around her waist, their laughter. This time she didn't speak.

"Here. Have some more." His warm Texas drawl urged her to the safety of the drink.

She started to take a sip, then realized how drunk she was.

"What's wrong?" he asked.

"I'll be right back." She rose unsteadily from the booth. "I have to powder my nose."

She found the hall leading to the ladies room. It looked like a tunnel with a narrow circle of light at its end. Shadows loomed out. She tried to dodge them and stumbled.

"Hang onto me," Sean said, too close now. "Let me help you."

■ ■ ■

Dorothy needed sleep, a pill to push back the morning and give her time to catch up. The elevator creaked with its load. Had to get it fixed. Just spend the money and do it. Old and ugly as it was, the lift had remained the thing she'd always loved about the house. She pressed her cheek against the elevator's cold wall, closed her eyes, and sailed straight up.

■ ■ ■

Dorothy twisted under the pressure of the unfamiliar covers. How did she get in bed? Something was wrong.

She raised her head and felt warm fingers on the back of her neck. "Be still. It's all right."

"But the bed, why here? It's not mine."

She twisted in the darkness, and something pressed down against her chest. "Stop," she gasped. "You're hurting me." She looked above her into the darkness. "Not my bed," she repeated, her breath gone. This was the master bedroom, not her retreat on the fifth floor. And her eyelashes. She must remove them. Dorothy Kilgallen never slept in her false eyelashes.

The pills appeared, offered on an imaginary tray. Her fingers fumbled, then pressed the tablets into her mouth. Thick fingers. Were they really hers? She saw flashing montages of Jack Ruby's hands and her own. No, someone else's hands, ghostly in a fragment of light.

"Wait," she said. "It's too early. I need to think."

She heard a chuckle, then another tablet. She tried to argue, to ask questions, but the night fell over her like a blanket. No more fight left. Fingers at her lips. She went ahead and swallowed.

Like pillskies, Johnnie would say.

"Johnnie, why aren't you here? Johnnie, I'm afraid."

Johnnie

She's dead.

She died in her sleep. News of it above the fold of the *L.A. Times* stopped my hand mid-way to my mouth. The piece of toast I'd been holding fell slowly in distorted time. I felt it land lightly on my blue pants, part of the suit she liked so much.

I knew I was in The Pantry, corner of Figueroa and Olympic, not far from where we last loved so hard that Halloween dawn. I knew the printed words meant she was gone. I knew that I was alone. I saw my hand still in front of me, felt the warmth of the sourdough toast in my lap, heard the clatter of plates and the clink of utensils.

But I couldn't move and hadn't since I read those words.

"I need some help over here," I finally said.

"Be right with you," replied one of the ancient waiters. "They sign up for life in this jernt," Morrie used to say. Soon the waiter appeared at my side, a kindly man in a tuxedo shirt, bowtie, waist-to-shoes apron. His hands were firm and helpful.

"I need the phone."

"Whom do you wish to call, Mr. Ray?"

"I don't know," I told him.

■ ■ ■

Someone estimated that ten thousand people had come. Old Roland said they darkened the eastern seaboard last night in her memory. I thought of that and hoped somewhere she knew about the scope of that honor.

Out of respect for the family, I waited with Phillip across the street from the funeral home. Clarice and Roland joined us. She had pulled her hair back in a tight knot. His eyes were bloodshot, and not from drink for once.

"She looked beautiful, Johnnie," Clarice said. "All cream and gold. A pearl rosary in her hands. How can it be?" She collapsed in tears against my shoulder. "I should have listened to her."

"Listened to what?" I asked.

She went silent and moved away from us.

Julian urged Dotty's three kids along protectively. The sight of their progression made me ache for her and all the times I'd kept her from them.

Anonymous mourners moved in slow motion like extras in a movie. One little shit quoted what Sinatra told a reporter. "Guess I'll have to revise my act." That's what the fucker had said when he heard the news.

Dotty's interior designer, the big guy who helped her with my apartment, stood with Clarice, Roland, and other arty types. He wiped his eyes with a large white handkerchief. Stars of film, television, and world affairs meandered in the ugly beauty of daylight, not once interrupting the dirge, the promise from the church of St. Vincent Ferrer, that behind our dark glasses, we were all known to God, and our day too would come.

Phillip helped me.

Babe and Cornshucks helped me.

I saw Dick Kollmar, and I felt a rush of pity until his stare met mine. In the time it took for the look between us to connect and fade, I promised myself to call on him.

Not long after, the contradictory facts began to emerge. She had died in that master bedroom she never used. She still wore full makeup, including her false eyelashes. The book she had been propped up holding was one she had mentioned finishing a couple of weeks ago. Every time I heard the question, "How did she die?" and every time I heard the answer, "No one knows," I vowed to face Kollmar again.

And I did. A few weeks later I walked into his nightclub. I let my eyes adjust to the smoke-stained dimness of the bar. He was there, waiting, an apparition. His edges bled into the gloom. He wore a gray suit and guarded a tumbler, its contents as dark as the bar he sat hunched over.

"You're early." He lifted his glass. "Chivas, straight up. Ice maker's on the fritz."

In the wicked light, he looked haggard, even tragic. I wondered how I must look to him. That thought made me lift his offering and drink half of it.

"That's the way, friend," he said.

"I'm not your friend."

"No, you're not."

His voice was resonant, a radio voice like those I remembered coming to me when I was a kid, the dial's glow soft and intimate against my white pillow, my mind spellbound, wondering why no one in real life sounded like that.

I squeezed the glass, swallowed hard, and screwed my gaze into his. Fear struck, but not the sort I felt when he'd threatened to kill me months before.

"Another?" He didn't wait for my answer and poured. The sound of the liquid was enormous in the stillness. He could murder me now, and not a living soul would know.

"Who killed her, Kollmar?"

"I did."

I didn't say a word, but my face, even in the light, must have given away my suspicions that he knew more than he was saying.

"And so did you," he added. "I kept her nightstand plied with the dope you started her on. We all three drank enough of this—" he raised his glass "—to sail the fucking Atlantic and Pacific."

I set my glass down with a vengeance. "You're hiding something."

"Bullshit."

"Why wasn't she in her own bed that night?" When he didn't answer, I stayed on him. "Where were you?"

"In my own bed," he said. Then, as if he had found a fact in his booze-warped brain, he added, "She had her own way of sneaking in at night. She'd even handed out several keys to the kingdom. To hairdressers, both men like you, by the way." He choked out a radio laugh. "And one man not like you."

I didn't take the bait. "Her files, Kollmar. What happened to her files?"

He pulled in his chin. "I destroyed them, burned every fucking note."

I pushed the stool out of my way. "You son of a bitch. All her stuff on the cover-up should be turned over."

"Turned over?" He was plenty drunk, but his voice came to me with conviction. "Who do you think I should have handed it over to?"

I tried to read him correctly, still unable to believe he'd destroy the words she'd risked her life for.

He swung his feet to the dark carpet and stood up. "I loved her." He jabbed a hand out between us. "Not like you think you loved her. You kept her around, hoping she'd make you look like a man."

He swayed, and I reached for him. "Her coffin," he said. "I saw that she got one of beautiful African mahogany. Do you know all of New York went dark for her?"

I turned from him and searched for a trail back through the sad-colored dining area. I saw shadows of Dotty and me touching under a table, daring the big man at the bar to catch us.

He must have been remembering too. His sobs ripped at the club's interior. His words, stage-trained as they may have been, were indiscernible, but as I started to leave, I felt his baritone voice vibrate through me like Babe Pascoe's drums.

"Come back," he called out. "Don't go. Have another drink with me."

■ ■ ■

Much, much later, I turned away from a mirror that didn't lie to me. I poured some whiskey in a glass and set it on the dressing table. Cornshucks came in and looked at it.

She made a thing out of busying herself with her gown.

"An hour to go," she told me. "Meantime, you can relax on the cot in my room."

"I'll be okay here."

"We can go right to your medley. I'll be by your side, throwing in some funk."

"That okay with Babe?"

"We'll be with ya," she said.

"I'll try not to parody myself and escape before they eat me. Then you can give 'em what they paid to see."

"Don't deal that fool hand." Her fingers caressed my cheek. Her lips made a kissing sound, then the glorious aura of her disappeared.

The drink watched me. I watched it.

Babe opened the door a crack as if he didn't want to bug me. Our eyes met in the mirror.

Something about his look jabbed me.

"What?"

"Dorothy's friend, the one she gave a chapter of her book to. She just died."

"Jesus. How?"

"Heart, they say, but no one's sure. Johnnie, some are wondering if Dorothy's death—well, you know."

I knew, all right. "She wouldn't have been that reckless," I told him. Not with the pillskies and the booze. "She and I had been doing that dance too long for her to screw up."

"You want us to cancel your numbers?" Babe asked. "Rose Helen and I are cool with that."

"No way."

"Want to be alone?"

"Yeah," I said. "I do. Just for a moment."

January, the bitch, came cold and sharp through cracks in the tiny room, from under the door as Babe closed it.

I drew a triangle in my mind—equal angles for perfect strength. I pictured me in one of its corners, for some reason lower right— crouched, alive, poised to escape.

"Fuck it," I said. "I'm not finished yet."

I sprung from my chair and left the room without touching the drink.

In the narrow hall, I walked fast toward the sound of musicians getting ready.

"Taste, J.R.?" The alto man offered a half-pint from his case.

"Maybe later." I didn't break stride.

Behind my back, I heard him say, "That's a first."

Afterword

Johnnie Ray did not stay sober for long. Dorothy Kilgallen's sudden death fueled his already out-of-control lifestyle. When asked about her in an interview years later, he replied. "Beyond question...I believe Dorothy was murdered, but I can't prove it."

Less than two years after her death, Richard Kollmar married the fashion designer who created the dress Dorothy had worn on *What's My Line?* the last night of her life. Four years later, at the age of sixty, Kollmar died in his bed of a drug overdose. He had told friends he would take the truth about Dorothy's last book to his grave, and he did. Her notes were never found.

Ever the trouper, Johnnie Ray maintained a demanding schedule, most of his performances as a cabaret singer. In 1974, twenty years after the first time, he played the London Palladium again. At that moment, he was once more the Atomic Ray. His standing ovation lasted fifteen minutes.

In October of 1989, he performed at a benefit for the Grand Theater in Salem, Oregon, one of his best live performances in years, and his last. The following February, he died of liver failure at Cedars-Sinai Hospital in Los Angeles.

In a televised interview in 1981, he described Dorothy Kilgallen as, "the softest, tenderest, most thoughtful, most loveable, most memorable woman that I have ever known."

To this day, Dorothy Kilgallen's death remains a mystery.

Also by Bonnie Hearn Hill

<u>Adult</u>
IF IT BLEEDS
CUTLINE
OFF THE RECORD
INTERN
KILLER BODY
MISTRESS
LAST WORDS

<u>Young Adult</u>
GHOST ISLAND

<u>Nonfiction</u>
DIGITAL INK: Writing Killer Fiction in the E-book Age

Also by Larry Hill

STREAK HITTER

About the Authors

Bonnie Hearn Hill is the author of 7 novels of suspense, 4 young adult novels, and numerous nonfiction titles. She leads online and real time writing workshops. You can see more about Bonnie at www. BonnieHHill.com.

Larry Hill is a writer and artist. The author of two books and many stories, he has won awards including New York University's 2010 Goldenberg Prize for Fiction (final judge, Gail Godwin).

CPSIA information can be obtained
at www.ICGtesting.com
Printed in the USA
LVOW10s2317290817
546899LV00008B/163/P